Red

Kait Nolan

Red
Written and published by Kait Nolan
Copyright 2011 Kait Nolan

ISBN-13: 978-1468002102
ISBN-10: 1468002104

AUTHOR'S NOTE: The following is a work of fiction. All people, places, and events are purely products of the author's imagination. Any resemblance to actual people, places, or events is entirely coincidental.

Cover Art by Robin Ludwig of Robin Ludwig Designs

For Allen,
My everyday hero, who makes me laugh.
All my love,
K

Acknowledgements

As is always the case, this book would not be possible without the extensive brainstorming, pep talks, chocolate, and critiques of Susan "The Pink Hammer" Bischoff. Best crit partner EVER.

Additionally, thanks to my agent, The Magnificent Laurie McLean, for seeing *Red's* potential and mine and fighting to give us wings.

Also thanks to my fabulous beta readers Claire Legrand and Andrew Mocete. Your reading updates were treasured.

Chapter 1

Elodie

I was thirteen when I found out why my mother left me. It seems important to start my story there. The moment when everything changed and my life became a nightmare. The moment when my mother's madness began to infect my father. Infect me.

The letter that came on my birthday that year was such a shock to my poor dad. So many times, I've wished I'd thrown it away. That I'd never let him see it. But at thirteen, I couldn't wrap my brain around the enormity of what my mother was imparting. I thought it was a joke at first. A cruel one.

Dad didn't. Instead of believing that she was mad, he took her words as the cold, hard truth. That I am a monster, just waiting for the proper catalyst to be unleashed. That I am cursed as she was.

Today I know it's true.

I stared at the final line, the period a blotch of blue ink that bled into the page until I lifted my pen. It was worse, somehow, putting my fears into words. Words made a thing real, and I'd spent so long in denial. My ancestors all wrote of the curse in the weeks and months before they died, so it seemed fitting that I begin documentation of my own story to slip beside my mother's letter, behind the final pages of the thick, leather-bound journal that held my gruesome family history.

With a careful, slanting hand, I continued.

I am seventeen today. Older than my predecessors by a full year. Nothing happened the way she said it would. As far as the history goes, all of them had given birth by now. All of them were dead by now. Some hunted and slaughtered. Some, like my mother, dead by their own hand. Maybe it's because I haven't transitioned yet, but I cannot see suicide as a viable alternative. The book hints of madness that accompanies the curse, but my mother seemed right enough in her mind when she penned the letter explaining things to me, arranging for its safe-keeping and delayed delivery, and seeing that the trail to my father was obliterated before she walked away from us, away from life, when I was only three days old.

I cannot help but feel she took the coward's way out, even if she thought she was protecting us. But was it cowardice? Each year since I got the letter, I've come out here, to contemplate whether I could do it. Each year I've brought a different weapon, testing, if you will, my willingness to end my own life, should it come to that. Acclimating myself to the idea. Pills the first year, though I learned from this book that our kind has a stronger constitution and requires something more definitive than an overdose. A rope the next. I wound up making a swing from it. Last year was my father's pistol. The barrel tasted bitter and oily when I put it in my mouth. I managed to load the cylinder, but didn't get so far as cocking the hammer.

You see, I don't want to die.

I want a life, a future. I want to be normal. And I thought I was until yesterday morning.

Then I smelled it. The succulent odor of bacon frying. So innocuous, really. I thought Dad had decided to cook breakfast, like he used to on Saturday mornings before the letter. We made it through the worst year, the worst of the waiting, and nothing happened. Nothing changed. I had hope.

But there wasn't any bacon frying. There wasn't even anybody in the kitchen. Just a note from Dad that he'd been called in to work, and he'd be back in a couple of days.

I don't know what possessed me to follow the smell. I was hungry, I guess. I tracked the scent to the Redmond's open kitchen window. They are our closest neighbors. A full three-quarters of a mile away.

Humans do not have such fine-tuned senses of smell.
But wolves do.

What will be next? My hearing? My reflexes? The fevers that precede the first shift? How long do I have before I change? Before I lose my humanity like those who came before me.

Will I have the courage to do what must be done?

I glanced down at the bone-handled knife sitting beside me on the stone but didn't touch it. Of all the weapons I'd tested, this was the first one that truly scared me. Pills were relatively painless. A rope, well if you did it right, that was pretty instant. Same with eating a bullet. But a knife... A knife was something else altogether. A knife meant you had to be sure, had to inflict pain, had to wait and watch as your life bled out, heartbeat by heartbeat.

A knife had been my mother's choice, according to the coroner's report.

Setting the notebook aside, I rose and paced a restless circle around the clearing. I had privacy here, out in the depths of the park with the slopes of the Appalachians rising around me like giant hands curved to hold the mist of morning. I wasn't worried about being interrupted. None of the tourists would stray so far from the trails that snaked their way through the trees. And as far as I was aware, no one else knew about this place.

Which made it the perfect spot to challenge myself.

I circled back around, eyes on the knife. Even sheathed, it made my breathing hitch. It's not like it was the very knife Mom used. That one was still in an evidence locker somewhere. I'd filched this one from Dad's workroom, so it wasn't cloaked in bad juju or anything. But I couldn't look at it and not imagine blood. Oceans of it, spilling out of a warm body, skin growing paler and paler as the life pulsed across the stone in some horrible sacrifice.

Dad always said I had an active imagination.

I approached the knife, willing myself to pick it up. *C'mon Elodie, you can do this. You can face the knife.*

Closing my hand around the hilt, I could feel the pattern carved into the bone handle where it pressed against my sweaty palm. A howling wolf. The irony. I was sure Dad would never have bought it if he'd known what I was.

My heart hammered against my ribs, galloping with a fear I hadn't felt in all my other trials. I wanted to run. To drop the knife and flee back to the sham of a normal life I'd struggled to build over the last four years. Instead, I unsnapped the leather strap that kept the knife in its sheath and slipped the blade free.

It gleamed, polished and sharpened, well-kept as everything my dad tended, though he probably hadn't used it in months. Nathaniel Rose took care of things—whether he wanted to or not. Mouth dry, I set the sheath aside and crossed to a green sapling. Tugging on a branch about the size of my pinky, I drew the knife across it. Two swipes. That's all it took to sever the branch.

The Cheerios I'd had for breakfast threatened to make a reappearance.

I moved back to the stone and sat, propping my right arm in my lap, wrist side up. The faint tracery of veins stood out like blue lace against my fair skin. I lifted the knife, but my hand shook so badly I had to stop and rest it against the rock. No way in hell was I going to accidentally slit my wrist while I was facing down this personal demon.

This is a test, I thought. *This is only a test.* I imagined an annoying, high pitched *BEEEEEEEEP!* My snicker sounded muffled in the trailing wisps of fog. The sun would be burning it off soon, once it topped the eastern ridge. Best get this done with.

The near laughter steadied me. I lifted the knife again and brought it slowly and carefully to my arm. Gooseflesh broke out at the kiss of the blade, its tip the barest of whispers against my skin. I focused on that point of contact, shutting my eyes, and reminding myself to breathe.

I can do this.

~*~

Sawyer

"I'm not going."

I didn't yell it, but my dad immediately changed into the I-don't-know-what-to-do-with-you-anymore expression that had become the norm in the last eight months.

"Sawyer, you've got to finish school. You were so close to graduating when you got expelled. If you'd just go to summer school, you'd finish up, graduate, and be ready to start college in the fall like we'd planned."

Oh of course, The Plan. Dad had been big on trying to get me back on The Plan since our lives fell apart. It was his way of coping, I guess. Ever the scientist, he wanted to restore order out of chaos. Like that could possibly repair the massive hole that was blown in our lives.

I thought about the GED shoved under my mattress upstairs. It would be easy enough to settle this, but then it would look like I was on board with the program. He'd start trying to push me back into Normal Life, as if there was any such thing for people like us. Besides, it was something else to fight about, and these days, I needed to fight like I needed to breathe.

"I'm. Not. Going," I repeated, letting the edge of a growl seep into my voice and shifting forward into his personal space. My eyes held his in a dominance challenge that should have spurred him to action to knock me down a peg. I wanted the physicality of fists as a release from the pressure constantly building inside me.

But he answered in words.

"Your mother would be so disappointed in you."

My breath rushed out in a whoosh, as if he'd sucker-punched my gut. Because it was true. Then I leaned in, so close I could feel his shuddering breath on my face, and delivered the only retaliation I had against the accusation. "And whose fault is it she's not here to say so herself?"

The question slid home like a knife between his ribs, and even though I believed it, I still felt like a dick for sinking so low. His eyes shifted to gold, his lip curled in a snarl, and I knew I'd gotten what I wanted.

At last. I balled my fists, body tensing to move, to finally let off some pressure. But the punch never came.

"She wouldn't want this," he said, and his voice was guttural, already halfway to animal. He stepped back.

Fresh fury boiled up. I whirled toward the back door, needing to get out, to move, to run.

"Where are you going?" Dad demanded.

"For a run."

He opened his mouth, to issue a warning probably, and I lifted my shoes in a sarcastic wave. "On two feet."

"Be—"

I slammed the door, cutting off the caution and sprinted for the tree line. Once in the shadow of the trees, I paused only long enough to put on my shoes before resuming my futile escape. You can't run from what you carry inside.

My rage grew with every thudding step, the fog shredded by my passage. I was desperate to shed my human skin and hunt, but I didn't dare. Not here. Timber wolves hadn't been native to the area for at least a couple of centuries, and after what had happened to my mother in Montana, where we didn't stand out in the least . . .

I missed the rugged and unforgiving terrain of the Rockies. Not only because we blended in, but because it was wild. Everything here was too low, too worn, too soft, too *civilized*. I hadn't been anywhere near civilized since my mother died.

The air pressed close, humidity draping over me like a big soggy towel. A few more degrees and it would edge into truly hot and sticky. East Tennessee felt like a world away from home, where we were lucky if it got up to 70 as a high in the dead of summer. And I was stuck here. Even if I went along with The Plan and headed off to college in the fall, there would be conditions. Rules. Restrictions.

Wolves don't like restrictions.

Something moved to my left as I burst free of a cluster of pines. A young buck. It spun away, springing toward safety. Even on two feet, instinct demanded I give chase. I bounded after it, pushing myself beyond human limits of agility and speed to keep the powerful haunches in sight. My muscles ached, and the pain helped to burn off some of the anger. By the time I lost the deer at the river, I was somewhat calmer.

But it wasn't enough. Nothing was ever enough. Our kind require the tempering influence of mated pairs. Two parents when we're young and through transition. A mate when we're older. I was only a few months beyond my transition when Mom was killed, enough in control that I wasn't *technically* a danger. At least not once the blood rage had passed. But I certainly wasn't winning Son of the Year awards.

Dad had let the farmer live. The self-righteous, sanctimonious, son of a bitch who put a bullet through my mother's brain was still walking around, still breathing. Fucking *lauded* for his actions. Because he, like the rest of his ilk who head up the calls to "thin out" the number of predators in the area in the name of "protecting" livestock, saw a wolf, saw an opportunity, and took it. One shot. One shot that should never have happened because Mom should have smelled the farmer, seen it coming. Taken precautions. But she'd been careless. Furious and careless because of a fight with my father. She'd gone out for a run to blow off steam, as I often did, and she had strayed where it wasn't safe.

Maybe my father could have protected her. Maybe he couldn't. But as her mate, it sure as shit was his job to avenge her. To rip the bastard to shreds.

He said that would make him into the monster our kind is reputed to be in legend.

We weren't so great with the agreeing to disagree.

I didn't know what I hoped to accomplish by goading him. Provoking him to some kind of action that let me know he was still an alpha male I could respect? Forcing his hand to go back to Montana and do what needed to be done. Or maybe just fueling the fury that was my constant companion. Anger was familiar and in its own way comforting. It was so much easier to cope with than the grief that threatened to swallow me whole.

The sun peeked over the ridge, burning off the last of the morning mist. I wasn't anywhere near a path I recognized. My explorations of the Great Smoky Mountain National Park hadn't been too extensive in the month we'd been in Mortimer. Our house was just at the edge of the Park proper, which made for easy access—something I'd have to take more advantage of in the future.

Rather than following my scent trail back, I stuck to the river. Might as well start mapping the area. I'd gone half a mile when I heard the hitched breath. Veering away from the river, I followed the sound into a copse of trees.

I stayed low to the ground and crept closer until I could see who it was.

The girl perched on a huge flat boulder on the opposite side of the clearing, her face raised to the sun so that her long black hair fell in shiny waves down her back. She was crying. Not that she was being noisy about it. She wasn't hysterical or red-faced and wailing. She was absolutely silent. I caught the faint gleam of tears on her cheeks, saw her shoulders shudder with the effort of holding in her grief. And it was grief. I recognized the expression on her face as one I couldn't bear myself, and I wondered who she had lost.

Conscience pricked. *I should get out of here. What kind of asshole sticks around and watches a girl cry?* But something about her pulled at me, so I stayed. It was as if her tears somehow released my own grief. I felt oddly soothed by it. Part of me wanted to go to her and offer…what? Comfort? I wasn't any good at that. And she wouldn't thank me for intruding. No doubt she came out here for privacy.

Feeling like a voyeur, I started to back away.

Spots of brighter sunlight flickered on her face, and I paused, looking for the source of the reflection. My eyes fell to her hands. The sun glinted off the blade of a knife where it lay poised against her wrist. She took a deep, shaky breath.

My heart jolted, a thunder of rage and horror. *No!* I scrambled up, mustering every ounce of speed I possessed to get to that knife. But my fastest wasn't fast enough, and the knife pressed into the white flesh.

~*~

Elodie

The knife was winning. Fear pulsed through me in waves, radiating from the epicenter where the blade pressed against my skin. I shook back my hair, trying to dislodge the sticky strands from my neck. And I thought of my mother.

Had she wrestled with the decision like I was? Or had she done it quickly? A vertical slash deep between the tissue, straight to the artery. No going back. How long had it taken her to bleed out? If they'd found her sooner, would she have stood a chance?

My stomach roiled. My shoulders bucked.

If it came down to me facing off with death, I wouldn't be doing it like this. But by God I was going to face down this knife and sit here until I got myself under control. I heaved a breath and repositioned the knife, steadying my hold.

Something hit my hand, a hard and fast strike that left my fingers stinging. I released the knife, my eyes springing open.

What the hell—

"—are you doing?"

I didn't register anything but the tone—furious and threatening. Still drenched in fear from my bout with the knife, I couldn't think, couldn't process. Some primitive part of my brain urged me into motion, and I scrambled backward and away, automatically looking around for a weapon before I even identified the threat.

My eyes lit on my knife, embedded halfway to the hilt in a flowering dogwood across the clearing. For a few precious seconds, I just stared.

How . . . ?

Then someone moved to my right, and I bolted back in panic. My heart kicked hard in my chest. He was *huge*. A great beast of a boy with linebacker shoulders and an expression of growling menace on his angular face. His hands were held up in a placating gesture, but everything in his posture screamed agitation and aggression. For every step I took in one direction, he countered.

Trapped.

My brain screamed at me to move, escape. But he was a good foot taller, with legs that would easily eat up any lead I would gain by surprise if I ran. I found myself lifting my head slightly and widening my nostrils to smell.

The stink of my own fear clouded everything else. I inhaled again sifting through the scents with some deeper part of my brain. Damp earth. Fresh cut green wood. And something else I couldn't identify.

The initial panic begin to ebb enough that I started understanding what he was saying.

"I'm not going to hurt you." That he snarled it in frustration didn't lend a lot of credence to the statement.

My breath was still coming fast and shallow. "You'll have to forgive me if I'm not inclined to believe you."

"I didn't mean to scare you, but I had to stop you."

"Stop me?" I asked blankly.

"I don't care how bad things are, that's not the answer."

"What . . ." Then I stopped, my brain catching up with what he was saying. "I wasn't trying to kill myself."

"You'll forgive me if I'm not inclined to believe you."

Having my words thrown back at me, I felt the urge to curl my lip in a snarl. I glared instead.

"What's your name?" he asked.

Did I look stupid? "You first."

"I'm—you're bleeding."

While my brain struggled to make sense of that, he sprang toward me, almost too fast to track. I tried to stumble back, but he had my hand in his, tugging me toward him.

"Hey!"

Then he pressed the tail of his t-shirt against the cut on my arm that I hadn't even noticed yet. His touch was firm but careful. The anger seemed to leech out of him, redirected into action.

I said the first thing that popped into my head. "You cut me!"

His face darkened again. "*I* cut you? I just stopped you from slitting your wrists. I saved your life."

My own temper started to emerge now that I was relatively sure he wasn't planning to kill me. "I wasn't slitting my wrists. You yanking it away from me nicked my vein."

"Not slitting your wrists. Oh, because there are so many *other* completely logical reasons for you to be out in the middle of nowhere *with a knife*, crying your heart out."

Had I been crying? I lifted my free hand to my face and found it wet. God, how mortifying. Then I stopped myself. This lunatic thought I was out here committing suicide and I was worried that he'd seen me crying? *Get your priorities straight, girl.*

"It's none of your damned business what I was doing, but I wasn't trying to kill myself."

"Right."

I glared at him but made no additional reply. He would either believe me or not. Repeating myself probably wouldn't help my case.

His long fingers were still curled around my wrist, keeping me immobilized, but oddly gentle in contrast to the storms in his eyes. It felt almost comforting. Which was just stupid given that he was some pissed off, misguided, wannabe hero. Still, my pulse slowed, my breathing evened out, and the fear of the knife finally ebbed. For better or worse, the trial was over.

He seemed to calm too as we stood there in awkward silence, him holding my wrist and staunching the bleeding. Whatever demons haunted him retreated so that, when he looked up at me, his face was no longer menacing. It was just heartbreakingly sad, marked by the kind of loss that scars a person. I knew it because I saw the same expression in the mirror every day.

My fingers itched to touch his cheek and smooth those worry lines away.

What the hell is wrong with me? I curled them into a fist instead and frowned.

He lifted the edge of the t-shirt, now stained with a darker spot on the black. "I think it's starting to clot." Working quickly, he ripped two clean strips off the bottom of the t-shirt. He folded one and pressed it to the cut and wrapped the other around my wrist to secure it. "Doesn't look like you'll need stitches."

My wrist felt suddenly cold without the pressure of his hand around it.

I am losing my mind.

I folded my injured arm across my chest and looked up at him. "Thank you," I said, though I didn't really know for what.

His eyes followed me as I moved back to the boulder, snagging the notebook and stuffing it in my bag. I picked up the leather sheath and looked at the knife buried in the tree. "How did you do that?"

His shoulders jerked in a motion that was half discomfort, half shrug. "Lucky shot. I can try to get it out if you want."

I lifted a brow at that. "Aren't you worried I'll use it?"

"Will you?"

"Not like that."

I guess he believed me because he crossed the clearing and reached up, wiggling the blade free of the tree. Then he walked back and presented it to me hilt first. "Be careful."

"Always." I slid the knife back into its sheath and slipped it into my bag. "Look, I need to go—" I trailed off, turning a fast circle.

The boy wasn't there.

I stood and listened for sounds of his passage. I heard nothing. Lifting my head and inhaling, I tried to find his scent. But other than a lingering trace of boy and sweat and that thing I couldn't place, there was nothing but the tangle of green and dirt that was summer in the mountains.

Gooseflesh broke out along my arms, despite the rising summer heat.

He was simply gone. Vanished into the woods he'd come from. Like a ghost.

Chapter 2

Elodie

I woke in the pearl gray light of dawn, my head still reeling from dreams of the ghost boy. I rolled over to turn off the alarm that would blare in twenty minutes and saw the scrap of t-shirt on my nightstand. Not a dream. Or rather, not *just* a dream.

I flopped onto my back and ran my fingers lightly over the clean bandage I'd applied the day before. It didn't hurt anymore. Carefully, I peeled up the edge of the First Aid tape and peeked. There was an odd sort of relief in seeing the thin, angry scab still stretched across my wrist. Accelerated healing was one of the signs of the change. After the bacon fiasco, I half expected things to start happening wham, bang, one after another even though I knew it should take more time.

The house was silent, a state of affairs I was becoming more and more accustomed to these days. As a firefighter, my father worked multi-day shifts on duty, staying at the fire station. When I was little, back when we lived in Texas, I had my own cot at the station and a platoon of unofficial uncles among the other firefighters. Since we moved here and I hit high school, that had stopped. Dad had gotten more comfortable with leaving me alone at the house. Or maybe he just wanted to get away from me. It was hard to tell. Either way, I was well-trained enough in The Rules that he knew I wasn't going to go do something that would get me noticed.

15

Which was exactly why he wouldn't expect me to be lying about my summer job.

I rolled out of bed and headed for the shower.

As far as Dad knew, I was spending my summer as a trail guide in the park. I certainly knew the area well enough, and it was the kind of job where I could disappear easily if something went wrong. Which really meant if I wolfed out and tried to eat someone. I suppose I should be flattered that he gave me credit for enough control that I *could* get away in that eventuality. I knew it was only because I'd made it through this year and because he didn't know about my new supernatural sense of smell. It was a job I probably would have liked, actually, but I had bigger plans.

Given my secret, Dad and I never talked about the future anymore. But I thought about it. One more year until I graduated high school. Then what? I wanted college and an education. I wanted a career. And this internship with Dr. Grant McGrath was a step in the right direction.

One of the foremost ethologists in the field, Dr. McGrath was in Tennessee to do a feasibility study on re-introducing red wolves into the park habitat. Others tried it back in the early '90s but it didn't take. Most of the wolves wandered out of the park, got killed by hunters, died of diseases that domestic dogs are vaccinated against, or wound up mating with coyotes or dogs. Eventually the researchers recaptured the remaining wolves and gave up the attempt. But a lot can change environmentally in twenty years, so Dr. McGrath was back to see if it was worth trying again.

My interest was two-fold: acquire field experience that looked great on college applications and learn as much as possible about real wolves from real life rather than just books. Granted, I was pretty sure that there would be a significant difference in the behavior of natural wolves and werewolves, but I couldn't see that educating myself about their behavior patterns could be a *bad* thing. Besides, maybe with my developing senses, I'd be able to find out something that the original scientists missed. Way to find the positive, right?

As I grabbed my keys off the nightstand, I stopped and stared at the scrap of cloth again. Then, without really knowing why, I shoved it into my pocket and headed out the door.

We were out of breakfast food at the house, and Dad hadn't yet conceded that I needed a car, so I was stuck with two-wheeled, self-powered transportation. The air was already sticky as I pedaled the mile and a half to Hansen's Quik Mart. By the time I rolled in to Hansen's and parked my bike, I could feel my t-shirt already sticking to my back.

Way to impress your new boss, I thought. But there was no help for it. We'd be mostly working in the field anyway. If Dr. McGrath didn't already know that Tennessee got knock-you-on-your-ass hot in the summer, he'd find out soon enough. I was willing to bet they didn't have this kind of humidity in Montana.

Inside the Quik Mart, the air was relatively frigid in comparison. I shoved both hands in my pockets as I trudged over to the aisle with the breakfast food. My fingers brushed the scrap of t-shirt and my mind snapped back to my errant "rescuer". I'd been doing that a lot since yesterday. It was stupid to dwell on what happened. I mean, the guy obviously thought I was some suicidal lunatic. And it wasn't like I'd ever see him again, so there was no reason for me to be intrigued.

But maybe that's why I *was* intrigued. I *wouldn't* ever see him again, so he was a safe fantasy.

Because of my condition—I really couldn't bring myself to think of it as a curse—a fantasy was the only kind of relationship I was ever going to have. According to the book, the final catalyst for the change was sex. So in real life, I had to stay as far away from guys and as below their radar as possible. Not as though that had ever been much of a chore. Like I was gonna give it up to somebody who required hand holding encouragement and a billboard stating interest? Please. High school boys were morons.

The jingle of the bell over the door and a peal of female laughter that was more like nails on a chalkboard drew my attention to the front of the store.

Case in point, I thought, watching Rich Phillips walk in with the Barbie Squad.

Amber Cooper, Deanna Jacobs, and Lindy Zimmerman were all part of the popular crowd in my class. Cheerleaders. Blonde. Beautiful. Bitchy. Pick your favorite teen movie and apply the popular girl stereotype, that was the Barbie Squad. Hey, the stereotype exists for a reason. And naturally, the favorite school year occupation of the BS—pun absolutely intended—was giving me crap. Because I was weird. Because I kept to myself. Because, according to popular rumor and the fact that I shot down the few guys with enough guts to approach me, I was an ice queen. I had only just recently managed to return to a low profile after a particularly vicious smear campaign they'd executed on Facebook earlier in the spring. Ah, social media. Ruining reputations everywhere.

I edged away from the powdered donuts and honey buns so that I was further down the aisle and less visible because of the tourist guy in glasses who thought Doritos were an appropriate breakfast food. No reason to get on their radar today.

Maybe I should disappear to the bathroom, I thought. *Surely they'll be gone in five or ten minutes.*

But then there was the possibility that one of them would have to use it, and I'd get stuck with a face to face in the tiny back hall, so I opted to stay put. I tried to focus on picking out something to eat so that I could pay and get out of here, but none of the over-processed, high sugar options really went with the churning of my stomach. I moved toward the drink cases in the back, circling around to the copious display of meat sticks. I didn't think too much about the fact that

Slim Jims sounded a lot more appealing than Hostess pastries.

"Meat for breakfast. A girl after my own heart."

I froze, my hand an inch away from the beef jerky. A big tanned arm reached past me to snag a couple of meat sticks. I chanced a glance up and caught the 180-watt grin of Rich Phillips. As casually as I could, I glanced the other way to see who was standing behind me, but no, it was just me. Rich Phillips was talking *to me.*

I grabbed a package of teriyaki flavored beef and turned toward him, automatically stepping back and not meeting his eyes as I mumbled something about the merits of starting the day with protein. To my utter horror, Rich didn't move on down the aisle to the cash register where two-thirds of the BS were motioning for him to hurry up. Instead he followed me to the drink cooler.

"So what're you up to this summer, Elodie?"

"Nothing much." I opened the case and grabbed a water.

He reached into an adjacent cooler and grabbed a Gatorade. "I've gotta drop my sister off for a Junior Explorers thing in the park, but after that we're all headed to the lake to go water skiing. If you're not busy you should join us."

The clear glass door fell shut out of my suddenly numb hand. He was inviting me to *hang out?* I shot a glance out the front window, searching for flying pork. Seeing none, I looked back at Rich and managed—just barely—not to gape.

"Um, that's nice of you to offer, but I really can't." I tried to step away again, but Rich countered, boxing me in against the glass doors with his bigger frame.

"What's the matter, El? I don't bite."

He offered up the grin again, but I was too busy trying to hold back a snarl. I was really particular about my personal space and having this big, testosterone-reeking boy invading mine was so not okay. All my instincts were screaming at me to shove him away and attack, but I held very still, even as his body pressed into mine, his scent—one of soap and sweat and some hideously overpowering boy deodorant—making my head spin.

Don't react. Don't draw attention. Don't react. Don't draw attention. The familiar litany ran through my brain as I kept my eyes on the Boar's Head Tavern t-shirt in front of me and struggled to keep my breathing even.

"Rich, what the hell are you doing?"

I closed my eyes. Oh God, this was worse. I was being *rescued* by *Amber*.

Rich finally stepped back and I could take a full breath. I edged away from both of them, fully aware of the daggers being mentally thrown at my back by the head Barbie, who totally had her sights set on Rich. And he was just hitting on me. In front of her. *Oh shit.*

It didn't actually matter whether he was being serious or playing some kind of joke. Amber's ire, once earned, was a thing of legend. So, really, I just needed to find a rock to crawl under for the rest of the summer and pray she found someone else to harass for senior year.

A girl can dream.

With Amber on duty, Rich rounded up his little sister, a skinny little girl of about ten who seemed to hide behind her curtain of sandy hair as soon as Amber got within ten feet of her. Poor kid. I totally related. The pair of them got hustled to the front of the store. I hung out by the coffee station, hardly daring to breathe until the lot of them paid and left.

Mr. Hansen eyed me as I brought my jerky and water to the register. "They givin' you trouble, Elodie?"

"No, sir."

The tilt of his caterpillar eyebrows suggested he didn't buy it, but he left it alone as he rang up my purchases.

Outside an engine roared to life, along with a radio cranked up to maximum volume. Stuffing my breakfast into my backpack, I looked out the window just in time to see

Amber's hot pink Jeep Wrangler back over my bike. This time I couldn't stop my mouth from falling open in shock.

Mr. Hansen swore and reached for the phone even as the Jeep peeled out of the parking lot. "I'll call the Sheriff."

"Don't bother," I told him, clenching my teeth to hold in the sudden spurt of rage. "I'm sure it was an accident."

Of course it wasn't. I'd seen Amber's self-satisfied smirk in the rear-view mirror. But maybe she'd consider us even.

I went outside to survey the damage. The bike was toast. The frame was bent, the front wheel now resembled a taco shell, and the sprockets were busted. The only place this thing was going was into the dumpster around back. And I was approximately seven miles from the research station.

Shit. I was gonna be late for my first day of work.

Elodie

Taking the road was not an option. Mortimer is a small town. My pulling an apparent hitchhiker routine on a stretch of pretty heavily travelled road was going to get me noticed, which was against The Rules. Plus, the last thing I needed was my dad finding out that I wasn't working where he thought I was working. Instead I struck out cross country, heading for the research station as the crow flew. It shaved off a mile and a half, but I was still forty-five minutes late.

The research station was housed in a trailer, one of those dealies you usually see at big construction sites. You know, where the foreman or architect or whoever hang out. This one was long and low, with corrugated tan walls and no sign to indicate I was in the right place. But this was the location Dr. McGrath had given me in his email, so after checking to make sure that my unscheduled hike hadn't totally blown my deodorant, I trudged across the gravel parking area, past a handful of mud-spattered vehicles.

21

Because they were shaking with nerves, I shoved my hands back in my pockets and started fiddling with the scrap of t-shirt. I wove the fabric through my fingers. *Please let me not have screwed this up.* I was just going to provide a calm, reasonable explanation for my tardiness, and hopefully Dr. McGrath wouldn't be so pissed he kicked me off the project on the first day.

At the door I hesitated. Should I knock? Just go in? In the end I opted for decisive and confident, even though I felt anything but. It was better than slinking in like a delinquent to the principal's office.

I stepped inside. Several people were clustered around a long table further down the room. All faces turned in my direction with expressions ranging from curiosity to irritation. *Too much attention. Too much focus.* In a moment of instinctual panic, my fingers tightened on the scrap of t-shirt in my pocket. It steadied me somehow, reminding me that I wasn't a coward.

Zeroing in on the older guy in glasses, I straightened my shoulders and said, in a voice that sounded a lot calmer than I felt, "Dr. McGrath, I'm Elodie Rose. I'm terribly sorry I'm late, but I had some transportation issues."

One of them stood up from the table and walked over. "Well, we're glad you made it, Elodie. I'm Grant McGrath. Come on in and join us."

I blinked, a little taken aback. Dr. McGrath wasn't the skinny guy in glasses who actually *looked* the part of a scientist. He was an enormous man, towering at least a full foot above me. His face was ruddy and windburned, with crinkles around his green eyes. *Indiana Jones, eat your heart out,* I thought, taking the hand he offered. His dwarfed mine.

"So did your car break down?" he asked.

"I don't have a car, actually. I had—" I paused, searching for words that did not reek of the angsty, teenage idiocy that had resulted in the destruction of my bike. "—a mechanical problem with my bike. So I had to hike in."

"Not too far, I hope," he said.

"Only five and a half miles, sir."

Now it was Dr. McGrath's turn to blink.

"Holy crap. You really just hiked nearly six miles to work?" This came from a pudgy, red-headed girl that I judged to be a grad student.

"The terrain is pretty moderate on this side of the park," I replied, shrugging.

"We'll see that you get a ride home this afternoon," said Dr. McGrath. "Come meet the team." He escorted me toward the table. Gesturing to the red-head, he said, "This is Abby Renfroe, one of my grad students. That's David Bryson, my post-doc." With his long, sun-streaked hair and hazy blue eyes, David looked like he belonged on a surf board instead of in a lab. "And this is Patrick Everett, my right hand man and co-investigator." The glasses guy nodded in my direction.

I nodded back to each of them in turn, relaxing a bit now that I knew I wasn't fired.

"We were just looking over a map of the park to start dividing things up into quadrants," said Dr. McGrath. "Part of what we'll be doing is tracking game patterns to establish prey density for the area. That was part of the problem when they did this the last time."

Taking a seat I slipped into a role I was comfortable with: attentive student. Some of what he told us I already knew from my research on the first attempt at reintroduction; some was new. I soaked it up like a sponge. School was something I was good at. When you have no friends and few activities to take up your time, there's nothing to distract you from your education. And when you've got a curse hanging over your head, you're pretty motivated to distract yourself by any means possible.

As I relaxed further, my brain began to register the scents around me. The stale, recirculated air. The rich scent of coffee. A sort of faint odor of mold. The various personal scents of the people around me. And somewhere layered over it all, a scent of something wild, with a trace of cedar. My nostrils flared, trying to capture and parse out the scent. The thing with the super nose was that I hadn't had it long enough to catalog stuff. I was scenting all kinds of things I'd never noticed before, and not all of them were familiar.

This scent tickled my brain, a teasing, fleeting recognition, then gone again. I lifted my head slightly, trying for a better whiff.

And then I knew.

~*~

Sawyer

You are turning into a stalker, I thought as I knelt to check the scent trail again. I'd been trying to convince myself otherwise for the last three miles.

After my questionable rescue of the girl in the woods yesterday, I'd trailed her home. It's not like I was turning into some sparkly, blood-sucker wannabe, who hung out staring into her room while she slept or something. Give me some credit. I just wanted to make sure she made it home okay and kept her word. As far as I knew, she had, and that should have been the end of it.

But she'd stayed with me. Or rather, what it felt like to be with her stayed with me. When I'd touched her, I felt calm for the first time in months. The bloodlust I'd been carrying around, that rage I'd been living with, finally took a break. And that really messed me up because that was *not* something that should happen from contact with a human girl. It freaked me out, and that's why I bolted from the clearing.

I spent half the night talking myself out of going back over to her house—on the grounds of that whole not being a stalker thing. Yet when I caught her scent on my run this morning, I couldn't help but follow. It lingered in my nose as I stared at the research station.

Not only was I a stalker, I was also going crazy. Because there was no way that this girl was hanging out in there with my father. Maybe my conscience was using the one positive thing I'd fixated on to fool me into doing the right thing by coming to help with Dad's research. I hadn't made up my mind on that front. It might seem too much like I was starting to get on board with The Plan after my rejection of summer school. Curiosity propelled me forward anyway. One way or the other, I had to know if my mind was playing tricks on me.

It was easy to slip in unnoticed, moving with my silent hunter's gait, up the steps, through the door.

And there she was. Impossibly sitting right there between Patrick and Abby, as if she was part of the research team.

My brain flashed back to the clearing, to the knife and the taste of fear that I wouldn't be able to stop her.

I gave myself a shake, trying to clear my head to address the more relevant question: What was she *doing* here? As I watched, she shifted in her seat, reaching over to rub a hand over her bandaged wrist. Then, as if she sensed I was standing there, she turned her head and met my eyes.

Her lips parted on a soft inhalation of surprise, and damn if that didn't make me wonder what she'd taste like.

Her eyes were a blue-gray with a darker blue ring around the iris. Witch eyes. The ones I couldn't stop thinking about. Yesterday they were filled with grief, today recognition and… anxiety? I had the urge to go to her, touch her, tell her it was gonna be okay. And what was that about? Not to mention that such a move in front of this audience would lead to a helluva lot of questions I didn't want to answer.

Everyone else shoved back from the table.

"Sawyer."

I jolted a little and shifted my attention to my father. "Sorry I'm late," I said.

"I wasn't sure you were coming," he said. His tone was pleased. That irritated me.

Whatever. I'd make the concession if it meant I finally got to meet this girl. Properly.

My eyes strayed back to Her. She was still watching me, but any traces of surprise had been replaced by polite curiosity.

So that's how you wanna play it. Never met before. Okay then.

"What'd I miss?" I moved over to the conference table, stepping out of the way as Abby and David headed to the other end of the trailer to start gathering gear.

"We've just been reviewing stuff you already know. We were about to head out into the field," said Dad.

I basically ignored him and turned to the girl. "You're new."

"Oh, right. This is Elodie Rose, our summer intern. Elodie, my son, Sawyer," he said absently, before turning to Patrick.

"Hi," she said, offering her hand.

I could smell some other guy on her and had to suppress a growl as I reached out to take it. "Nice to meet you, Elodie."

I curled my fingers gently around hers, clasping instead of shaking. God her hand was tiny. She frowned when I turned it over and brushed two fingers lightly over the bandage on her wrist. Her pupils sprang wide and the pulse beneath my fingertips jumped and skittered, which was awesome in the instant before the sudden scent of fear. I felt like a total jackass.

She seemed to relax a fraction as soon as I let her go, but I could still see the pulse pounding in her throat. She wanted to run. The desire to escape was clearly etched in every inch of her body. But she didn't move, a fact that I both admired and appreciated, given that my natural instinct as a predator would have been to give chase, which wouldn't have helped things at all.

"Sawyer, you and Elodie will go with Patrick over to Tremont to do some exploring of the original release area there. Abby, David, and I will check out Cades Cove."

"Yes, sir." I spoke quietly, not wanting to spook Elodie any more than I already had.

Dad shot me a look, as if wondering why I was suddenly noncombative, but I ignored him and headed for the equipment closet.

I sat in the back on the drive to Tremont and let Patrick do what he was best at. His absent-minded professor look was about as threatening as a flop-eared rabbit, and tended to instantly put people at ease. Elodie was no exception.

She was shy at first, something I found rather fascinating given how readily she'd sparred with me in the clearing yesterday. Then again, I'd clearly underestimated how badly I'd scared her. Note to self: Behaving like an enraged animal while on two feet is not going to earn Elodie's trust. Regardless of my issues with my dad, I was going to have to put a leash on my beast and turn back into something resembling civilized if I wanted a shot with this girl. A shot at what exactly, I chose not to analyze too closely just now.

"So where are you from originally, Elodie?" asked Patrick.

She looked faintly startled at the question, and I wondered why. It was a normal enough thing to ask.

"Your accent," he clarified. "Doesn't sound like you're from around here."

"Oh. No. I grew up in Texas."

When she said nothing else, Patrick shifted gears. "What got you interested in the project?"

"We went on a field trip to Alligator River Wildlife Refuge in zoology my sophomore year, and I was one of the lucky ones to actually see a few of the wolves while we were there. I just . . . They used to range throughout the entire south eastern U.S. and the fact that now there are comparatively so few . . . It makes me sad, I guess. I wanted to do something to help. So when Mr. Jorgensen told me Dr. McGrath was coming, I put in an application."

Well that shot down any crazy notion that she'd somehow discovered my identity and weaseled her way in to get to know me. Not that I'd seriously considered that as an explanation for more than half a second when I first saw her at the conference table.

"You must be quite the student," I remarked, reaching between the seats to snag a handful of chips from the bag of Doritos Patrick had shoved into the center console. "Dad doesn't usually take on anybody below the graduate level."

Elodie shrugged. "I'm good at school."

"More than good, I'd say. Grant said with your credentials, you could have your pick of top schools," said Patrick.

"Maybe if money wasn't an object. I'm hoping the experience I get on the project will help me when I start applying for scholarships this year."

Smart. Thinking of the future. Okay, she totally didn't fit the profile of somebody suicidal. Maybe she really *was* out there for some other reason yesterday. Which just sparked my curiosity all the more. Not that I expected her to actually, you know, tell me.

"So you're making the wolves your cause?" I asked.

"My cause?"

"Sure. Colleges love to see extracurricular causes. Habitat for Humanity. Literacy drives. Blood drives. Race for the Cure. You know, the stuff that says you have a life beyond school and that you're interested in the community or the larger world or whatever."

"You make it sound so bloodthirsty and calculated." Her offended idealism made me smile.

"College applications *are* bloodthirsty and calculated."

Elodie was quiet for a minute, shaking her head in what was probably disgust. "I've heard them," she said at last.

"Pardon?"

"The wolves," she clarified.

"At Alligator River?" asked Patrick.

"No. I mean, yes, I heard them there. But I mean I've heard them here. In the park."

We both looked at her.

"That's not possible," he said.

"I know there aren't supposed to be any wolves here. On our field trip, the guide talked all about the repopulation efforts in various parts of the South during the 80s and 90s and how Alligator River was the only place it had been semi-successful and that the remaining wolves from the last attempt here were taken there. And I know you're thinking it was probably dogs or coyotes, but I know the difference between them and a wolf howling."

Patrick absorbed that for a minute. "When was this?"

"Off and on over the last four years. Mostly at night or at dusk."

A muscle in Patrick's jaw started to twitch, a sure sign that he was excited. But his voice was still bland when he said, "That would be quite the scientific find, Elodie. Have you seen any?"

Elodie shook her head. "No. But they're out there."

I sat back in my seat, frowning. Claims of wolves where there should be none. I didn't like the sound of that. Either there were pups from the last attempt that had survived and reproduced without the original scientists being aware of it—which didn't seem likely given their vulnerability to canine diseases—or there were others of *my* kind in the area. Werewolves are rare and typically so dominant they can't live in packs like normal wolves. I wondered if Dad knew anything about this and if that's what had prompted him to sign on with Patrick to redo a study that had already failed. If he didn't know and there were others in the area, we could have problems.

Chapter 3

Elodie

"Good job today, folks. We'll see you back here bright and early tomorrow morning. Now who can give Elodie a ride home?" asked Dr. McGrath.

Please, please don't let it be—

"I'll do it," said Sawyer.

Nobody else volunteered.

Crap.

"Take the truck," said Dr. McGrath, tossing him the keys. "I'll hitch a ride home with Patrick. We need to go over some things."

Sawyer held open the door. "After you."

I took a firmer grip on my pack strap and went outside. It was just a car ride, I told myself. And a pretty short one at that. There was no reason to get all wound up. But as soon as he shut his door and started the engine, I felt my muscles coil up. Without any of the others as a buffer, there was nothing to distract me from *him.*

At the end of the gravel drive, he turned toward me with a soft smile that put Rich Phillips' grin to shame. "Which way?"

My stomach did a shimmy and my hands clutched my pack in a death grip. "Left."

Seriously, this was ridiculous. There was nothing about this guy that should impede my freaking breathing. He was just driving. In fact, he seemed to have been going out of his way all day to be non-threatening, always moving slowly and

31

talking in that soft voice like I was a skittish horse or something. And, crap, maybe I was. I was *nervous* with him. Not awkward or shy like whenever I was the center of attention, but straight up jittery and ridiculously aware of him at every moment. Ever since he'd taken my hand this morning, my body had been charged up like a freaking Duracell. It was nerve-wracking.

"I wanted to apologize," he said.

I jolted at the sound of his voice, then cursed myself for the reaction. This wasn't like me. Not at all.

"For what?" I managed.

"For scaring you," he said. "I jumped to conclusions yesterday and I reacted. I was really, really angry—not at you—but it just happened to spill over on you when I thought you were . . . Well you know what I thought." He lifted a shoulder in a half shrug. "I just wanted to say that I'm not going to hurt you, and I'm really sorry I freaked you out like that."

He thought I was afraid of him because of what had happened in the clearing. Well, that was a helluva lot less embarrassing than the reality.

"I'm not afraid of you, Sawyer." *At least not the way you think.* "I was just . . . really surprised to see you today."

"That makes two of us. But I have to say that I'm really glad to see you again under less . . . dramatic circumstances."

He was glad to see me? Well didn't that just make my heart go pitter pat? What *was* this? Where was that whole, perfectly-honed ice queen routine I'd perfected over the last three years of high school?

Rather than responding to his comment, I said, "Can you pull off here at Hansen's for a bit?"

Sawyer spun the wheel and whipped into the parking lot.

"Just over to the side of the building, thanks."

"What are we doing?" he asked.

"I need to pick up my bike."

I slipped out of the truck and made a beeline for the dumpster. I'd stashed what was left of my bike behind it when I set out for work. As soon as I dragged it around, Sawyer was out of the truck.

"What the hell happened to it?"

"A classmate of mine backed over it this morning. That's why I was late to work."

He picked it up and hefted it into the bed of the truck. "Were they just not paying attention? Because, damn, you'd think they'd notice this."

"Oh no, she knew exactly what she was doing." I grimaced as the bike clattered into the back. But really, being banged around in a truck bed wasn't gonna do it any further harm.

"Someone did this on purpose? Why?" There was a little growl in his voice that made my belly jump again, but not with nerves. I could tell he was angry on my behalf and, for some reason, that pleased me a great deal.

"She thought I was poaching on her territory. As if I would even look cross-eyed at the likes of Rich Phillips." I could see Rich's truck still parked on the far side of the lot, so I guessed the Barbie Squad hadn't dropped him off from their little water skiing excursion. I shook off the desire to growl myself and climbed back into the truck. "It's a long-standing war—one that's always been one-sided. Her against me."

"Every school's got one."

I directed him back to my road.

"So are you uninterested in this Phillips guy because you're seeing somebody else or because he's a douche?"

I thought of Rich boxing me in this morning, getting me on Amber's radar. "He's attractive, charming, and completely full of himself. And he can't stand the idea that someone won't fall at his feet and be grateful for the attention he pays." I scowled, wishing I had said or done *something* this morning instead of just standing there.

"He hassling you?" The fury from yesterday was back in his voice. When I glanced over, his jaw was tight, his hands in a white-knuckled grip on the steering wheel.

"He's harmless. An idiot, but harmless." But I had a feeling that Sawyer wasn't harmless. I could see so much rage simmering beneath the surface, just looking for an outlet. I wondered where it came from.

Sawyer visibly reeled his temper back in, then shot a half-smile in my direction. "So he is a douche. Although that doesn't rule out option A."

"Option A?"

"That you're seeing somebody else."

It took a minute for my brain to catch up to what he was saying, and when I did, all I could do was stare at him. I'm pretty sure my mouth was actually hanging part-way open, but I couldn't seem to help it. Sawyer McGrath was fishing to find out if I was dating somebody. Which presumably meant that he hoped I wasn't.

"I . . . uh . . ." Oh great. Now I was reduced to monosyllabic stammering. Yes, here sat the future valedictorian of Mortimer High School. Aren't we all so proud?

"It's okay. That's not really any of my business," he said. "I mean, I guess it's weird that I'm asking after how we met yesterday and all. Forget it."

"No," I said.

"No, it's not weird?"

"Yes. I mean, no." Crap. Why couldn't I get my brain to work? "Maybe it is a little weird after yesterday, but no I'm not. Seeing anybody." *And why did you tell him that, genius? Where exactly do you expect this to go? That's right. The train is pulling out of the station to Nowheresville, where you can't date. So stop encouraging him.*

"Good to know," said Sawyer, pulling into my driveway.

Anxious, I looked toward the garage, but Dad wasn't back from his shift yet. He would flip his lid if he saw some guy bringing me home.

I unbuckled my seatbelt. "Thanks for the ride," I told him, hoping my face didn't betray the schizo conversation I was having with myself.

"No problem." Sawyer got out of the truck and retrieved my bike from the back. "Where do you want it?"

Seeing him holding the thing with the taco shell front wheel and the bent frame, I frowned. "I guess I probably should have just had you toss it in the dumpster. Even if I got a new front wheel, I probably won't be able to straighten that frame out."

Sawyer studied it. "Doesn't look good," he agreed.

"I guess just lean it against the wall of the garage there. I'll let Dad decide what to do with it. Thanks."

Relieved of the bike, he seemed not to know what to do with his hands, so he shoved them in the back pockets of his shorts and rocked back on his heels, looking at me.

I felt the blood rushing under my skin and prayed to half a dozen deities that I wasn't blushing like a fire engine. "Um, I'd invite you in for a Coke or something, but my dad is kind of over-protective, and I'm really not allowed to have guys over while he's out." According to The Rules, I really wasn't allowed to have *anyone* over while he was out, but that sounded even more lame and hard to believe. I gave an awkward shrug and half-smile. "Only daughter, single parent, and all that."

"S'ok. I need to get home myself." He took a few steps toward the truck. "Since you're kind of sans transportation, why don't you let me pick you up for work in the morning. It wouldn't be any trouble. We don't live too far from here."

Oh, no. No. I could not have a guy coming to my house to pick me up. Dad would freak and probably put me on house arrest. But it's not like I could hike six miles to work every day.

"Do you think you could pick me up at Hansen's?"

If he thought that was an odd request, he let it pass.

"Sure. Say seven-thirty?"

"I'll see you then. Thanks."

I fiddled with my keys as he climbed in the truck, waved, and drove away.

What. The. Hell. Am. I. Doing?

I was half numb with shock as I unlocked the door and headed for the kitchen to start something for supper. This was stupid. I was acting like a normal girl with a normal crush on a cute guy. It wasn't just stupid, it was dangerous. Both to him and to me. It wouldn't matter if he was a hulking giant of a guy if I wolfed out. Strength was nothing against razor sharp teeth.

I'd spent the last four years of my life doing everything in my power to *avoid* that eventuality. And here Sawyer comes and wrecks my "all high school boys are morons and assholes" rule to live by in just over twenty-four hours, such that I'd gone and accepted a ride to work and *was looking forward to it.*

I pulled some chicken out of the freezer and tossed it in the microwave to defrost. If I didn't get a handle on this and put a stop to it *fast*, this chicken wasn't going to be the only thing that was cooked.

I replayed our conversation from the ride home, reliving every awkward moment in a loop as I gathered ingredients for dinner. On the third time through, I stopped, my hand inches from the bottle of Italian dressing.

He'd just whipped into my driveway. I'd never given the address or pointed out the house, and our name wasn't on the mailbox.

How had Sawyer known which house was mine?

~*~

Sawyer

Elodie Rose is available. I caught myself drumming a cheerful beat on the steering wheel and grinning like a dumbass at the thought. The expression felt so foreign that it kinda hurt my face. There hadn't been much to smile about since Mom died.

And then I stopped.

"What the hell are you doing, McGrath?"

I'd done what I set out to do. I'd apologized for my behavior from the day before. And then I'd *flirted* with her? Poked around to find out if she was dating anybody?

She'd entirely missed the first subtle query, and I could still see the shock on her face when she'd realized what I was asking. That was the expression of someone not used to such attentions. Which just went to prove that the guys here were grade-A, class act fucktards if they hadn't recognized that she was amazing.

She was so cute when she blushed.

But what did it matter if she was dating somebody? It's not like *I* could date her.

Hello? Werewolf. We don't mate outside our own kind. I guess it's not technically impossible. There aren't any genetic incompatibilities. But I never heard of anybody doing it. I mean, it's not like that's a third date confession. "Oh by the way, I can turn fanged and furry at will. That's not a problem for you, is it?" How many humans—given their fear of what they don't know, don't understand—would actually say, "Yeah okay, I can deal with that"?

No, they'd be calling up the men in white coats and trying to have you put away. Or locking you in a cage to test and poke and prod and probably dissect.

It was far smarter to stick to our own kind.

I'd done what I meant to. She wasn't afraid of me. I'd apologized. Mission accomplished.

The best thing, at this point, would be to cut this off before it started. I mean, nothing had been started, really. It's just that we had amazing, off-the-charts chemistry, and she had the power to soothe the savage beast.

Well, we didn't have to be dating or together for her to do that. Just being around her seemed to do the trick. So I'd make nice, be her friend, and squash any idea that this could be anything more. It would be fine.

By the time I took the turn at the end of the road, I was scowling again.

My brain ran back over our conversation on the drive home. If she wasn't dating anybody, then who had I smelled on her this morning? That Rich Phillips guy she mentioned? The one her bike got ruined over? She'd said he hadn't hassled her—or more properly she'd said the guy was an idiot and harmless. I got the feeling Elodie was prone to both understatement and a tendency to handle things herself.

A jackass unable to comprehend the meaning of "No" was not something she should have to handle herself. It wasn't safe. Someone should be watching out for her.

By the time I approached Hansen's again, I felt the beast pacing within me.

A truck pulled out into traffic a few cars in front of me. The same truck Elodie had been scowling at when she'd talked about this Phillips guy. I couldn't see the driver well enough to tell anything but that he had blond hair.

When he turned off into the park, I peeled off and followed.

I don't know why I did it, but I was too cagey and restless to head home, so driving a while longer wasn't a bad thing. Even after my morning run and a day spent hiking, I needed to move. Needed out of the confines of the truck, of society. Of my body. I was desperate to shift and *hunt*. But there were at least a couple of hours until sunset, and I just couldn't risk it.

God, I couldn't *stand* it here.

It'd been bad when we first moved to Mortimer. But it was worse now that I'd met Elodie, to have felt the calm and have it disappear again. Worse now that I'd released some of the chokehold on my instincts. I was going to go mad from inaction. And then where would Dad be with all his careful planning and restriction if I wound up hurting some innocent bystander because I hadn't been allowed to take care of business. Case in point. Why the hell was I following this guy?

The truck pulled off at a trailhead, and I started to slow. Then I saw the little girl get out of the passenger seat and rolled on by. None of my business, and in my current filthy temper, if it *was* Rich Phillips, I wasn't entirely sure I could keep a lid on it. No reason to risk losing control via fists or fangs when there was a child involved. Better that I find some way to decompress.

I could be careful. Hike in deep, find some cave to shift in and leave my clothes. Keep well away from trails. People would be hiking back at this point in the day, if they hadn't already. Wanting dinner, a cool drink, a shower.

I parked at the next empty overlook. There was no formal trailhead here, but I could see a path through the underbrush that had been worn by some intrepid or foolish hikers before me. Lifting my nose I tested the wind, but there were no signs of people. The sounds of other vehicles were faint, far enough away that I could slip over the railing and into the foliage without being seen. Circling around, well out of the view of anyone from above, I pushed my way through the undergrowth until I came out on the forest floor more than a quarter mile below the overlook, hidden by the canopy of trees.

For more than two miles, I kept up a steady lope. It helped a little, burning some of the pent up energy as I kept my nose and ears open for the presence of others, my eyes scanning for a good place to hide and shift. It wasn't a cave that I finally found, but a thick copse of trees that grew so close together, the branches practically knit to form a wall. I pushed through and stripped, then crouched to let the wolf take over.

It had been too long since I last shifted. My muscles bunched and cramped, twitching beneath my skin like a full-body Charlie horse. I gritted my teeth as my frame rearranged itself, bones lengthening to accommodate the additional muscle. Finally with somewhere to go, the clenched muscles loosened, the pressure eased. My claws dug into dirt as I stretched my new form, pushing and dropping my haunches, then dropping my front end low and stretching my hind-quarters all the way down to my toes.

Holy God, that felt good.

I pushed out of the thicket and into the long shadows of dusk. Night wasn't far off and the forest was stirring. It was finally safe to be myself for a while. Suppressing a howl of joy—I had enough human intellect left to know not to push it—I took off at a sprint.

I ran for miles, free for the first time in months to just *be*. Free of rules. Free of restrictions. Free of my father. I wasn't free of the anger, of course. It pulsed below my skin like a second heartbeat. But as a wolf, it felt more manageable, channeled into healthier pursuits, like hunting.

I cast about, testing the air for deer or rabbit, something that would give a good chase. And then I caught the scent. The same male I'd smelled on Elodie this morning. My lips peeled back in a snarl as I lifted my nose, determined direction. East. Toward the trailhead where the other driver had parked.

I shouldn't have followed the scent. Even with some of the pressure released, my temper was still volatile. But I found myself tracking him as the sun sank behind the mountains and the sky bled with color.

When I realized I was hunting, I stopped short, my human intellect throwing on the brakes before I did something irrevocably stupid. I was not in control enough to do this and trust that I wouldn't act. Yet instinct demanded that I do *something* to this asshole for hassling Elodie. Scare him. Rough him up. Teach him a lesson. I needed to protect her.

As if he'd make the connection between a wolf attack and his actions earlier in the day.

I threw back my head and howled in frustration.

And in the distance, I heard a long cry of response.

~*~

Elodie

It was a supremely lousy morning. My body was swamped with the kind of edgy, dragging exhaustion that made me wish I actually liked coffee. The problem of Sawyer had kept me awake into the deep hours of the night when even the crickets and cicadas had gone to sleep.

He'd followed me home from the clearing that day. It was the only explanation for how he'd known where I lived. Combined with his mysterious disappearing act after our confrontation, it added up to one thing: creepy. I wasn't sure which part disturbed me more—that he had followed me or that I hadn't sensed it. I should've been able to smell him at least. Of course I'd been so rattled, it's not like I was paying all that much attention.

He knew where I lived.

Well, duh, he'd have known from dropping me off anyway, but that wasn't the same. He wasn't just my boss's son, a cute guy giving me a ride. He could be a stalker. And contrary to the heroines of some popular teen fiction, I wasn't into that.

I called myself an idiot for my paranoia.

Sure, I felt nervous as hell around Sawyer, but it had nothing to do with fear for my personal safety. I felt jazzed around him, electrified and attracted in a way I'd never felt before. But what if my attraction to him was making me blind to something more dangerous? I couldn't help but think about all the anger I sensed simmering just below the surface. Sawyer was not someone I wanted to piss off. I tried to imagine that rage directed at me, but I wound up less afraid of him and more afraid of what I might to do to defend myself.

I admit that I'm more paranoid than the average teenager. It's kind of a natural byproduct when you're forced to pick up and move across several states, change your last name through less than legal channels, and start a whole new life because your dad believes just enough of your mother's crazy for "just in case". But the idea of somebody I didn't know just standing out there *watching* me, *following* me, freaked me the hell out.

I was glad we were meeting at Hansen's where there'd be people and video footage.

Sawyer was leaning against the back bumper of an ancient brown Jeep when I walked up, his face set in a scowl. His was a real CJ-7, not one of those toy Barbie Jeeps like Amber drove. He was upwind, and I could smell him—that curious mix of evergreen and sweat and wild. And something else that I thought was maybe irritation. The scent made my pulse speed up a notch. I took a firmer grip on my pack strap, as if the gesture was somehow going to steady me.

His gaze swung my way, and I felt the punch of it in my gut, my heart thumping like a tympani in my chest. His mouth curved in a smile that had me thinking all sorts of inappropriate thoughts about what I wanted to do with it.

No. *No.* You do *not* want to make out with the hot stalker guy. The *creepy* stalker guy, I amended.

"Hey," he said.

I tried to relax the white-knuckled grip on my pack, while attraction and paranoia warred inside me. "Hey."

Sawyer tipped his head toward the store. "You need anything?"

A new brain? A boost to my will power? For you to do something unutterably disgusting or hateful so that I don't find you so damned attractive despite the fact that you may have been hanging around outside my house watching me? I shook my head, more in an effort to shake the absurdity out of my brain than an answer.

"Let's go then."

As I climbed into the passenger seat, I glanced around, on edge for a whole other reason as I looked for evidence of the Barbie Squad. The last thing I needed was another run-in with any of them. On that front, at least, it appeared I was safe. Once Sawyer pulled out onto the road, I kept my eyes on the tree line. Maybe if I didn't look at him, it wouldn't be so bad.

The wind whipped my hair, bringing with it a plethora of scents that my brain automatically tried to categorize. My own nerves. Trees. Freshly turned earth. Exhaust from other cars. Some kind of animal. It seemed my nose was getting more sensitive. Or maybe I was getting better at separating things out. I tipped my face up to get a better whiff.

"Morning person," said Sawyer.

"Sorry?" I asked.

"I was trying to figure out if you're a morning person or a night owl. If you weren't a morning person, you'd be hiding behind sunglasses and a thermos of coffee," he said.

I glanced at him, taking in the dark wrap-around shades he'd slipped on and the to-go cup of java from Hansen's in the cup-holder. Covering bloodshot eyes because he'd been up all night hanging outside my house? Ridiculous. "You're speaking in something other than monosyllabic grunts. That must make you a hybrid."

His lips curved in that half smile that shot my internal temperature up five degrees. "Something like that."

I had to look away again, grateful for the cool morning breeze against my hot cheeks. I really, really had to get this under control. What there was of my blunt cut fingernails, I dug unobtrusively into my leg as a distraction. God, at least it was only another couple of miles.

When he passed the turnoff for the research station, I turned back to him. "Where are we going?" The question came out a lot sharper than I'd intended.

Sawyer glanced at me, a frown line between his brows. "Dad's having us meet in one of the north quadrants. He wants to start doing some prey density analysis."

"Oh." I had to work to make my shoulders relax. I could do this. Really, I could.

"You okay, Elodie?" There it was again. That talking to a scared animal tone he used all day yesterday.

Relax. "Fine. Just didn't want to be late two days running."

Huh. Was that weird metallic scent on my skin what a lie smelled like?

His irritation was back again. Good. Maybe he'd get annoyed with my hot/cold routine and decide I wasn't worth the effort.

"You're a lousy liar," he said.

I didn't dare look at him because I didn't have control over my face. "Wh . . . what are you talking about?" *Damn it, damn it, damn it.* Why couldn't I keep my voice steady?

"You're afraid of me again."

Damn straight. Panic fluttered in my belly, and I coiled my muscles prepared to . . . To what? Jump out of the Jeep if he made a move? That was insane. We were going nearly fifty miles per hour.

"What did I do?" he asked.

"You followed me home." The words popped out before I could stop them. Well hell. I'd opened this can of worms. I might as well follow through. "I never told you which house was mine, but you already knew because you followed me home the other day. Didn't you?" My voice didn't squeak as I delivered the accusation. Bonus.

When he didn't immediately respond, I got up the guts to glance at him.

He looked . . . sheepish? Contrite?

"Yeah, I did," he admitted.

Wouldn't an actual stalker be trying to deny the allegation?

"Why?"

"I was worried about you. For all I knew, you were unstable and were just going to pick back up where I'd stopped you. I wanted to make sure you got home okay."

Well didn't that sound reasonable? It was exactly the kind of logical explanation a stalker would come up with.

"And disappearing like some kind of ghost and playing the creepy stalker was a preferable alternative to actually walking me home?"

"Would you have let me?" he countered.

Okay, no, I wouldn't, because I'd thought him every bit as unstable as he'd thought me. "That's not the point."

"What *is* the point, Elodie? I screwed up. I admit it. I freaked you out and followed you home all while trying to do the right thing. End of story."

My head hurt from trying to analyze his scent and tone and words. He was angry, but not enraged. Defensive, but who wouldn't be against such charges? Sitting next to him in silence, the whole thing felt stupid. He probably was telling the truth. A nice person probably would have followed a presumably unstable person home just to make sure they got there without killing themselves. Right?

Before I could make any kind of reply—as if there was an appropriate reply for this situation, we turned into the parking area beside the trailhead, suddenly confronted by dozens of cars and milling people.

"Something's up," said Sawyer.

In a glance I took in the half dozen dogs and the deputies from the Sheriff's Department. "That's the K-9 Search and Rescue Unit. Somebody's missing."

He wheeled into a space beside a park ranger's truck and I leapt out, striding over to where a series of tables had been set up with radio equipment, coffee, and snacks. I recognized Eileen Nichols manning the home base and organizing the tracking log. A dispatcher for the county, I'd known Eileen for years because of Dad's job with the fire department. As she finished giving orders to the assembled K-9 unit, I looked around to see if Dad was here. He was still on duty at the fire station, but that didn't necessarily mean he hadn't been called in for this. Eileen dismissed the assorted dogs and their handlers. I waited until she'd finished making notations in the log before I stepped up.

"Oh good. Somebody on the phone tree got you." Eileen glanced over my shoulder, raised a brow. "And you brought reinforcements. Even better."

I didn't bother to look as Sawyer stepped up behind me.

"I didn't get the call," I told her. "What's going on?"

"Missing kids. One your age. You probably know him. Rich Phillips and his little sister Molly."

My mouth dropped open. "What happened?"

"His truck was found at the trailhead by patrol at dawn, and his parents say he didn't come home last night. Last anybody saw him was when he picked Molly up from her Junior Explorers hike yesterday around 4:30."

"His truck was at Hansen's when I passed by a bit after 5 yesterday. There might be something on the security cameras," I told her.

"We'll get somebody to check, see if we can verify when he left and if anybody else was with him. Your dad's already out in the field with Eddie Richenbach, but I can radio to find out their position if you'd like to join in," said Eileen.

"No!" I said. God, the last thing I needed to do was run into my dad right now. "There's no need to pull him from the search or hold him up waiting for me. Where is he?"

She tapped a finger on his last reported location and showed me his assigned sector.

"And what's not currently being covered?"

She pointed to a couple of other areas. "Can you search?"

I hesitated, spotting Dr. McGrath and the rest of the team on the far side of the parking lot, talking to a couple of park rangers. "Not sure yet. I'm technically working right now."

"That's right. Your dad said you were working as a guide this summer. Well, I know you won't steer anybody wrong. You keep your eyes peeled out there today for that Phillips boy."

Sawyer waited until we started toward his father. "You're part of Search and Rescue?" he asked.

"Yes," I said, my mind already on the search to come.

"And what's this thing about being a guide?"

"What my father—and yours—don't know, won't hurt them." When he said nothing, I felt a spurt of panic and turned toward him. "Sawyer, please. I have my reasons."

He studied me for a long moment before dropping his gaze. I followed and saw that my hand was clutched around his forearm. Horrified that I'd touched him without realizing it, I pulled back.

"Please," I said again.

"Give me your reasons, I'll give you my silence," he said.

I grit my teeth, bit back a growl. "That's blackmail."

"I call it curiosity, but hey, potato, potahtoh."

Narrowing my eyes, I said, "There's no time now."

"Later then."

Chapter 4

Sawyer

Of course Dad and the others agreed to search. One of those missing was a child. Research could wait.

After briefly conferring with the woman who seemed to be organizing things, we were split into groups—Dad and Abby, Patrick and David, me and Elodie—and assigned search sectors. Elodie passed out radios and explained the check-in procedure.

"Be sure to keep a close eye on your heading and make notes on your map." She turned to the other woman again. "Have the dogs alerted anywhere along the trail yet?"

"Here in sector three was the last strong alert. They found Molly's windbreaker. That was about forty-five minutes ago. The Junior Explorers troop leader thinks she left it when they stopped for lunch."

"So maybe Rich brought her out here to find it before they went home," said Elodie.

"That's the thinking. It's the damnedest thing. The dogs were able to follow their scent from the parking lot to about a hundred yards in, then lost it. It's like they up and disappeared."

"We'll find them." She said it with a grim determination that made me suspect she'd stay out as long as it took.

I waited until we were away from the group and into the park before breaking the silence. "So riddle me this, Miss Rose. You can't possibly be old enough to be certified in search and rescue, yet you very definitely seem to know your shit. How is that?"

She was so focused on looking for signs of passage. I wasn't sure she'd heard me. "I'm as close to certified as I can get. My dad has made sure of it. I've passed all the classes and the tests. I just need to be eighteen. When they have searches like this, it's all hands on deck."

"So this is something you and your dad do together?"

"Yeah."

"That's kind of a strange father-daughter bonding exercise," I observed.

"It's practical," she said. "Mountaineering. Survival skills. Tracking. He's been teaching me how to do all of it since—" She cut herself off abruptly. "Since I was old enough to train."

I really wanted to know what she wasn't telling me. but I didn't need my superior senses to tell that avenue of questioning was totally cut off. At least this morning's bout of fear seemed to have abated now that she had something else to focus on besides my questionable behavior.

"Well that's cool. So you and your dad are like the Bear Grylls family of Mortimer?"

She glanced back at me, a trace of amusement on her face. "Do you see me jumping unnecessarily off a cliff or being trailed by a camera crew from the Discovery Channel?"

"Hey, the day's still young."

Her lips curved in a smile that was gone so fast. I almost wasn't sure I'd seen it.

"So what's this whole deal about you lying to everybody about your summer job?"

For a few moments she ignored me. making notations in her notebook. She stalled a little longer by checking our heading on her compass and comparing it to the topographical map she carried. I had a feeling she didn't actually need either. As far as I could tell, she was as at home out here as any of the native wildlife.

When she started moving again, she was agitated, her shoulders stiff, her stride jerky. "I couldn't tell my father about this job. He wouldn't approve."

"Why not? Does he have something against science?"

She took her time answering, hopping down a rocky incline like a mountain goat. I followed fast enough to catch her quiet response. "No. He has something against college. He doesn't want me to go."

"But that's nuts. You're brilliant. If anybody should go to college, it's you. Is it a money thing?"

Elodie glanced at me, her face twisted in frustration. "No. Or it's not just that." She fisted her hands. Flexed them. Fisted them again. "He's afraid."

"Of what?"

She dropped her eyes down to her bandaged wrist. "That I'll turn out just like my mother."

The subtle pain in her voice throbbed like an old wound. There was something here, something to do with what happened in that clearing. The wolf in me wanted to touch and nuzzle, to soothe. Instead, I stayed quiet, waiting for her to continue.

"My dad didn't go to college. He never got the chance. He's been saddled with me since he was seventeen."

"Young to be a dad," I said. I tried to imagine having a kid now. That kind of thing would be life altering in a way I couldn't even fathom.

She flashed me a bitter smile. "Yeah, my parents were a good illustration for the 'Why' of safe sex campaigns everywhere."

"So he's worried about you repeating their mistakes?" That didn't seem to fit with the grief, but single dad of a teenage daughter—it wasn't an unreasonable fear. And it would explain why she hadn't wanted me picking her up at her house.

She was quiet for so long, I didn't think she was going to answer me.

"Three days after I was born, my mother handed me over to my father, checked out of the hospital, and disappeared into the mountains." She stopped, crouching to check something that might have been the heel of a boot print. It must have been nothing because she straightened again and moved on.

"When you say disappeared you mean . . ."

"Disappeared."

"Like the kind of disappeared they'd be calling out search and rescue for?"

Elodie spared me a glance, nodded.

Well that explained the unusual father-daughter bonding.

"I'm not sure how long it took them to realize she was missing, and I don't know that it would have made any difference if they'd gotten a search team out sooner. It was days before anybody found her. By the time they did, animals had savaged her body pretty badly. But it was still obvious that she'd slit her wrists." Elodie absently traced a finger down the veins in her forearms.

The gesture chilled me to the bone.

Jesus. I was devastated by the loss of my mother, but at least she hadn't chosen to die.

"So the other day in the clearing you were . . ."

I didn't really think the prompt would work, but she kept talking.

"Every year I go out on my birthday and I test myself, to prove that I'm not like her. That I'm strong enough to deal with the reality of my life."

I wasn't sure whether to be horrified or humbled.

I did the math. "Wait, three days after you were born . . . so that's today. Today's the anniversary."

She nodded and sucked in a breath. I could hear the tremble of tears when she spoke again. "It's twisted and morbid but there you have it. That's what I was doing when you found me. And that's why I didn't tell my dad about this job. Because he'd have said no as a means to keep me close. And as it happens, I'm more like my mother than either of us realized."

"No you're not." I couldn't help myself. I had to touch her, to brush away the tear that glittered on the curve of her cheek.

"How would you know?" she demanded, rubbing angrily at the stream of others that followed.

I ran a hand down her arm and curled my fingers around hers. "Because you're still here."

She shut her eyes, and I was already cursing myself for sticking my foot in it. But it was the right thing to say. On a sigh, the tension seemed to seep out of her body, her hand squeezing mine for the briefest of moments before she pulled away, moving again in an obvious effort to shake off the mood. "So," she said. "There you have it. That is why I am lying to my father. Satisfied?" There was an edge to her voice that let me know she was still pissed I'd cornered her.

"No."

Elodie whirled and glared at me.

Before she could spew forth what was no doubt an impressive display of temper, I said, "Now I owe you. Fair's fair. So here's a secret nobody else knows: I'm lying to my dad, too."

She shut her mouth, waiting.

It was my turn to feel caged and restless, so I took the lead on the trail. "I got expelled from school eight months ago. Dad keeps pushing me to go to summer school so I can go on off to college in the fall. I haven't told him I already got my GED."

"Why?"

There was the $64,000 question. "I'm not what you'd call 'on board' with his plan for my life."

"You don't want college?"

"I don't know what I want right now. He thinks everything can just go back to normal. That he can just move us across country and start over like nothing happened."

"What happened?"

"My mother was shot." The pain was bright and hot in my chest, and it woke the rage. The beast bristled, and I clenched my teeth, reaching for control. I was not gonna spill this shit on Elodie.

A tiny hand slipped tentatively into mine, squeezed. "I'm sorry."

Anybody else tried to give me sympathy, the beast would snap, but for Elodie, it settled down. So we walked for a while in silence, hand in hand, until I was back in control.

"It shouldn't have happened. She shouldn't have been there. But she was so angry. She and Dad had some kind of fight, and she'd gone out to blow off some steam. Just for a run. And this trigger happy farmer thought she was . . ." I had to stop myself from spilling out the full truth. "I don't know what he thought she was. They said it was an accident."

"You don't think it was?"

I thought of the farmer, shooting at what he thought was a predator. "He didn't see her for what she was."

Elodie said nothing, but I could feel her thumb lightly rubbing the back of my hand. I wondered if her hands stroking through my fur would feel as nice.

"What was she like?"

Her words jolted me out of the alternate reality where she might ever actually see me in fur. I jerked my shoulders, restless as I tried to come up with the words. "Smart. Beautiful." I frowned. All true, but not the essence of her. "She was a free spirit. Didn't like being caged by society." Neither did I. "She had a temper, like I do. But she seldom lost it without really good reason. She was a supreme champion for the underdog in all situations. There was this one time when I was a kid when she went to bat against the town council for a moose." My lips curved at the memory.

Elodie looked a bit perplexed at that. "A moose?"

"You really had to be there, I guess. Anyway, she was . . . grounding. When the world was nuts, she had this way of centering me. Dad too. Of making things feel okay." I looked down at our joined hands. "She was a lot like you actually."

She stumbled and stopped.

Well shit. Two steps forward, three steps back.

But she didn't pull away as I expected. When I looked over in question, her face was tipped into the wind, her gaze unfocused. At that moment, I'm not sure she even remembered I was there.

As I watched, she tilted her head, angling her nose more fully into the wind, and she sniffed in a decidedly canine gesture. *What the hell?* Could she possibly be *scenting* something?

I turned my face into the wind to do exactly that.

And I smelled Rich Phillips.

It made no sense. We were miles from where I'd tracked him last night. And yeah, okay, I didn't actually know where he'd ended up because I'd been busy trying to find that other wolf. What the hell was he doing so far from the original trailhead?

Elodie's expression was uncertain, as if she wasn't sure of her own reaction. Hell, *I* wasn't certain I'd actually seen her do what I thought she'd done. It was completely insane and I was probably just engaging in wishful thinking. She couldn't possibly be . . . like me.

"You okay?" I asked.

She shook her head as if to clear it and flashed an embarrassed smile. "Yeah. Woolgathering. Hearing you talk about your mom makes me wonder about mine. Dad doesn't talk about her much, so other than the bad stuff or whatever they reported in the papers following her death, she's a blank. I don't know what she sounded like, or what her favorite foods were or what kind of music she liked. All I really know is that I look like her. And according to Dad, I'm starting to act like her, which scares the shit out of him."

"That must be hard."

"We have a weird relationship." Now she pulled away, releasing my hand and starting to trudge up upwind in the direction of the scent.

It had to be a coincidence.

~*~

Elodie

I was losing my mind. There was no other answer. We were miles away from the trailhead where Rich and Molly had gone missing, so there was no way that I'd actually caught his scent. And way to take a trip into Weirdsmoville by totally zoning out while Sawyer told me about his mom. Yes, invite deep, personal sharing and then ignore it as if you can't be bothered to pay attention.

The wind shifted and I caught the scent again, jerking my head in that direction to get a better whiff. I wouldn't be sure except that Rich had been so in my face yesterday that I couldn't help but get the smell of him imprinted in my brain if for no other reason than to be able to identify and avoid him for self preservation in the future.

I searched the ground for the usual signs of passage, something to corroborate the idea that they'd passed this way. But there was nothing. Frustration simmered, and I wished I'd been paired up with one of the handlers with a dog. Sawyer wasn't trained for this, and I couldn't track them when there were no physical signs.

The next trace scent proved me a liar.

Okay, so I could track them if I gave in and tried to actually use my newly sensitive nose, but what would that mean for me? Would intentional use accelerate the change? Could I really risk that? This could be, probably *would* be my last summer. Did I want to risk shortening that time on behalf of arrogant, entitled Rich Phillips?

Unbidden, an image of Molly hiding behind her curtain of hair sprang into my mind. She was a child. Innocent. No matter what kind of an asshole her brother might be, she was out there. Tired. Likely dehydrated. Hungry. Probably terrified.

The radio crackled at my waist, pulling me out of my thoughts. "Elodie, do you copy? What is your position?"

I tugged it off my belt. "I copy. Just a sec." I checked the compass and the topographical map and relayed the coordinates back to base camp.

Eileen repeated them back to me, then asked, "Any signs?

There was nothing I could officially report back. Not yet anyway. "No. Have there been any alerts from the other searchers?"

"Bill Throckmorton's Lucy alerted to Rich in Sector Four, but the trail's gone cold. It's looking like a vehicle may have been involved." She paused. "There were traces of blood on the scene. You and Sawyer stick close together. Check in every ten minutes."

"Will do." I dialed the radio volume back down and looked over at Sawyer. His face was grim.

"Foul play," he said. "Has to be."

"Not necessarily," I said, running alternate scenarios through my head. "If someone came across them and they were injured, they could have been a Good Samaritan and taken them to the hospital or something."

"Then wouldn't the hospital have reported back? They'd be notified of the ongoing search, right? That the police are looking. If Rich and Molly had turned up that way, we'd have heard by now."

He was right. I didn't want to think about what that meant. It was one thing if Rich and Molly had gotten lost in the park. It was something else if someone had harmed them.

Screw it, I thought. I was trained to use every resource at my disposal. Now that included my nose. And I had to face it, the change was probably coming anyway. At the very least, maybe I could do something good with it before the end.

I spread out the topographical map and studied it.

"What are you looking for?" asked Sawyer.

"Vehicle access. The alert came in from somewhere in this general area—" I tapped the areas in Sector Four that had access roads. I had to tread carefully here. There was no overt evidence to suggest that they were in our area. "—that would mean there's something of a limit to where someone could take them, if they were inclined to move to some other area in the park. The terrain severely limits vehicle access. I don't know why they'd do that except for privacy. But if they did, there's only a couple of access roads in this area. A couple miles north. Here." I pointed again. "If they came back into the park in a vehicle and came through our sector, it has to be on one of them." It was a decent theory—at least based on all those episodes of CSI I'd watched—and that was the general direction Rich's scent led.

"You're the boss," said Sawyer, grabbing my hand.

I looked down, frowning at how much I liked the feel of his hand around mine.

"We're doing like she said and sticking close," he explained.

"Not gonna argue with that," I told him.

"Lead the way."

I tried to remember what the trainers had said in the two canine search and rescue classes I'd audited. There was something about how scent travelled in a cone, very focused at the source of the trail, and spreading out like a funnel from there. The scent cone was affected by stuff like wind, temperatures, barometric pressure, dust—every little thing changed the edge of that cone and made it harder to track for dogs with a less sensitive nose. Heat made scent rise, but humidity was supposed to be good for enhancing scent. Certainly the early morning damp on the ride in had been full of bright, clear scents. So I just had to keep moving and find the center of the scent cone. Then there should be other physical signs of his passage, like tracks and disturbed vegetation. Those I had a lot more experience following.

I looked up at Sawyer. "Keep your eyes peeled for tracks, any snagged threads of fabric, anything that might suggest people came through here."

"Got it."

When I was sure he wasn't looking at me, I closed my eyes and took another deep inhale. The myriad of scents were so tangled, so *many* that it almost made me dizzy with sensory overload. It was the olfactory equivalent of stepping out in the middle of rush hour traffic in down town Atlanta. *Focus*, I ordered myself. I inhaled again, tugging at the thread I recognized as Rich and teasing it out from the others. Angling my body, I steered us both in that direction.

My shoulder bumped companionably against Sawyer's arm as we moved. Last night's suspicions seemed paranoid and stupid now. Of course he wasn't a stalker. He was a nice guy with protective instincts a mile wide and maybe a little bit of an anger management problem. That was it. I actually felt better having him with me out here, which was weird because I was usually perfectly at home in the woods. Dad had made sure of that.

I looked down at our joined hands and frowned again. Dad would very much *not* approve of this. My better judgment didn't approve of this either, but I still wasn't pulling away.

Rich's scent petered out, and I came to an abrupt halt.

"Damn it," I muttered. I'd been too busy thinking about Sawyer to keep my brain fully on the search.

"What's wrong?" he asked.

"Nothing. Just stubbed my toe." I looked around as if getting my bearings and carefully tested the air. No trace.

"C'mon." He tugged me up a rise.

Frustration simmered. I was angry that I'd let this thing with Sawyer, whatever the hell it was, distract me. Lives were at stake.

Focus came easier this time. Inhale. Sift. Exhale. Repeat. Sixty yards on, my pulse leapt as I caught Rich again, stronger now. My eyes stayed glued to the ground, looking for trampled vegetation or other signs of passage, my attention fully zeroed in on what my nose and eyes were telling me. Everything else was just noise.

The scent pulled me like a beacon, and I started moving faster, until I was the one tugging Sawyer. He kept up with the pace I set, letting me do my thing. If he thought it was weird, he said nothing, and I was grateful for not having to give an explanation because I couldn't think of one.

The scent was so strong now there had to be some kind of physical sign nearby. Urgency beat in my blood. *Close now.* I charged up the hill, Sawyer right with me. We stumbled out onto the narrow access road, and I came to an abrupt stop at the end of Sawyer's arm. I nearly growled in annoyance at the interruption of the hunt.

No, I thought, startled. *No, not the hunt. The search.*

"Where to next?" he asked.

His voice sounded strange, somehow deeper than usual, or more guttural, but I didn't have time to analyze it. I was distracted by a new and more terrifying scent.

Blood.

The world seemed to shrink down to that one focal point. My jaw began to ache, and I realized it was because my teeth were clenched to hold back the growl that wanted to roll out of my throat.

A bolt of panic shot through me.

Sawyer squeezed my hand. "Elodie?"

Ruthlessly I shoved the panic back. I was not going to wolf out. There were too many other signs, other steps, and I hadn't had them yet. It was just instinct, that was all.

I had to find the source of that blood.

"East," I said. My voice came out husky, but still sounded like me.

I followed the pull, my hand gripping Sawyer's as if my life depended on it. I prayed he didn't ask what was wrong because there was no way I could tell him. We moved up the road a few dozen yards. The scent was all but screaming at me. Without it, I don't know that I'd have noticed the navy blue threads snagged on a branch. As it was, I all but pounced on them, tugging off my pack and pulling out a roll of bright orange flagging tape.

"What are you doing?" asked Sawyer.

"Marking the trail." I pointed to the threads. "Might be nothing—" It was definitely something. "—but Rich was wearing a navy t-shirt yesterday."

I circled around from the snagged threads until I found what I was looking for—drops of blood spattered in a single boot print.

Sawyer came around and knelt beside me.

"This isn't Rich's boot. He was in flip flops yesterday, and his feet are bigger," I said. My mouth was dry. "If those threads belong to Rich's shirt, he didn't come through here under his own steam."

"He wouldn't have dripped blood into his own print either," said Sawyer.

I closed my eyes and inhaled, tipping my head toward the bright, copper scent.

No. No, that was wrong. This blood was at least a few hours old. Where was that fresh source coming from?

I opened my eyes and rose, moving in the direction the boot print pointed, looking for more signs.

"Shouldn't you radio into Eileen?"

I should. I was breaking protocol. But I had to find the source of that scent. "In a minute," I said.

The wind gusted, bringing with it a blast of copper-scented air that left me dizzy. I stumbled and went to one knee, my hands fisting in the vegetation around me.

Prey. Fresh kill. Blood. East.

Run.

~*~

Sawyer

Elodie shot up from the ground and bolted.

"Hey!" It was all I could manage when the wolf pressed so close to the surface.

She didn't slow, just continued to run as if the devil himself were right behind. Straight in the direction of the blood source.

I took off after her, viciously suppressing the urge to howl at the chase, at the hunt. She was *fast*, leaping and dodging brush and fallen limbs with the agility of a deer. Fast enough to be like me?

The wolf rose just enough to let me catch her. I started to call her name, to reach out and stop her before she stumbled headlong into what was probably going to be a nightmare. But my mouth was crowded with extra teeth, and I had to fight my own reaction to the rising scent of fresh blood.

So it was Elodie who broke the tree line first. Elodie who stumbled and fell. Elodie who screamed.

I leapt after her, not caring at that moment that I was seconds from shifting, needing only to get between her and whatever had frightened her.

Blood. So much blood and carnage. My head reeled from it until I collapsed to my knees, fingers digging into the earth, curving to claws. Terror sliced through me as I fought the wolf for control, the human part of my brain assessing the scene.

Not now. Not here. The threat is already past. It's over.

The wolf didn't like my logic.

Behind me, I could hear Elodie losing whatever she'd had for breakfast. Then she crawled past me, through the bloody dirt, toward the body, where it lay propped against a tree. She didn't even glance my way, and I wasted precious seconds watching as she reached one shaking hand toward his neck to check for a pulse.

His eyes snapped open and Elodie shrieked, falling back.

"Jesus. Oh Jesus," she said, scrambling to her knees and going back to him.

My hands were still tipped with brutal claws, the wolf not willing to give up its hold in the face of all the blood, so I had to stay put. Even as I fought for control, Elodie seemed to find hers, looking past the gore to assess the situation. That was confirmation enough that my hopes were dashed. No young werewolf could control herself in the face of this.

I beat down the disappointment and wrestled for dominance.

"It's gonna be okay," she said. Her voice was strong, confident as she slung off her pack and began taking stock of his injuries.

She didn't ask him what happened. That's what I wanted to know. There was no way all this blood was his. The scent was too muddied, but there was simply too much of it for him to still be breathing.

Oh Christ, where was the sister?

Elodie's voice jerked my attention back. "Rich, where's Molly?" I didn't need the quaver in her voice to know her thoughts had flown the same way as mine.

"Not . . . make it," he mumbled, eyes starting to roll back.

"Rich!" she snapped, and his eyes focused on her again. "We need to know where Molly is. Was she with you?"

"Got away," he said.

"Got away from where? From who?"

"Don't know. Left her in a cave. Told her to hide. Wait for me. But he found me."

"He who?" she demanded. When that didn't get a response, she shifted gears. "What cave, Rich? What was nearby? Help us help Molly."

The beast was starting to calm down at the sound of her voice, at her rationality.

That's right. Let her do her thing. Settle down so I can help her.

"Was cabin . . . by the river. Where he took us. Got away. But not far enough."

"Do you remember any distinctive features of the landscape. Anything that might narrow down where you were?"

But Rich's eyes rolled back into his head as he passed out again.

Elodie swore a blue streak as she snagged the radio off her belt and turned it back up. "Base this is Elodie Rose. We have Rich. He's alive but badly wounded and only semi-conscious. He's sustained a head wound, probably a concussion. His leg is . . . it's caught in a bear trap."

Bear trap?

I could just see the edges of mangled flesh and the white gleam of bone beyond where she knelt. A growl built low in my throat, and I missed the dispatcher's reply.

"I haven't attempted removal, as I think the pressure from the trap is the only thing that's kept him from bleeding out. Molly is not with him. Over."

There was a crackling pause.

"What is your position?"

As she passed on the coordinates, I staggered to my feet and over to them, pretty sure the wolf would let me have control now. The leg was bad. With no pants or boot to stop the teeth, the trap had dug deep into tissue, shredding muscle and possibly cracking bone. But though he was bleeding, it was evident that Rich's leg was not the source of all the gore.

"Can he be transported to the access road?"

"Not without help," she replied. "We'll need bolt cutters to cut through the chain. The trap is attached to a tree with a spike."

I followed the coil of chain from the trap to where it was pinned to the tree, calculating whether I could yank it loose.

"Patrick and David are nearest you. I'm rerouting them to assist in stabilization. Lynn Petersen and Ralph Fleming will be en route with medical. Is there any sign of Molly?"

Elodie took in the remains around us. She swallowed. "No."

Well that was one fear I could put to rest. I was dimly aware of Elodie relaying what Rich had said about his sister as I paced the clearing, examining the carnage with a more critical eye. Something had been butchered here. Organs and blood were scattered in a wide perimeter around the tree where Rich was trapped. Why? To attract predators? To confuse the scene? I sure as hell couldn't parse out the kidnapper's scent amid all these competing odors.

Elodie was tugging at the chain, when I turned back. The muscles in her back strained with the effort, but the spike didn't budge.

"Help me," she snarled. Her face was white, her jaw clenched.

I crossed to her, laying a hand on her shoulder. "It's not human," I said quietly. "Whatever this is, it's not human remains. It's not Molly."

She closed her eyes and inhaled a shaky breath. "Okay." Another breath, then she took a firmer grip on the chain. "Help me," she said again, calmer this time.

"Let me up front. I'll have more leverage." I nudged her back and took the chain in my hands, wrapping it around my fists. Behind me, Elodie did the same. "On, three. One. Two—"

"Don't move!" she hissed.

I saw it, even as she spoke. A huge black bear shuffled along, sniffing at the remains about a dozen feet beyond the tree. It hadn't noticed us yet, probably because all the blood and guts masked our scent. I hadn't noticed it for the same reason.

It noticed us now, freezing to the spot.

We held perfectly still, watching the bear. The chain links dug into my palms as I clenched it, fighting the wolf for control. A cool head needed to prevail here. This wasn't a grizzly. Black bears weren't as aggressive. This one might just walk away as long as we didn't do anything to antagonize it.

Through the length of chain, I could feel Elodie trembling, and I couldn't stop the growl from rumbling in my chest. If the bear noticed, it gave no sign. Instead, it paced to the side, circling the tree, eyes fixed on us. We should've been backing slowly away, getting out of the bear's territory. But that left Rich. Bleeding, unconscious Rich.

Sure enough, the bear's attention shifted to him as it came around.

Shit.

It lowered its muzzle to sniff at Rich's leg.

Naturally, the idiot chose that second to open his eyes.

"What the fuck?" The words were quiet, slurred with shock, which was probably the only thing that kept the bear from noticing he was no longer playing dead. But his eyes went wide, consciousness seeming to hit him like a freight train.

"Don't move," I gritted out.

I don't know if he heard me. At that moment, the wind shifted, coming from our backs. The bear snorted, clearly catching our scent. The tiny, dark eyes snapped back to us, and I knew then that this thing had never smelled a werewolf before.

Shit, shit, shit.

The bear reared up with a roar.

I shoved Elodie behind me and jumped over Rich, toward the towering bear.

"Sawyer!"

I couldn't reply to Elodie. The wolf had had enough of waiting, enough of the threat to *her,* and rose to the surface, claiming my vision, my teeth. This thing would not touch her.

You wanna dance? Let's dance.

The bear roared again.

I drew breath to reply in kind, to hasten the shift. A shot rang out, dust puffing up at the feet of the bear. It shuffled back on its hind legs. A second shot, another cloud of dirt. Behind me, Elodie began to yell.

"Go on! Get out of here! Get!"

From his spot by the tree, Rich joined her with his own shouts, and since I couldn't yell myself—at least not with a voice sounding remotely human—I waved my arms, even as the third shot was fired.

Deciding it was outnumbered, the bear dropped back to its paws and lumbered off through the trees.

I stood there, panting, staring after it while I struggled to pull back to fully human. Horror came swiftly on the heels of relief. I'd nearly shifted in front of Elodie and Rich. Yes, it would have been to protect them, but holy hell, how *stupid* could I be? What the fuck was wrong with me? The shock was enough to finish the change back to human.

Feet crunched through the brush and a hand fell on my shoulder. "You okay?"

I swung my head around to meet Patrick's worried gaze. My voice was gruff, but human when I replied. "Yeah. Yeah, just kinda shaken up."

I didn't ask where he'd gotten the rifle. I was just grateful he'd shown up when he did.

Elodie and David where kneeling by Rich as another couple materialized from the trees. Lynn and Ralph, I presumed, taking in the bags emblazoned with a big red cross on the side.

"What happened?" Ralph demanded. "We heard shots."

"Bear," said Patrick. "Fired some shots to scare it off."

The pair of them stopped, taking in the carnage of the scene.

"Holy hell," said Lynn, her face going two shades paler. She shook herself and crossed to Rich, unshouldering the bag.

Somebody's radio crackled. "Transport is on the access road due west. What's your status on getting that trap loose?"

"We just arrived," answered Lynn.

"Bolt cutters are coming to you. Sit tight."

Ralph unpacked a collapsible stretcher. "Gonna need this to get him outta here."

I felt useless as the trained personnel came in and took over. Even Elodie was nudged back as Lynn took over. She stood there watching, face drawn, arms crossed over her torso. God knew what she was thinking. My brain scrambled over what had happened, trying to figure out what she might have seen of my partial transformation.

Taking a bracing breath, I walked over to her. She turned to face me and the color that had returned to her cheeks faded again.

"Elodie," I began.

But she wasn't looking at me. She was looking past me, toward the tree line where a tall, sandy-haired man stood with a pair of bolt cutters in hand, staring right at her, a grim expression on his face. Who the hell was this? His eyes flicked to me momentarily, and I felt the chill even across the clearing. Beside me, I felt Elodie draw herself up, square her shoulders, waiting as the man crossed over to us.

I could smell the anger on him, and my protective instincts were roused. But before I could do anything like step in front of Elodie, she opened her mouth to speak.

"Hi, Dad."

Chapter 5

Elodie

Despite the sticky summer air, I felt chilled as I faced my father. He took a pointed glance around at the carnage then looked back at me, gray eyes as hard and flat as gun metal as they searched my face.

"You okay?"

I heard what he was really asking. *Are you feeling wolfish? Are you going to change?*

I thought back to my mad dash toward the scent of blood. The temporary loss of control before I pulled myself together again. "Yes, sir, I'm fine."

He nodded once. Momentarily satisfied with my answer, he crossed over to Rich and applied the bolt cutters to the chain. I wrapped my arms tighter around my middle. There were so many opportunities for this lie to blow up in my face. Patrick was a dozen feet away from my father, talking to Ralph. What if he said something about the project? About my internship? And, dear God, what happened if Dr. McGrath showed up? He'd probably do something really horrible, like compliment my dad on having such an academically accomplished daughter. Jesus. There was a distinct possibility I was going to be sick again.

Sawyer was watching me, but I didn't dare look at him. I could tell he wanted to say something, and I really, really needed him to be a stranger right now. Just some guy I was supposed to lead on the trails today, who'd decided to help with the search.

With a metallic clink, the chain slithered to the ground. All the grownups converged to move Rich, trap and all, to the collapsible stretcher. I felt really superfluous now. As he helped heft the stretcher up, Dad shot me a look that clearly said, *Don't go anywhere.* They disappeared into the trees, back toward the access road where a transport waited to take Rich to the hospital.

Unable to be still any longer, I moved over to the tree, running my fingers over the spike and the short bit of chain still dangling from it. There were too many scents competing now. Everybody had touched it, compelled to test for themselves how stuck the thing really was while we'd been waiting for the bolt cutters. I began to circle the tree in an ever widening radius, keeping my eyes on the ground, my nose open, looking for something, anything that might be a clue to who had done this or where Molly might be.

Sawyer fell in beside me. "You okay?"

Unlike my father, I knew he really was asking how I was coping with all of this. Because he seemed to care about my well-being. Was it just my well-being? He had, after all, freaking thrown himself *in front of a bear* to protect me. I was torn between admiration at his bravery and horror at his utter stupidity. I wondered if it was symptomatic of his apparent hero complex or if there was something more to it.

"I don't know," I admitted. "We found Rich. Great. Molly's still out there, somewhere. And there's obviously some kind of psycho out there too because nobody sane or normal did this. So, I really don't know what to think."

"They'll find Molly," he said.

He didn't say what I knew we were both thinking. *In what condition?*

My stomach rolled again.

We made it outside the worst of the charnel stench, and I still couldn't find signs of anyone's scent but those people already present. I didn't know anything about how somebody might cover that kind of trail or why they'd think to, unless they knew about the search and rescue dogs and were trying to throw them off the scent somehow. Maybe that's what that butchered animal was about. Confusing the dogs. I really hated the implications of that. That it could be someone related to K9 Search and Rescue. I'd known those people for years, and I couldn't imagine any of them being off their rocker enough to have done this.

I glanced up at Sawyer. He'd been affected as strongly or stronger than I was when we'd stumbled into this mess, then put it away, as I had, to do what needed to be done. He seemed to be making a concerted effort *not* to look at the butchery now. A muscle in his cheek twitched and his Adam's apple bobbed as he swallowed. He was clearly fighting to hold it together.

And then I remembered.

My mother was shot.

Dear God, had he been there? Had he seen his mother's body?

For all my research into my mother's death, I really only had my imagination and the coroner's report to tell me what it was like. But to actually see it happen or see the immediate aftermath . . . If he had, then this whole disgusting mess was bound to remind him.

"Sawyer—"

"Elodie."

I snatched back the hand I'd been reaching toward Sawyer and scrambled to wipe the guilt from my face as I turned toward my dad's call. My pulse beat fast and thick in my throat, but my voice came out normal. "Yes, sir?"

I searched his face, looking for any traces of condemnation, of disappointment. Mostly he just looked pissed and worried. But he wasn't hustling me away, so maybe Patrick hadn't said anything.

71

"The sheriff is here. He wants to talk to you." Dad's attention shifted to Sawyer. "Both of you."

"The sheriff?" Okay, yeah, that squeak didn't sound at all nervous. Not.

Sawyer shifted beside me, the back of his hand brushing mine. Probably it wasn't intentional, but it steadied me. He seemed to have his own issues with the idea of law enforcement. Though he didn't outwardly react, his scent changed. Not nerves or fear. Something else. A quick reaction, gone almost before I could catch it. I filed it away as something to analyze later.

Dad just gave me a *hurry up* look.

Okay, suck it up and deal. You haven't done anything wrong. At least not in the eyes of the sheriff. Squaring my shoulders I started trudging through the trees.

I don't know why the idea of talking to the sheriff made me anxious. It's not like I've ever been in trouble. But the whole purpose of my life was to stay below the radar, so being put in the spotlight with an authority figure, even when I didn't do anything wrong . . . well, it made me nervous. It didn't help that I was totally flipping out that my dad might find out my lie, and if I didn't get a handle on this *stat*, I was going to look like I *really* had something to hide.

Dad fell into step behind me, shoulder to shoulder with Sawyer, like some kind of entourage. They were both looking at me. I could feel it, like an itch between my shoulder blades.

I'd met Sheriff Beasley, of course. He was a routine fixture on all search and rescue operations. But he'd never actually, you know, talked to me before. Then again, I'd never been the one to find the missing person before, so I guess he'd never had reason to.

A couple of deputies passed us as we emerged onto the access road. One carried a roll of crime scene tape. Usually at this point in a search, the mood was jubilant, with everybody looking forward to a shower and good food as a celebration of victory. But this search had only been half successful so far, and the deputies' grim expressions reflected that.

A small group of people gathered around the sheriff's cruiser, studying a map. A fresh bout of nerves started bouncing in my gut as I saw Patrick and David among them. Not like it was a shock. Where were they going to go? As I neared, I could see that someone had made markings on the map in red Sharpie, showing where the search had begun and all the points where the dogs had alerted. It was a duplicate of the one I knew Eileen was maintaining at the base camp. I buttoned down the panic. I was definitely not the object of conversation here, so it was unlikely that my internship was going to come up. Right?

"You wanted to see me, sir?" I said.

All eyes turned to me, and it was like a repeat of walking into the research station yesterday. *Too much attention.* My palms started to sweat.

"You're the one who found the Phillips boy?" asked the sheriff.

"Yes, sir. Sawyer and I did."

Sawyer stepped forward. *That's right. Don't leave me standing here by myself. You were there too.*

"What did he say about what happened to him and his sister?"

Sawyer let me do the talking. The more I told Sheriff Beasley, the deeper the creases around his mouth became, until he resembled nothing so much as an angry English bulldog who'd aged a decade before my eyes. He didn't ask me anything about how I'd found Rich.

When I finished, he radioed back to base and had them reorganize the search along the river.

"Where do you want us to reconvene?" I asked.

"Nowhere," said Dad. "We're done for the day."

"But Molly—"

"The rest of the team is still out there looking. They'll find her. You're done. We're going home," he said.

73

The chill crept back. The search wasn't finished and Dad was pulling us both out? Crap, this couldn't be good. The sheriff was thanking us for our efforts, telling me what a good job I'd done, but I heard almost none of it. I was too busy trying to figure out what this meant and how I was going to cover my butt.

Patrick walked over, and I felt a fresh spurt of panic. *Oh God, don't let him ask if I can come to work the rest of the day.* Instead he looked over at Sawyer. "Give you a ride back?"

"Sure."

Sawyer turned to me, looking again like he wanted to say something. Instead he said, "Later," and pulled one of those male head jerks that's supposed to count as a wave.

Okay, good. Great. One potential threat down. Two more to go.

I made a generic wave to everybody, and walked past David and Patrick without catching their eyes as I made my way up the road to where Dad was standing by our ancient Ford pickup. He said nothing as I climbed in, just cranked the engine and pulled a three point turn to head back toward home. I quietly watched him out of the corner of my eye and tried to figure out exactly how deep in it I really was.

~*~

Sawyer

No, really, I'm not a stalker, I thought as I crept through the woods to the edge of Elodie's property. There were so many things *wrong* with what I was doing. It was broad day, and I shouldn't be on four feet, but I could move faster this way and I trusted that my fur gave me enough natural camouflage that no one would notice me. I shouldn't be here again, particularly after Elodie had busted me this morning. I knew that. But, she was afraid again. And this time it wasn't of me. She was scared of her father.

I didn't like it. And maybe she hadn't asked for a guardian werewolf, but if something was going on with her dad that shouldn't be, I wasn't going to leave her to face it alone.

I'd watched the old black pickup disappear from view, already calculating how I'd get away. The opportunity presented itself when we'd returned to base camp so I could pick up my Jeep. The call came in that they'd found Molly Phillips, alive and terrified, but unharmed, somewhere along the river, exactly as her brother had said. It was easy to lose myself in the midst of all the celebration.

The argument was in full swing by the time I got within listening range of Elodie's house.

" . . . the hell did you think you were doing?" Her father, showing none of the emotional control he'd displayed in public.

"I was on the search just like—"

"No. No, it wasn't like any other search because you were not out there with an adult. You were on your own with some other *kid.*"

Never mind that this "kid" can do more to protect your daughter than any member of that search team, I thought.

"And we found Rich," said Elodie in a reasonable tone. "What are you so upset about?"

"What am I upset about?" His voice went up several decibels, and I found myself leaving the shelter of the trees and slinking closer to try and peer in the picture window on the back porch. "There's some kind of lunatic out there and you're just wandering around with no protection. I don't know what the hell Eileen was thinking."

They were in the living room, squared off on either side of a coffee table. Mr. Rose paced in agitation, rubbing both hands over his short hair. By contrast, Elodie was still. I could read the tension in her body, see the temper she was holding back as she tried to stay reasonable.

"What would you have had me do, Dad? Nobody knew it was as bad as that until after we were already out. I followed protocol. I radioed in as soon as we found him. I stayed with my partner. There was nothing about that search prior to finding Rich that indicated we were in any kind of danger, so you can't go blaming Eileen for sending me out. This is what I've trained for, what you've made me."

"I did not train you to put yourself at risk."

She folded her arms, the first suggestion of belligerence I'd seen. "And exactly what risk would you be referring to? The idea that I was out in the park, off trail and unarmed, or the fact that I could have been compromised?"

What the hell did she mean by compromised?

Her father whirled at the statement, his face going pale. "Were you?" he demanded.

She spread her arms and pivoted once before walking over to get in his face. "Do I look compromised?"

He stared at her, looking for . . . I didn't know what. She just looked like herself.

"Would you tell me if you were?" he asked.

Something flickered across her face. "Of course. I'm not Mom."

Mr. Rose flinched. Obviously Elodie's mom was as big a sore point with him as mine was with my dad. His shoulders slumped and he reached out, curling a hand around the back of her neck. "Ellie," he sighed, drawing her into a hug. "I just don't want to see you—"

"I know," she said.

"I can't go through that again. Not with you."

Go through what? The suicide?

"Look, no more going out in to the park on your own. No going off trail."

Great, finally the man says *something* I whole-heartedly agreed with. Elodie being out on her own was reckless and unnecessarily risky.

"I'll talk to your boss—"

"*I'll* talk to my boss," she interrupted. "I'm sure he'll want to change procedure, be sure we keep to large groups. There will probably be a staff meeting in the morning after the sheriff makes whatever proclamations he's going to make about safety in the park."

"Okay, fine. But I'm serious. Be careful. Regardless of our own personal . . . problem, there's still some nut job out there who kidnapped Rich and his sister. They're lucky to be alive. Promise me you won't take any unnecessary risks."

"I promise."

He kissed her forehead. "You wanna cook or call for pizza?"

Food. The universal sign of truce.

"Pizza," she said. "Double pepperoni. We're celebrating a successful rescue."

"I'll call it in," he said.

"Okay. I'm going up to change." Elodie started across the room.

"Elodie."

She stopped in the doorway, carefully wiping the expression of *oh shit* guilt from her face before looking back at him.

"I love you, honey."

Why did that sound so hard for him to say?

Judging by the look on her face, it wasn't something Elodie was used to hearing. "Love you too, Dad." Then she went on and bounded up the stairs.

That was possibly one of the strangest conversations I'd ever overheard between a parent and kid. Clearly *something* was going on, but I didn't think it involved her dad being some kind of abuser or molester, so I slunk back into the trees and began to make my way toward home.

What was Elodie hiding?

This obviously went well beyond the bounds of an over-protective, single dad looking out for his teenage daughter. *I could have been compromised.* It was such a strange thing to say. Whatever she meant, it wasn't a matter of her virtue. It had something to do with the scene where we'd found Rich. Something other than the obvious threat of whoever had done it still being loose. But how could that have compromised her?

Was it her emotional stability he meant? That somehow the blood and death would send her over the edge like her mother?

No. Elodie was clearly rock steady on that front. It had to be something else. Yet still something to do with her mother. Some secret she'd kept from Elodie's father. What was the connection between her mother, who'd killed herself seventeen years ago, and the bloody scene of today?

Dad was waiting in the garage when I drove up, perched on a stool at the makeshift lab that lined one wall. A half empty bottle of water sat on the table in a ring of condensation. He didn't turn as I walked in, but I knew by his too careful stillness that something was wrong. Tension coiled in my muscles as I prepared myself, though I wasn't sure if it was to receive bad news or for a fight of some kind.

He didn't turn as he spoke. "Where have you been?" The question came out weary rather than accusatory, so I unbent enough to answer with semi-honesty.

"Elodie's."

"Why?"

Okay, this whole talking to his back thing was annoying me. "I went to let her and her dad know that the little girl had been found. Elodie was really worried about her."

"And what about last night?"

"Excuse me?"

"Where were you last night? You didn't come home until hours after you dropped her off."

A fight then, I thought. "I didn't realize I had such an early curfew," I said, crossing to the mini-fridge and grabbing a bottle of water for myself.

"You didn't answer the question."

"I was out."

"Out," he repeated, a low thrum of anger seeping into his voice. "And I suppose that's why I found *this* on our search today?"

He swiveled and held out his hand. In the center of his palm lay a large tuft of grayish white fur. Mine.

Shit.

"So I went for a run. So what? I was careful."

"And what exactly would you have done if it had been Patrick who'd found this?"

I jerked my shoulders in a shrug. "It's fur. There are no timber wolves in this area naturally, so logic would dictate that it was from somebody's Malamute or a wolf-dog hybrid. Occam's Razor. The simplest explanation is usually the right one. There's no reason why he should think it was from a wild wolf and no reason why he or anyone else should connect it to me."

"You were out near where that boy disappeared. Your scent trail crossed his."

I shrugged again. "I scented him while I was out. Followed his trail for a while, then got distracted." By that other wolf, which I still hadn't told Dad about. Now didn't seem to be the time. I twisted off the cap of the water and took a drink, waiting to see where he was going with this.

He said nothing, just continued to stare me down, his gold eyes the only sign his patience was waning.

I lowered the bottle, slowly. "You don't think I had something to *do* with this, do you?"

"Did you?"

"No!" I exploded. "How could you think that? What motive would I have for stalking some guy and his kid sister?

They were both attacked and drugged. I don't have access to that kind of stuff."

Except that I did. I realized as soon as it was out of my mouth that we had tranquilizers both here and at the research station.

Still, he said nothing. Watching me. Waiting for me to slip up. My temper spiked. I couldn't believe he was accusing me of this. But blowing up at him wasn't going to help my case. So I thought of Elodie and searched for patience. "I didn't drug them. I didn't even see them. And I sure as hell didn't modify a bear trap to hack halfway through that guy's leg, then tear up a deer nearby for shits and giggles in order to attract predators. All I did was go for a run. That's it."

Dad let out a breath and his eyes faded back to their usual green. "Okay."

I blinked at him. "Just, 'okay'?"

"You say you didn't do it, I believe you. But son, you've got to be more careful."

"Is this the part where you point out that there's some psycho out there like a normal parent? Because we both know I can protect myself."

"We both know that doesn't necessarily mean jack shit. You have to see the threat to defend against it."

The stab of pain hit just below my breastbone. Mom. If she'd been attacked directly, she probably would have survived.

"I can't take it if something happens to you too," said Dad quietly. "So please, promise me you'll be careful."

"I promise."

~*~

Elodie

By some miracle I held it together through dinner. Dad didn't seem to catch on to all the lies I was spouting, so clearly I deserved an Oscar for my performance. Bully for me. I even managed to scarf down three slices of pizza, though the meaty, cheesy goodness sat like lead in my stomach. He'd have noticed if my appetite had changed. And while I could have blamed it on Rich and what I'd seen, I knew he'd pay more attention if I did. So I stuck to the everything's fine, everything's *normal* routine until I got upstairs to my room. Then I promptly shut and locked the door, went into the bathroom, turned on the shower to mask the noise, and lost my dinner.

The shakes started then. Full body tremors. I wanted to fight them, to tense up my muscles and simply *refuse* to give in to my body. But after the day I'd put in, I just couldn't. I stripped out of my clothes and crawled in the shower, sinking down to sit beneath the steaming spray. Jesus, I was cold. And achy. Like that time I'd had the flu when I was twelve. The last time I'd been really sick.

I'd forgotten how much it sucked.

As long as I was wrapped in the cocoon of steam, my senses focused on the drumming spray, I didn't have to think, didn't have to consider what I'd done today. But eventually the hot water ran out. My skin was all pruney and sensitized from the beating as I stepped out, still freezing. Quick as I could, I toweled off and bundled up in my flannel pjs, buried deep in the drawer from winter. Then I practically hurled myself beneath a mound of blankets on my bed and lay there, shaking.

Oh this was not good. This was *so not good.*

If the fevers were starting, there was no denying that I'd pushed the envelope today.

Who was I kidding? I'd been pushing the envelope for days, ever since I woke up smelling that bacon. The change was coming. After all the years of being so careful, of doing everything right, it was happening anyway. All I'd managed to do was delay the inevitable.

My mother had been right.

I'd never *really* believed it. That I was cursed. I mean, seriously, who honestly believes in *curses?* That's the stuff of fiction and fairy tales.

Which is fitting, I suppose, since my family spawned a fairy tale. You know the story of Red Riding Hood? Yeah, that's my great, great, many times over great grandmother. The original version, before it got diluted and Disneyfied, was a morality tale, meant to keep good young women chaste and obedient.

According to the story I'd parsed out from the journal—which had been a slow process, as I'd had to translate some pretty archaic French—this all started with a girl named Sabine. Sabine was a good girl, pious, devout, submissive. A real testament to her family. Then she fell in love with some guy. They met on the road outside her village. She was on her way to visit her grandmother, who was ill. He was, well, I couldn't quite figure out the translation. It was something like "wanderer." I'd always romanticized it to him being some sort of Gypsy. But whatever he was, her family didn't approve. So they forbade her from seeing him. Of course. Because *that* always stops headstrong women from doing whatever they want. She had an affair. I don't know how long it went on, but eventually, Sabine's wanderer convinced her to run away with him.

Her family found out and intercepted them, killing the wanderer for besmirching their daughter's virtue. Sabine got shipped off to relatives in some other part of the country. Right around that time, it came out that she was pregnant. She was married to some other guy in a hurry. Sabine's husband was a good guy by all accounts, a widower with a son by his first wife. When Sabine's daughter was born, he took her as his own, and everything was hunky dory for a while.

But the daughter, Brynne, was wild, even more so than her mother. By the time she was fifteen, she'd gotten involved with some guy. She was brazen about it, which really flew in the face of the morality of the time. Her stepfather decided to put a stop to it, and I don't know what exactly that he did, but I can guarantee it wasn't some emotionally touchy feely intervention Dr. Phil style. Things got physical and she . . . well, she changed. That went over like a lead balloon and he attacked her. According to the journal, she killed him in self defense, then left her village alone, scared, and—like her mother before her—pregnant. It pretty well went that way from generation to generation—not with the killing part, but with each generation bearing a daughter who also reached sexual maturity and turned into a werewolf. I'm really not clear where the whole idea of a curse entered into things, but the story perpetuated in various versions throughout the journal was that Brynne was Sabine's punishment for her lack of virtue.

Nobody really talked about love until my mother.

According to her, she and my dad were a Romeo and Juliet, wrong-side-of-the-tracks, love story. They fell in love in high school—a blistering, lightning-strike, love-at-first-sight kind of thing. They kept their relationship quiet because their families would never have approved. When Mom got pregnant, she went through hell keeping my father's name a secret, no matter what her dad said or did, she held her silence, and they planned.

She was supposed to give me up. It's what her father was expecting. One of those private adoption deals to a couple in another town. Her mother, of course, wasn't around anymore to issue an opinion. But instead of some strange couple, she handed me over to my father. He took me, left town, and waited for her. She was supposed to take a Greyhound bus to meet him a few days later, once she was out of the hospital. But she never showed.

He told me she'd died from complications. That's less scarring, I suppose, than telling your child that her mother slit her wrists, which is what I found out after some unauthorized snooping in his room turned up the newspaper articles about her death. I was ten. It was kind of hard to keep believing the illusion of their love story after finding out she'd made the choice to leave us. The fact that Dad still believed it made him seem kind of sad and deluded. I didn't have the heart to bring it up. But even he didn't know the real truth. Not until the letter. Now I wonder if he wishes he left me behind.

I knew Dad believed. Or believed enough that he was willing to uproot us and force me into this fringe existence where the most important Rule was to remain unnoticed. He'd been *scared* after we got the letter and the journal. He'd never told me why. I'd gone along with it because it's what he wanted. I figured I would pass the age that Mom died and he would finally accept that the only thing that was being passed down the female line was some kind of mental disorder. Because, seriously, which is more logical: that I was the latest generation of a curse that follows the female line of the family because some long distant ancestress couldn't keep her skirts down or that my mother was a raving lunatic?

I'd been all prepared to admit my own insanity if it came to that. Because surely if I'd begun to think that any of these physical changes were truly happening, it would be nothing more than a delusion.

But I couldn't argue with what I'd done today.

Apparently great-great-great—however many greats— Grandma Brynne had passed on something worse than big feet or an overbite or any of a million other inheritable genetic traits. Because it had to be genetic. I was too much a scientist at heart to believe in anything like curses. Looking at this story as a true scientist, it wasn't Sabine but her lover who'd introduced the werewolf gene. And evidently it was dominant. Like how the offspring of a brown-eyed person and a blue-eyed person was probably going to be brown-eyed, unless the brown-eyed person had a blue-eye recessive gene to pass on. My AP Biology class hadn't covered genetics in enough detail to explain why only daughters had been born from the line, but I figured there was some scientific principle out there that covered it.

Punnett squares weren't going to fix my problem, though.

In the end, it didn't matter whether it was genetic or a curse or straight up magic. It was *happening*. To. Me.

And I didn't know how to stop it.

Chapter 6

Elodie

Someone is watching me.

I twitched my shoulders and resisted the urge to look behind me. Again. Because that would be too much of an admission that in the last two weeks, I'd turned into a paranoid freak. Okay, maybe not so much a freak. The whole town was on edge. It wasn't a shock, really. We'd gotten Rich and Molly back, but nobody had been caught and punished for it. Whoever had snatched them was still out there. Somewhere. The sheriff was hypothesizing that whoever had done it had moved on when his plans were spoiled. Lots of people wanted to believe that, for obvious reasons. No one wanted to believe that one of our own was responsible for instilling night terrors in a ten year old or for Rich being laid up in the hospital still after having reconstructive surgery on his leg.

The part that made me a paranoid freak was that I was starting to wonder if the kidnapper was after me. Which was crazy. Because why would someone target me? I was nobody. I mean, unless you were a werewolf hunter who somehow managed to track my family line down despite all the ridiculous precautions my dad had taken to make us disappear. And what was the likelihood of that? The journal didn't report any hunters for at least three generations. The entire point of my life was to stay off everybody's radar, and I was really good at it. Well, except for the Barbie Squad, but who listened to them? No one noticed me.

"Yeah, that's the girl that found the Phillips boy."

I froze, my hand inches from the pack of paper towels. Okay, nobody had noticed me before I rescued Rich. Since then, I seemed to have acquired a certain level of notoriety, which Dad was less than pleased about. Given my aversion to being the center of attention, I didn't care for it either. But that didn't mean that someone was out to get me. What happened to Rich and Molly had absolutely nothing to do with me.

I looked casually down the aisle, first one way, then the other, frowning when I didn't see anybody. Weird. She'd sounded like she was *right there.*

I grabbed the paper towels and stood, scanning over the top of the shelves for the others. Sawyer, David, and I were on a supply run at McIntyre's Grocery and Mercantile. I'd learned a lot in the last two weeks on the job with Dr. McGrath. Not the least of which was the fact that, no matter how smart I might be, I was still even lower than an undergrad intern on the totem pole, and that meant I was a grunt, often relegated to the simplest and most boring of jobs. Any dreams of making some glorious scientific discovery that would immortalize my name in scientific journals had pretty well evaporated by now.

Still, I liked the work. I learned a lot through observation, and at least I got to be outside in the park. And I got to be with Sawyer. Not like anything had happened. No matter how I might wish otherwise, we were just friends. I knew that's all we could be. Whatever was happening to me, I wasn't willing to risk that final alleged catalyst. But hanging out with him was my guilty pleasure. Despite his protestations to the contrary, he was smart, almost reluctantly so, and he had a wicked sense of humor. When I was with him, I didn't feel paranoid and freaked out. And strangely, I thought I was a good influence on him. Which sounds totally arrogant and stupid. But the anger he carted around like a shield seemed to take a backseat when he was with me, and it seemed like, maybe, he was starting to heal from his mother's death.

On the far side of the store, I spotted two women looking at me and whispering. They were trying to look casual, glancing down at the end cap display, then back at me. I recognized them in that way that you recognize the faces of people you pass on a semi-regular basis in a small town, but I didn't know them.

"I heard he was just covered in blood and gore—from some animal that maniac killed and spread around, but still—and she just radios in, calm as you please. That girl's got ice in her veins." The voice was as clear as if she'd been shouting.

Oh shit. The words sounded almost like praise, but were layered over with disgust. I wasn't sure if that was for the maniac, the gore, or my professional attitude. I shouldn't care. I didn't care. I just wished she would shut up and leave.

"You okay?"

I jolted, bumping into Sawyer, who'd come up behind me with that curiously silent gait of his.

He put a hand briefly on my arm to steady me. "Bit jumpy today?"

Immediately I mourned the loss of his touch.

"Everyone's jumpy," I retorted.

His dark eyes searched my face, and I felt, not for the first time, as if he could see past all the walls and armor and defenses. Past the bullshit that kept everybody at arm's length.

"What's wrong?"

I really needed to work on my technique. "They're talking about me." I jerked my head toward the two old biddies, whose teased up hair seemed to bob with the animation of their conversation.

He lifted a brow. "And we have super hearing, do we?"

Apparently yes. "They keep looking over here while they're talking," I said defensively. "So unless I have something on my face that merits a distraction from their true conversation, they're talking about me."

Sawyer gave them a withering look. Both women's cheeks reddened, and they moved on down into one of the taller aisles. He turned back to me and smiled. "Problem solved."

My pulse skittered. "My hero," I said.

"C'mon. David's waiting at the register."

We added our purchases to the pile and checked out, each of us grabbing a couple of bags to lug back to David's Explorer. We'd had to park a couple of blocks away because they were doing some kind of work on the utilities under the street. The whole thing was a mess, with a clump of workers drilling down with jack hammers to get past the pavement. The noise was deafening, a staccato rumble that made my ears ache. The hammering stopped, but there was no silence. Cars drove by with a roar. Somebody coughed and sounded like they were right beside me. A shop bell jingled somewhere over a door. Down the street a kid shrieked and sprinted away from his mother.

"Tommy!" The mom tone snapped out, stopping the kid in his tracks. I could hear the crunch of his shoes on the grit and bits of gravel on the sidewalk across the street.

My head felt swimmy with too much input. Holy crap, how did Superman deal with this? *Focus on something*, I thought. That had worked with my sense of smell.

"They say that it'll be months before the Phillips boy will walk again. And the little girl refuses to leave the house."

I cocked my head, tuning in to another conversation from somewhere up the street.

"I heard the parents are considering moving the whole family away."

"Well who could blame them? I sure couldn't rest easy if my child was kidnapped and drugged and who knows what all and nobody was caught for it. It's such a shame, really.

Mortimer was always such a peaceful place. There's not supposed to be any of that kind of nastiness here."

"As if bad things never happen in small towns," I muttered.

Something jerked me backward. My heart jolted, and I flailed, dropping the bags and slamming into something just as a pickup careened by, inches from my feet.

David shouted something profane and flipped off the driver. I couldn't say anything for the arms clamped around my midsection. Sawyer's breath seemed to be caught in his throat, and I could feel his body trembling against my back. He was . . . panicked?

"Elodie, you okay?" asked David.

Sawyer still wasn't letting me go, and while I was really enjoying having him wrapped around me, people—okay David—was starting to stare. I laid my arm over Sawyer's and rubbed lightly, trying to soothe. The muscles beneath my fingers were hard as oak.

"I'm okay," I said. I squeezed his arm. "I'm okay."

"Let's try not to walk in front of traffic, shall we?" His tone was light, but he was still slow to release me.

"I'll try to remember that. Thanks for stopping me from becoming road kill."

"It would have been a terrible waste," he said.

One of the bags I'd dropped had split on impact, so we took a minute to gather up its contents and redistribute them among the remaining bags. The hair on my arms was standing on end and my head was starting to ache, a sharp, lancing pain that made my vision flicker. I made another casual scan of the street expecting—hoping?—to find someone watching. But, though there were a few glances our way, nobody seemed to be watching us.

I didn't know if I was disappointed or relieved.

"Earth to Elodie."

I looked up at Sawyer and blinked as he looped another bag around my fingers. David was already half way up the next block.

"What is your current location and where can I get a ticket, because you are definitely not here today."

"It's stupid," I mumbled, rubbing at my temple and checking both ways this time before I crossed the street.

"Lemmings following each other off a cliff to drown in the sea are stupid. You are anything but. What gives?"

"It's just . . . I keep having this feeling that someone is watching me."

"You're beautiful. Of course people watch you." He said it so matter-of-factly that I stumbled.

Naturally he somehow managed to get a hand under my elbow to steady me, despite the bags in his hands. I never used to be this klutzy before.

I was saying something before he distracted me with compliments . . . Oh right.

"I mean like creepy watching me. Skulking around corners and staying hidden kind of watching."

"Are we on that stalker thing again? Because I've been with you the whole time." His face was set in an *I'm completely innocent* expression. I knew if he was joking about it, he'd forgiven me for my misgivings when we'd first met.

"No, not you. I just . . . Ever since we found Rich. I've felt like I'm being followed."

Sawyer said nothing.

"I told you it was stupid."

"It's not stupid," he said, all traces of teasing gone. "Just because you may be paranoid, doesn't mean you're wrong. You're not going out on your own, are you? You promised your dad."

I arched a brow at him.

"What? If you were my daughter I'd have made you promise not to go out alone after all this."

92

"Fair enough. And no, I'm not breaking my promise and wandering around the park on my own. The only stretch of alone I've got is when I drive to and from work."

Dad had been so freaked out by what happened to Rich and Molly, he'd finally broken down and bought me a second-hand car. Well, okay, really it was probably more like a fifth-hand Toyota that was closer in age to my dad than me. It was pushing 250,000 miles and had paint so faded I couldn't tell you what the original color was. But so far it ran reliably, got me where I needed to go, and made me, in theory, less accessible than my bike, which he'd agreed was a lost cause.

"I just . . . I don't know. I feel really unsettled, I guess. I think everybody will until someone is caught and punished for this." Jesus, I needed some painkillers. This headache was brutal.

"Maybe I should start following you to and from work," said Sawyer, chucking his bags in the back of David's Explorer and reaching for the ones in my hands.

I waved him off. "I'm just being nervy, and it's out of your way. Forget I said anything. Let's just get back to work."

I climbed into the backseat and rubbed my arms until the gooseflesh was gone.

~*~

Sawyer

I was getting desperate. My fascination with Elodie was starting to edge dangerously close to obsession. It was as if my world had narrowed down to tunnel vision where all I could see, all I could think about, was her. I hadn't crossed any truly creeptastic lines—yet. But I had to know what her secret was, what she was hiding. I'd been watching her like a hawk during work, and following that rattletrap car of hers home after, hoping to catch some glimpse of a clue that would prove definitively that she was or wasn't like me.

Was she or wasn't she? It's the question that kept me awake at night. It shouldn't be possible. Her father was one hundred percent human. I'd briefly considered that she wasn't his child, but despite the difference in coloring, it was obvious they were related, so that was out. Her mother was an unknown. If she'd been a wolf . . . I'd never heard of such a pairing, but that didn't mean it wasn't theoretically possible. And it would explain why I couldn't sense it with any certainty. I wanted so badly for it to be true that I couldn't be positive if the things I'd seen were real or a product of my own imagination.

Like today. Just before she nearly walked out in front of that truck—holy crap my heart still hadn't quite slowed down from that scare—she'd been muttering what sounded like a reply to a conversation up the street. Which, of course, she shouldn't have been able to hear. Just like she shouldn't have been able to hear what those old women were saying about her. But I wasn't *sure*. The explanation she'd given me in the store was perfectly plausible. And given where her mind was these days, she could've just been talking to herself on the sidewalk.

I needed something that was absolute proof. Hence the near obsession.

But damned if I knew what that proof would be.

She was younger than me. Which meant that if she was a werewolf, she should have been unstable enough to shift in the middle of all that blood and gore where we found Rich. That scene was practically tailor made to flush a werewolf, a fact that had given me more than a little pause and a half a dozen nightmares in the three weeks since. But Elodie hadn't shifted. She'd been sick, but hell, anybody would've been. Instead, I was the one who barely held it together.

Elodie was worried. She'd been worried ever since we'd found Rich, which was a normal enough reaction that I

hadn't given it too much thought. *Everybody* was worried.
Dad had made sure we weren't out in groups less than three
for any assignment. Reasonable precautions. If someone *else*
was following her, I hadn't noticed. But I'd been so focused
on her, I hadn't paid enough attention to be sure, something I
would be rectifying immediately.

I wondered if I looked guilty. I felt it. Especially since
two hours ago I'd just flat out lied about the fact that I'd been
following Elodie for the last couple of weeks. Hell, I was
doing it again right now. Dad and Patrick had cut us all loose
early for the day. I figured Elodie and I would hang out, but
she had to get home to catch up on chores. Not in that scared
rabbit with a predator way—we were past that thankfully—
but still nervous. I wondered if she was in trouble with her
dad again and he had her on some kind of lockdown except
for work. But she wasn't going home. She bypassed the turn
at Hansen's and circled around a few more miles to a
trailhead I hadn't used before.

There was an overlook on the opposite side of the road
several hundred yards back, far enough that I didn't think
she'd see me. I pulled into it beside a Suburban and watched
through its windows as she got out of the car and circled
around to the trunk. She hefted out a full frame backpack,
balancing it on the edge of the trunk as she buckled it on.

"Elodie, what are you doing?" I muttered.

She'd promised her father she wouldn't go into the park
alone. From what I knew of her, she wasn't a person to break
promises lightly. She was clearly up to *something*. That was
no day pack she was hauling. If she was hiking into the park
now, she had a reason.

I left the Jeep parked at the overlook and slipped into the
woods across the road, setting a path to intersect hers. I could
have just straight out caught up with her, demanding to know
what she was doing or that she let me accompany her
because there was safety in numbers. But I needed answers,
and putting her on the spot wasn't likely to get me any, so

instead I adjusted my path so I ran parallel and well behind her.

The air was hot and sticky. God, would I ever get used to the humidity in Tennessee? It certainly didn't seem to bother Elodie. Even with the loaded pack she moved at a steady clip up the trail, never slowing to take in the scenery or to catch her breath. I got the sense that wherever she was going, she wanted to be there before dark. Which was—I checked my watch—in approximately three hours. Maybe she planned to be there and back again by sunset. I hoped so. I didn't relish another confrontation with my dad about my post-work whereabouts.

Elodie left the trail after half an hour. I didn't have her knowledge of the park, but my general sense was that we were starting to curve back slightly toward her house. Of course that was miles and several ridges and hollows and peaks away. Maybe access to wherever we were going was easier from this side. Not surprising, the terrain got rougher the further we went from the trail, and I had to fall back further to keep from being seen or heard. It was much harder to be silent on two feet amid all the leaves and deadfall. The wind was on my side, at least. When I lost her by sight I could still keep track of her scent.

I didn't like having her out of my sight. Not with some potential, unknown threat hanging out there. I had this gut feeling that as long as I could see Elodie, I could keep her safe. As long as I could see her, nothing could harm her. Which was totally stupid. Even if I or my father had seen my mother, been with her, we still couldn't have stopped the bullet. It was truly an accident. I was starting to be able to admit that now. That still didn't mean I was ready to forgive my father for whatever fight he'd had with her that sent her out there in the first place.

When I crested the next rise and didn't immediately catch sight of Elodie, I felt a spurt of panic. Where was she? I lifted my head, sniffed. I could still smell her, like honeysuckle and rain. Nothing like the coppery tang of blood to suggest she'd been injured. So I shoved the panic back and followed the scent trail as quietly as possible.

I nearly stumbled headlong into the cave. It was partially hidden by a pallet of interwoven branches that, when fully in place, would mask it from the eyes of casual onlookers. The cover was partially askew, and inside I could hear Elodie moving around. Unpacking? Since I couldn't just go in and ask her what she was doing, I withdrew to the cover of trees and hunkered down to wait.

It didn't take long, maybe fifteen minutes, before she emerged again, the backpack empty. I tried to read her expression as she fitted the cover back into place, effectively concealing the entrance to the cave. Was she guilty? Pleased? Somehow afraid? But the only thing I could detect was the perpetual sadness that fit her like a second skin.

The melancholy really bugged me. It lingered, even when I managed to make her smile, which was a rarity. She had this quiet acceptance, like somebody who was battling a terminal disease and had only a few months to live. She had her whole life ahead of her once she got out of this town. Maybe, with her dad's reservations, she didn't feel like that was possible. We'd see about that.

She didn't linger. As soon as the cover was back in place, Elodie was on her way back the up the hill. I waited until she'd crested over to the other side before easing from my observation point and heading down to the cave. Naturally I didn't have a flashlight, so I moved the cover entirely away to catch as much of the lowering afternoon light as possible. After a quick check over my shoulder to make sure Elodie hadn't come back for something, I slipped inside.

I had to stoop. The front of the cave was maybe five feet high. Making my way through a combination of squinting and feeling with my hands, I discovered that after about fifteen feet, it opened up enough that I could stand. I waited for my eyes to adjust, my internal clock winding tighter with each minute Elodie was ahead of me, unprotected. Gradually I started making out shapes.

Stacked neatly in a corner between the cave wall and a huge rock that had, at some time past, fallen from the ceiling, were a dozen gallon water jugs. Beside them was an equally organized collection of canned goods. I moved closer and found all sorts of other non-perishable food staples—jerky, beans, rice—most of it in containers designed to keep out the critters. Along the opposite wall, I found a small camp stove, some of that compact cooking gear that multi-tasked as cook pots and plates and stuff, fuel, and a propane lantern. Some of it was covered in dust, enough that I could tell it had been here a while. Some was new, presumably what she'd brought in today. There were enough supplies in here that someone could last for several weeks at least. Longer if they supplemented with fish, game, and other sources of food out in the wild. Given everything *else* Elodie knew about mountaineering and survival, I suspected she was perfectly capable on that front too.

What the hell was all this? I mean, it was obvious what it was, but why was it here? Why was she stockpiling supplies in the middle of the park? She struck me as the kind of girl who always had a contingency plan. But contingency for what? Running away? What reason would she have to do that, unless things at home with her dad were worse than I realized. No. This struck me as something he might have taught her. What was it she'd said yesterday?

This is what I've trained for, what you've made me.

He was preparing her for something. But what? Surely this wasn't all some excessive response to her mother's death. From what Elodie had said, she'd died at her own hand, not because she had no wilderness survival skills. It all seemed to circle back to the secret she was keeping. Which was evidently cause to be prepared to run and hide. I'd hoped that following her out here today would shed some light on things, but all it had done was stir up more questions.

I touched nothing, instead backing out of the cave and replacing the cover exactly as she'd left it. Then I struck out behind her, intent on seeing her home before darkness fell.

~*~

Elodie

"C'mon baby, just get me to the pump." I glared at the needle hovering *below* E, as if that would somehow scare the car into making it up the road to Hansen's in the event my encouragement failed. I'd never had a car. I wasn't used to keeping an eye on the gas tank. Sue me.

As my tires bumped across the dip at the parking lot to Hansen's, I could swear I heard a sort of gasping hiss, as if the car were dying of thirst. But I rolled up to a stop beside the pump. I thought about cheering, but that would draw attention. Instead, I got out, cool as a cucumber, and set the gas to pump. Then I grabbed the squeegee thing and started cleaning the windows. My car might not win any beauty contests, but she deserved to be treated well. That was a Rule in the Rose household.

"Well, well, well, look who has new wheels."

My hand fisted around the squeegee. Amber. Just what I needed to start my day. I hadn't seen her car as I rolled in. I pretended not to hear her and continued on about my window washing. Swish in the cleaning fluid. Swipe across the window. Scrub the dirty spots. Squeegee dry. Swish. Swipe. Scrub. Squeegee.

Amber circled on around, and I noted in my peripheral vision that she seemed to be without her entourage this morning. Perhaps with no audience to her torments, she'd finish up this round of insults and leave.

"It's a good thing you spend your money on your wardrobe instead of your car. Oh . . . Oops."

Insults about my apparel weren't new, so there was no reason to dignify them with a reply. *She is not in my dimension,* I told myself, *therefore, she cannot bother me.*

Swish. Swipe. Scrub. Squeegee.

She clearly wasn't taking the hint. She continued to circle around, taking in all sides of the car. "Seriously though, I love your car. It so fits your thrift store reject chic."

Bully for me. I didn't even roll my eyes, just continued washing windows. Swish. Swipe. Scrub. Squeegee.

"I mean, rust is so your color."

Swish. Swipe. Scrub. Squeegee. I realized I'd moved on around for a second cleaning, but I kept going because I needed something to keep me from interacting with Amber. And by God, these windows were going to freaking *sparkle.*

"I bet it'll go zero to sixty in however long it will take you to get a date. Never!"

I could ride my bike even faster before you fucking destroyed it, you bitch. My knuckles were white on the handle, but I kept moving. Swish. Swipe. Scrub. Squeegee.

"But you obviously haven't given up hope of that, have you. I mean look at this new look you've got going on. You're making an *effort* to actually look like a *girl* instead of a refugee."

I gritted my teeth. I had no idea what she was talking about. I was dressing exactly as I always dressed. Low-key, neutral colors, no makeup. Nothing that said, *Notice me.*

Swish.

Amber moved directly into my path back to the car, forcing me to face her. I didn't look her in the face, keeping my eyes on the tiny diamonds glinting in her butterfly necklace. Submissive, though I felt as if I would burst from my skin any moment.

"Maybe you're thinking that saving his life means you can actually get somewhere with Rich. But let me tell you something. A guy like Rich would never be interested in a girl like you for real. All he and any other guy wants from you is to get into your pants, just like your daddy did with your mama. He just didn't count on getting stuck with you."

All the suppressed and diverted emotions from the last four years coalesced into a pure, boiling rage. Her neck felt small and fragile in my hand, and her body made a satisfying thump against the gas pump as I slammed her against it. My lips curled in a snarl and a low growl rumbled in my throat. Amber's eyes bulged with shock. Her hands scrabbled frantically at my wrist. I could feel her rabbit fast pulse beneath my fingers and almost smiled. After all the terrorizing she'd done to me and to others, the scent of her fear was incredibly gratifying. For once I was the one in control.

"Elodie, let her go."

The voice was calm and low. For a minute I thought it might be the distant voice of my conscience, which had taken a back seat to this show. Then a hand gripped my shoulder. I growled in warning.

"She's not worth it."

What was he talking about? Of course it was worth it. This bitch had made my life a living hell for the last four years. I was going to sleep like a baby with the sounds of her gasping panic in my ears.

"Ellie. Look at me."

I cocked my head at the name. No one called me Ellie except Dad. A trickle of *oh shit* bled into the satisfaction of my power trip as I turned my head slowly.

Not Dad. Sawyer.

A little bit of sanity started limping through my brain. I was assaulting Amber. In a public place. And I was growling like an angry dog. No, like a wolf.

If Sawyer was alarmed at my behavior, he didn't show it. The hand he'd curled around my shoulder began to rub rhythmically, his thumb making circles in the knot of my shoulder muscles.

"You've made your point. She deserved it. Now let her go," he said.

I looked back at Amber. She was whimpering. Just a scared, weak thing at my mercy. Behind me, the gas pump clicked off, my tank full. The sound was the last thing to snap me back to reality.

"You are a self-absorbed, entitled bitch," I told her. "You lift yourself up by tearing everyone else down because that's easier than turning yourself into an example of a decent human being. I don't know what I ever did to get on your radar, but I swear to God, now you're on mine. Stay the hell away from me."

Reluctantly, I uncurled my fingers from around her throat.

She stumbled back, gasping. "I'll . . ." Wheeze. "I'll press charges!"

A cold wave of dread washed through me.

"You and what witness?" asked Sawyer, putting an arm around me.

Amber looked over toward the store. Slowly, I followed her gaze. Mr. Hansen stood on the sidewalk in front of the door, arms crossed, bushy eyebrows drawn down in a scowl.

There was no need to worry about the best means of ending my own life to wipe out the curse. Dad was absolutely going to kill me.

Mr. Hansen looked at me, then looked back at Amber. "I didn't see nothing."

Amber gaped at him, sputtering in protest. I gaped at him, too, in utter disbelief. He was willing to cover for me?

"I reckon you oughta start shoppin' at the Double Quick on the other side of town. I hear they even got security cameras there." He jerked a finger at the glowing red eye pointing down from the awning. "Mine're just for show."

I started muttering silent prayers of thanks to every deity I could think of as Amber got into her Barbie Jeep and drove away.

Sawyer used the arm around my shoulders to maneuver me into a hug, and I let him. Because now that it was all over, I was shaking like a leaf. All that adrenaline had dumped into my system and no longer had anywhere else to go.

"You okay?" he asked.

A bark of laughter escaped before I could stop it. The question was so ludicrous. I'd just accosted someone, and he was asking if *I* was okay? But the patent truth of the matter was that I was most definitely *not* okay. I'd just broken every Rule my father had ever given me, including some that hadn't been covered because their eventuality was so outlandish, he hadn't felt the need to mention it. Well, every Rule but one.

I pushed away from Sawyer, letting my hand linger on his chest before I dropped it and looked over to Mr. Hansen. Time to face the music.

"She likely *will* press charges," I said. "I don't want you getting into trouble for protecting me."

"Anybody asks, she started it," he said. "Ain't nobody gonna fault you for finishin' it. It's about time you stood up for yourself. Now go on, get to work. You'll be late."

"I still need to pay for my gas."

"On the house," said Mr. Hansen, his face breaking into a wrinkled grin. "That's the best entertainment I've had in months." He made a shooing motion, then went back inside.

I scrubbed both hands over my face. *Oh, what have I done.* I wasn't an aggressive person. I *wasn't.* I'd never been in a fight in my life. Never *not* backed down from a confrontation. And yet for a few fleeting moments, I had actually considered . . . killing her.

Whatever blood was left, drained out of my face at the thought. I reached for the gas nozzle.

"It isn't true," said Sawyer.

"What isn't true?" I asked, carefully replacing the nozzle and screwing on my gas cap. Anything to keep from looking at him.

"What she said about your mother and about you."

Well I just didn't know what to do with that, so I shoved it on some shelf in the back of my brain to think about later. "Doesn't matter whether it's true or not. I shouldn't have let her get to me. I shouldn't have done . . . that. Whether she presses formal charges or not, she'll find some way to retaliate. It's how she operates. And I just really didn't need that."

"Elodie . . ." He snagged my arm, turning me toward him, tipping my chin up so I had to meet his eyes. He looked grave and intense and . . . I don't know . . . purposeful in a way that made my mouth go dry and my stomach drop somewhere around my feet.

"You are amazing," he said in a measured voice. "You're smart, funny, beautiful, and any guy would be lucky to have you in his life. You have no idea how lucky I am to have you in mine."

I swallowed. Where was he going with this?

His hand shifted to cup my face, his thumb tracing my cheekbone. I knew I should put a stop to this. Pull away. Deflect. *Something.* But all I could do was stare up at him and pray I wasn't gaping like a fish.

"Sawyer!"

I jolted back, guilty, as Dr. McGrath rolled to a stop on the other side of my car. He looked pissed. Not in the thundercloud hovering over his head furious way my dad was prone to, but a definite expression of disapproval was etched on his weathered face. There was probably a Rule against fraternizing with your boss's son. I didn't know whether to be embarrassed or grateful that he'd saved me from . . . well. I didn't know exactly what he'd saved me from other than something that probably would have headed toward breaking that last Rule.

Sawyer dropped his hands, disappointment and annoyance warring in his eyes before resignation beat them both. "Yes?"

"Coffee, son. Let's go. We've got a lot to do today."

"Yes, sir," Sawyer muttered.

I reached blindly for my car door. "I'll see you at work," I muttered.

"Yeah. Okay," he said.

Dr. McGrath sat there, truck idling until Sawyer trudged toward Hansen's to make the morning coffee run. Apparently it was his turn. When he turned his gaze on me, his expression softened. "Good morning."

Okay so maybe he wasn't pissed at *me?* I mumbled something that I hoped was good morning, then gave a half wave and escaped to my car.

Chapter 7

Sawyer

Elodie was gone by the time I made it out with the two cardboard trays of coffee.

Damn it, damn it, damn it. I was finally getting through her defenses. We were having a frigging moment. Dad just *had* to show up *right then*. Not that I knew exactly what I was going to say or do if he hadn't. I was too busy trying to keep my emotions, my reactions in check so as not to scare her. Again.

Because now I knew for sure. I wasn't crazy, and I didn't have to stay away from her. When she'd turned from the bully girl to look at me, her eyes were gold.

Elodie was a wolf. Like me.

Or she would be very soon. I didn't think she'd shifted yet. She was late. Not unheard of, but not common either. Maybe it was because she was half human. I wasn't all together sure if she truly knew what was happening to her. She certainly didn't seem to recognize me for what I was. But it fit with her strange behavior. She was coming into her sharpened senses. And the aggression . . . I didn't want to think what she might have done to that girl if I hadn't shown up. No matter that the bitch deserved it.

Elodie needed to be taught. Trained to control the wolf. I couldn't imagine facing the change without having both parents to explain and support me. Up to now she'd had no one.

Well now she had me. And I had to find a way to talk to her about it. In private.

How was that conversation liable to go, I wondered as I headed toward the research station.

I know you're a werewolf. So am I. Let's talk. Direct much? No.

Is there something you've been keeping from me? That could cover any number of things. Not specific enough.

Have you been having headaches? Body chills? Super sensitive hearing and smell? I know just the diagnosis for you. Please dial 1-800-456-WOLF. Infomercial cheese. I think not.

Do I smell different to you?

After trying out and rejecting another dozen possibilities by the time I made it to the lab, I concluded there was no good way to broach this subject. I'd just have to wing it. Grabbing the coffee trays, I headed for the door.

The trailer was empty but for my father, who sat looking over some report or other.

"Where's Elodie," I asked.

"Out in the field with Patrick and the others," said Dad. "They're up near Tremont today."

I turned to go, coffee trays in hand, already calculating how much lead time they had. "Okay. I'll catch up with them before the coffee gets cold."

"No." He didn't shout it. That wasn't Dad's way, it was mine and—had been—Mom's. But dad didn't have to. I felt the full force of an alpha behind the command, so I stopped, facing the door and scrabbling for some kind of hold on the instant roar of temper.

"No?" I said, aiming for casual. I missed by a mile and came somewhere closer to belligerent.

"No," he repeated. "You're with me today. I need to talk to you."

"About?"

"Elodie."

My hands curled to fists before I could stop them. "What about her?"

"Son, what the hell are you doing with that girl?"

I turned, wielding the comfortable shield of sarcasm. "I believe the popular term for it is being her friend."

"That's not what it looked like this morning."

"And what did it *look like*, Dad?" I spat in exasperation.

"Like she has feelings for you. Like you were going to act on it."

My brain circled around that. *Shy, fantastic, funny Elodie Rose, who I can't stop thinking about, might actually be into me too?* I'd been so focused on protection detail, on confirming whether she was or wasn't a wolf, that I hadn't given much thought to how she felt about me other than making sure she wasn't afraid of me. Could it really be true? I mean, maybe. She'd relaxed enough to flirt back some. And—I really couldn't think about this right now because here was Dad staring me down and looking all grim and disappointed and shit.

"Sawyer, you can't play with her. She's a bright, talented girl, and I won't stand for you to use her as some kind of distraction or toy."

The wolf pressed close to the surface, offended at the accusation, furious at the order to stay away. "What do you take me for?" I growled. "Do you honestly think I would be so cruel to her?"

"I wouldn't have thought so before. I thought you were better here."

"I *am* better here. Because of *her*. I'd slit my own wrists before I'd deliberately cause her any kind of pain."

This was the wrong thing to say.

Dad's face shifted from stern to alarmed. "You can't be with her like that, Sawyer. You know that. She isn't like us."

I could tell him about her. Clear this up, avoid the lecture. Do something really radical and bring in an adult to help me teach her. But it wasn't my secret to tell. And since when did I ever do things the easy way?

"I know exactly what she is. She's a brilliant, amazing, lonely girl, who deserves better than the likes of this hick town. I'm not crossing any lines, not doing anything that would jeopardize her future."

"So long as we're clear."

"We're clear."

Dad nodded, as if satisfied with my response. But I couldn't leave it at that. I stepped toward him, back into his line of sight so that he made eye contact again. "Now make sure you're clear on this. She's been humiliated and ostracized by her classmates since she moved here, with nobody to protect or stand up for her. I am her friend, and I'm not walking away and abandoning her because you think it's best."

I could see him considering responses, rejecting them, trying to assess whether an alpha smackdown was going to deter me from my path. Whether it was necessary. But I'd framed it right. Protection was one of our highest priorities, one that he and I both felt he'd failed at with Mom. Whether Elodie was wolf or not, mine or not, he understood that need.

"Be careful, son. This is a dangerous path you're walking."

"I'm fine. No one's trying to kill her. I just want to have her back if any of these assholes from her school try to hassle her again."

"Fair enough." His eyes shifted back to green. "Now grab that pack. We're headed out past Kephart Prong today."

I squelched irritation. Evidently my punishment was going to be busywork for the day. Instead of arguing, I schlepped to the supply closet and grabbed the pack. Maybe by tonight I'd have figured out what to say to Elodie.

~*~

Elodie

Dad was gonna kill me. If he hadn't called out search parties already. The sky was fading from a wash of red and orange to the purpling of night. Which meant it was really freaking late. No trail guide would still be at work this late. And that meant he was bound to have called the park looking for me. My cover was gonna be blown, all because I'd stayed late to help secure the station for the night because it was the first chance I'd had to see Sawyer since the incident at Hansen's this morning. God, I was a moron.

I took one last glance at the research station before climbing into my car. For all I knew it was the last time I'd see Sawyer. Dad might put me under house arrest when I got home. Sawyer was still in there with his dad working on the map and the plan for tomorrow's work. We'd both been kept busy today. Separately. Maybe it was nothing and Dr. McGrath just wanted us to work on different things, but I couldn't help but feel like he wholly disapproved of the idea of Sawyer taking more than a friendly interest in me. I mean he'd been nothing but kind and professional all day. Nothing had really changed in how he acted toward me. But his manner with Sawyer was different. Gruffer. Shorter. I wondered why. Did he think Sawyer was somehow bad for me?

My car sputtered a bit when I cranked it, but she caught and purred to life. Okay perhaps purred was euphemistic. Whimpered maybe. I really needed Dad to get under the hood and tinker. After he was done flaying me alive for lying to him.

I wasn't used to being out this late. Even before Rich and Molly's kidnapping, standard operating procedure in our household meant that I was in before sunset, period. Not like the chances of me wolfing out were greater after dark, but Dad *was* a single parent of a teenage daughter and, curse aside, it was a reasonable precaution.

111

Shadows of trees and boulders stretched long across the road into deeper pools of blackness. My headlights cut through them, a narrow swath of light leading me home. There wasn't anybody else on the road. Which wasn't a shock. There wasn't much *on* this road other than park access, and everybody was gone for the day.

My heart jolted as something jerked in the beams. I jammed my foot down on the brakes, tires screeching as I slid to a stop. But it was only a deer, wheeling away from the road and back into the trees.

The breath whooshed out of me in relief.

Then the car died.

I patted the dash, as if it was an animal that needed soothing from the encounter. "It's okay, baby. It was just a deer. It wasn't hurt. I didn't wreck. You weren't hurt. This is not a problem."

I turned the key. The engine sputtered and coughed. Nothing. I cranked it again. Cough. Sputter. Wheeze. Die. It occurred to me the fourth time I tried that I might be flooding the engine. Could you do that with an automatic? It didn't matter, really. Either way, the car apparently wasn't going to start.

"Shit."

I turned on my emergency flashers.

I was halfway home. I could chance walking back to the lab, but Sawyer and his dad would probably be finished and gone by the time I got there. Probably the best thing to do would be to head for home. At least it would give me a valid excuse for being late. And if I was lucky, somebody I knew would drive by and could maybe give me a lift.

This was one of those occasions I *really* thought Dad should rethink his no cell phone policy. I'd never fought it before because, really, who would I call? It's not like I had friends. But the prospect of hiking home in the dark was so not thrilling me. Maybe I'd start a campaign for one of those pre-paid burner phones.

I climbed out of the car, grabbed my day pack, and locked the door.

For about two seconds I considered hiking cross country. I could shave off a mile probably. But though I knew practically every inch of the park in the daylight, I wasn't comfortable trekking through at night. I hadn't forgotten our encounter with the bear, and predators aside, even an almost werewolf was subject to sprained ankles or broken bones as a result of a fall. So road it was.

I hugged the left shoulder, keeping as much out of the road as possible. I'd see and hear any oncoming traffic well enough in advance to get out of the way. To the right there was no shoulder for the most part, just sheer walls of rock of varying heights where the mountain had been blasted to make way for the roadbed.

Now that the sun was down, the oppressive heat of the day had waned. It was actually almost pleasant to be outside under the stars. Except for the mosquitoes. Tipping my head back, I peered up at the swatch of sky visible through the trees where the road cut through. Now that I'd walked far enough that my headlights had disappeared, I could see hundreds of pinpricks of light in the black. It's one of my favorite things about living in a podunk town. No city lights to drown out the night sky.

Dad and I used to have a telescope when I was younger, and we made stargazing a big thing. He taught me all the constellations, let me stay up late for those rare astronomical events. Since we'd come here, the telescope had stayed packed in its crate and the only star related stuff we'd done was navigational. I could find my way around without a map or compass. In theory.

My dad. Always about the practical.

It hadn't seemed worth the hurt to mention the fact that getting lost hadn't been why Mom died.

A distant rumble separated itself from the noisy song of crickets and buzz of cicadas. An engine. I tipped my head, listening. Was it coming this way? Hard to tell. The new super sensitive hearing seemed to be coming and going, and I really had no idea of the range. I could be hearing a car on another road entirely.

I stopped walking to listen again, turning around to face the direction I'd come from. It occurred to me that the mobility of canine ears would be much more convenient for locating the direction of sounds. Not that I really wanted to sprout a pair, but I could just see the utility of that particular trait.

The vehicle was definitely getting closer. I could hear the rise and fall of sound as it rounded the switchbacks coming down the mountain. Great. Maybe it would be someone I knew or at least someone Dad knew. Maybe it would even be Sawyer or his dad. They had to come this way to get home.

I thought of Rich and Molly as I turned back toward home and started walking again. What if whoever kidnapped them had been someone who they knew? They hadn't seen his face, but it might've been. It was coming from behind me, from the direction of the park. There were a few other things on this road than the park, but I found myself picking up the pace. A prickle of unease skated up my spine. Okay maybe I wouldn't take a ride from anybody. It was only about a mile and a half to Hansen's and from there another mile and a half home. Me and the mosquitoes would be fine that far.

I passed into one of the long, stone corridors with rock rising up on either side. It made me feel hemmed in. Trapped. I didn't like closed spaces of any kind, so I broke into a jog. The sooner I came out the other side, the better. Maybe the driver of the approaching vehicle would think I was just out for a run and drive on by. Yeah, just out for a little nighttime exercise. With a backpack. On a random, dark, mountain road. Well, if they stopped to ask if I needed help, I'd just say I was fine. I kept my pace steady and unconcerned. Just jogging here.

Headlights cut through the dark as the car entered the pass, and as soon as they struck me, I froze like some kind of moronic deer, then turned around. Stupid, stupid! My night vision was blown. The car got closer. Surely the driver had seen me. Just in case, I edged over well into the oncoming lane, out of the way so the vehicle could pass.

I lifted a hand to shield my eyes from the glare, but I couldn't see squat except that it was some kind of truck or SUV. And it wasn't slowing. In fact, the engine revved. What the hell? It wasn't that much of a straight away. What lunatic would be speeding up on a mountain road at night? When a pedestrian was in the road? Was he drunk?

The car *switched lanes* and started to barrel toward me. Oh shit. *Oh shit.* Oh shit!

I started to run, my pack bouncing against my back as my legs pumped, propelling me down the road. Needed speed. Needed distance. Needed to get to the end of the pass so I could dive off the road and into the trees.

Behind me the engine revved again, a rising whine as the driver pushed the truck even faster, eating up the meager distance between us even as my lungs burned and screamed for air. Thirty feet. Twenty. Fifteen. I tried to push faster, harder, but it wasn't enough. I wasn't gonna make it.

In a moment of startling clarity, I was grateful I wouldn't have to pull the trigger myself, that the curse would be ended with me, and that my death wouldn't be tainted by the stain of suicide.

Then it hit me, and I was flying through the air, pain a bright blossoming in my ribs. The impact didn't come from the expected direction. I had just enough time to register that fact before I crashed back to the ground, rolling, sliding in sticks and leaves and rocks, until I slammed, back first, into a tree. Everything exploded into a burst of white.

~*~

Elodie

Being dead was not at all what I'd expected. Instead of the proverbial white light and warmth, after that initial flash everything went dark and cold. Agonizing. It occurred to me then that maybe werewolves go to hell, and I had skipped right on by the pearly gates.

Well damn, that sucked.

Something moved beside me. I heard it shift, heaving a great weight to its feet and making the leaves crackle. That startled me enough to suck in a breath and try to pry my eyes open.

Wait, a breath? Did you need to breathe in the afterlife? Maybe old habits died hard. But no, once my lungs got a taste of oxygen, they started heaving to suck in more. I was still working on the eyes, but they really were not wanting to cooperate.

The thing took a step toward me. Then another. I could feel my heart racing in my chest. That was another weird thing. Why was my heart beating? Surely I didn't need that in hell. But maybe it was to feel the full impact of the paralyzing terror as you were eaten alive. I had visions of great, scary hell beasts a la Buffy, only less campy and more terrifying. That really didn't help with the eye opening agenda.

Oh God. Oh God it was coming. I'd totally missed the pain of being broken in half by that truck, so this thing was here to make sure I paid my dues. It came closer, and closer, and I couldn't get my eyes to freaking open, couldn't move because my body refused to frigging obey the frantic commands of my brain, and this thing was going to—

—whine at me.

Wha—?

The rabid hamster that was apparently running my brain simply stopped on its little wheel. Then the thing snuffled me with a cold, wet nose, whining more as it seemed to check out my face and shoulders before finally nudging at my cheek. I managed to crack an eye open.

It wasn't a hellhound crouched over me, but it was a dog. A really freaking *big* one that seemed very insistent that I wake up. Because apparently I was not, in fact, dead.

"Hey!" I croaked. "That nose is *cold*."

The dog chuffed and licked my face.

"Yeah, yeah, okay. Not dead. Get off. You weigh a ton." I shoved at his shoulder—Hey look at that, my arm worked—and the dog backed up a couple feet.

Pain radiated out from my back. But pain meant the nerves were still intact. I took inventory of my other limbs, carefully testing to make sure they still moved. Nothing broken. I wasn't paralyzed. I guess since I wasn't dead, that was a good thing.

But how was this possible? That truck had to be going at least sixty. I shouldn't be in one piece. Speaking of which . . . yeah . . . I needed to get vertical in case the lunatic who'd tried to run me over decided to come back and finish the job. Not like I could run or fight if he did but it was the principle of the thing. Since it seemed safe to do so, I curled my legs up and tried to roll to my knees. Crap, that hurt.

The dog crouched, shoving his head under my arm. He chuffed again until my fingers twined in his fur. It was a strange combination of soft and rough and a part of me just wanted to collapse around him. When he lifted his head, it helped me straighten. Then I tipped back, sprawling with total lack of grace, to fall against the offending tree. If I was flat on my ass again, at least I was upright this time.

"Thanks," I muttered, closing my eyes again to try and catch my breath since that single effort had wiped out whatever energy I had left.

Okay, so I could add being hit by a motor vehicle as yet another ineffective means of killing a werewolf. Check. Not an option that had been on my list to try.

117

I struggled to remember clearly what had happened. I'd been in the pass. The truck had started gunning for me. I started running. Obviously I had somehow made it out of the pass, or I'd be smeared against one of those rock walls instead of leaning against this tree. I felt gingerly along my ribs. Definitely bruised at the very least. I'd really expected to be hit straight on from behind, which would have tossed me forward. Instead, the impact had come from the side, sort of diagonal and under my right arm. That didn't make any sense. The driver was headed right for me. Had he fishtailed at the last second?

I didn't think so. I couldn't remember any squealing of tires.

So the only other option was that something *else* had knocked me out of the way.

I peeled my eyes open again and got a good look at the dog, standing only a few feet away, studying me. He was tall and kind of grayish white, broad in the chest. Enormous, but not built like a malamute. Definitely big enough to have hit me like a freight train.

As my eyes adjusted to the dark and focused, I went cold. It was no dog that had rescued me. It was a wolf. No hypothetical, small-boned red wolf like we were wanting to reintroduce. This was a fully-grown, two hundred pound timber wolf, as out of place in Tennessee as a bespectacled librarian in a mosh pit.

Maybe I should have been afraid. I mean, it was a *wolf* only three feet away. But if he'd gone to the trouble to knock me out of the way of an oncoming vehicle, it didn't seem like he had plans to eat me. Not that wolves usually did that to humans. Mostly they avoid us altogether. Except, I wasn't human anymore. Not fully. So maybe that explained why he didn't appear to be wary of me. Or maybe he was someone's pet? I knew there were some people who kept wolf-hybrids or even full blooded, domesticated wolves as pets sometimes. But I didn't see evidence of a collar. And nothing about him seemed tame. His long body was tense, quivering, his ears turning this way and that, taking in the sounds of the night, alert and ready for action.

"I'm okay," I told him. "I don't think he's coming back." It was probably stupid talking to a wolf. It's not like they spoke our language. But I was hoping my tone would help calm him. I thought about Sawyer's voice and how he spoke to soothe whenever I was upset. How he always knew when I was, I had no idea. God, how I wished he were here. He'd probably make some joke to try and lighten the mood. Elodie Rose, Wolf Whisperer.

"Are you the wolf I've been hearing all these years? Do you have a mate somewhere? A pack? The people I work with thought I was crazy for saying there were wolves in the park. But I know what I heard."

Of course he didn't actually respond to that. But as I talked some of the tension seemed to leak out of him, so I kept going. "You could have been hurt, you know. Knocking me out of the way like that. I don't know why you did it, but thank you for saving me."

The wolf inclined his head, as if in acknowledgement.

Tentatively, I held out my hand. Without hesitation, he took a stumbling step forward, dipping his head to nuzzle my palm.

"Oh! You *were* hurt!"

I scrambled stiffly to my knees, reaching toward him before my brain could telegraph that this was a bad idea. But the wolf held still, letting me examine him. Nothing seemed to be broken, but he whined a little when I felt my way down his right flank. My hand came away bloody.

"Looks like the truck clipped you," I said. I don't know why I kept talking, except that it seemed to keep him calm and make me feel less panicked. "You could use stitches."

He looked at me steadily, intelligently. Surely he wasn't understanding what I was saying? His gaze stayed on me as I made it to my feet. Would he follow me?

"I could clean you up at least. Disinfect the wound. Which is stupid because you'll never follow me all the way home."

And how was I going to get home anyway? Obviously the roads weren't safe. Whoever was driving that truck had *tried to hit me.* Deliberately. I still needed to think about what that meant. But first I had to get home where it was safe. I guessed it was time to test out my nighttime navigation skills.

Feeling like an idiot, I patted my leg. "C'mon. Come with me."

I retrieved my pack and took a few steps. The wolf followed. It went on that way for a couple of long miles. I'd go a few feet, then check to make sure he was following. He had to be someone's pet, I decided. No way would an actual wild animal freaking *follow me home.* I kept up a steady stream of inane chatter the whole way. The wolf patiently limped after me. Maybe I could get in and grab the first aid supplies and slip back out before Dad noticed. Sure. And maybe pigs would fly. I was so dead.

But the house was dark when we broke the tree line. I slumped with relief. I didn't know where he was, but I'd worry about it later. For now, I owed my rescuer some first aid. My brain was too addled to think about how that was going to work just yet, so I kept moving forward, doing the next thing, as if he were a person.

I opened the back door. "Wait here," I called.

The first aid kit was in the bathroom. There was no way to know how much time I had, so I needed to be fast. I raced through the house, slapping on lights as I went. When I ran back into the kitchen I found the wolf slumped on the floor next to the kitchen table, blood dripping out on the tile. He didn't even lift his head when I came in.

"Oh, God, no." Was he dead? Passed out? I started to lunge forward, then checked myself. *Possible wild animal. Wounded. Don't be an idiot.*

I approached him slowly. He was still breathing. When I laid a hand on his shoulder, he peeled open one eye and looked at me as if to say, *Do what you have to.*

I flipped open the first aid kit on the kitchen table. Because it was Dad's it covered practically every eventuality other than field surgery. Which meant that there were actually sutures. I didn't really think we'd get that far, but maybe I could at least disinfect the wound and get some antibiotic ointment in it before the wolf ran off again. Not that he seemed like he'd be running anywhere any time soon.

"Okay, easy now." I knelt to examine the flank. It was steadily leaking blood, staining his fur, the floor. "Easy." With one eye on his head and those teeth, I dabbed carefully with a clean cloth, trying to see how bad it was. The three inch gash *did* need stitches, but it didn't look like any major arteries had been cut.

"I'm going to disinfect this now. It's going to sting." I crouched, armed with the bottle of hydrogen peroxide, prepared to spring back if he lunged. I tipped the bottle, splashing peroxide into the wound.

The wolf didn't make a sound and didn't make any effort to attack. I eased forward and flushed the wound some more. There was an awful mess on the floor as the blood and peroxide poured down. Thank God for tile. When the disinfectant no longer bubbled, I pressed a towel against the wound to staunch the flow of blood. The wolf turned his head to look at me.

"I know it hurts, I'm sorry. But I have to get it to stop bleeding."

I held his eyes and thought of Sawyer, of the first time we'd met when he'd used his t-shirt to stop the bleeding of my wrist. The bit of t-shirt was still in my pocket.

"I think it's starting to clot," I said.

Beneath my hands the wolf began to tremble.

"Shhh," I murmured. "I'll be done in just a bit."

The bleeding had slowed to a trickle, but as soon as he moved, it was going to start bleeding freely again. I was not so insane as to push my luck by trying to stitch up the gash. Even domesticated animals were put under for that kind of procedure. But I had to do *something*. Maybe I could get him to hold still long enough that I could put on some butterfly strips? They wouldn't hold long but maybe long enough.

"Okay, look. I've got to do something to close up this wound," I told the wolf.

Before I could present his options—as if he was going to answer me one way or the other—headlights swept over the wall in the living room.

"Oh shit! Oh shit, my dad's home!"

There was no possible way I could explain why I had a *wolf* bleeding in the kitchen.

I whirled around, intending to find somewhere to hide him, but the wolf was nowhere in sight. I raced around the island, peeked into the laundry room. No wolf. Then I spotted the open back door. I ran across to shut it, peering into the yard. The wolf was simply gone, the only signs of his ever having been here the pile of bloody rags on the floor.

Chapter 8

Elodie

Outside the truck door slammed shut and I turned to face the mess in the kitchen. Panicked, I dumped a towel on the floor to sop up the mess in a hurry and gathered up the other bloody cloths, racing to toss them into the washer. I came back for the towel, hurriedly swiping the floor and turning off the big overhead light, leaving only the light over the kitchen table where the First Aid kit was spread out. Maybe he wouldn't notice the floor in the shadows.

No time, no time. I got the towel and chucked it after the others in the washer and managed to collapse in a chair as the front door opened. In a spurt of inspiration, I doused a cotton ball with peroxide and was dabbing my own injuries with a shaking hand by the time Dad came into the kitchen.

"Where the hell have you—" He broke off and took one jerking step toward me before his EMT training kicked in and he stopped to assess me. "Are you okay?" Beneath the level, professional voice, I could hear the effort it took him to control himself.

"Bruises and scrapes mostly," I said. Like him I tried to keep my voice matter of fact, but it trembled.

Dad dragged out the next chair and took the peroxide from me, grabbing some fresh cotton. "What happened?" I winced as he gently daubed my upper arm. Evidently I'd lost a good section of skin there, probably on my landing. I hadn't even noticed it until now.

"My car broke down on the way home from work."

"Broke down or wrecked?" he asked skeptically, looking over the rest of me.

I glared at him. "If I'd wrecked it, I would have said so. No, it broke down. Just kaput. Since I didn't have any means of calling anybody, I left it locked with the emergency flashers on and started walking home. Then someone nearly ran me over."

"What?" Dad's voice chilled, and I recognized the Scary Quiet tone.

"Someone in a truck or SUV nearly ran me over."

"On purpose?" he demanded.

If I told him this now, he would jump to conclusions and I'd be put on house arrest at the very least. I needed time to figure out what it meant for myself.

"The driver was probably drunk. I dove off the side of the road and got banged up. The truck kept going. It might not even have seen me." Total, bald-faced lie. The driver had to have seen me.

"Did you get a license plate? Make and model of the vehicle?"

"I hit a tree, so I didn't get anything."

"We'll make a report anyway. Where did you hit the tree? Does anything feel broken?"

"My back. No, I don't think anything's broken."

"Let me see."

I swiveled around so he could lift my shirt and check out the damage. Dad swore viciously, and I knew then it must look pretty bad.

"We're taking you to the hospital." He was already up, grabbing his keys.

"Dad that's completely unnecessary. Really. It's just bruising. Seriously, I *walked* all the way home from the site. If something was seriously wrong, I wouldn't have been able to do that. It's just bruised. I'll be sore for a few days."

He grunted. "We'll let it go until tomorrow, then reassess. Where's your car?"

I told him where I'd left it.

"I'll call for a tow. Finish cleaning up."

I'd familiarized myself with all my visible scrapes and bruises by the time he came back. I was afraid of what I was going to see when I undressed and checked my back in the mirror.

"I'm gonna meet Jim up at the car. Will you be okay here for a little while?"

It was such an uncharacteristic thing for him to ask. Multiple sarcastic replies sprang to mind, but instead I said, "Yeah. I'll be fine. I think I'm gonna go up and have a bath. Clean up. Then take some aspirin and go to bed early."

"I'll check in when I get back."

Not until he'd walked out the door, cranked the truck and pulled out of the driveway did I budge from the table. Now that the adrenaline rush was wearing off, the pain was coming back, and along with it a vicious headache, so I moved a lot slower as I finished cleaning the floor properly and packing up the First Aid kit. Once I was satisfied that all traces of the wolf were gone, I dumped some detergent and Oxiclean into the washer and started the load. I thought about adding what I was wearing to the mix, but I wasn't even sure yet if it was salvageable.

Upstairs I stripped out of my clothes and swiveled in front of the bathroom mirror.

"Holy shit."

The deep purple bruise ran in a diagonal stripe from my right shoulder down to my hip. It was nearly five inches across in places. It was a miracle my spine hadn't been broken on impact. The skin of my back was abraded from the bark of the tree, and my t-shirt was ripped in several spots. Not salvageable then. I was missing the top layer of skin from much of my right arm and leg, as if I'd skidded along the ground. Maybe I had. Maybe that's what had slowed my impact enough to save me. I couldn't remember.

I stepped into the shower to wash off the ground in dirt as best I could. The immediate sting of water and soap made me grit my teeth and whimper, but it cleared my head enough to think again.

Someone had tried to run me down. Deliberately. He'd sped up and changed lanes. But he hadn't made it. Despite the relatively short distance between us, he hadn't actually hit me. I didn't know what kind of truck it was, but an engine that big should have been able to make up the distance. So why hadn't he? Sure, part of it was that the wolf had knocked me out of the way, but I should never have been able to make it to the end of the pass in the first place. So if the driver hadn't intended to kill me, what purpose would nearly running me down serve? Some kind of sick joke? Let's terrify the lone walker for kicks. Or maybe . . . maybe it had been more personal. Maybe it was to see exactly how fast I could go.

A werewolf should be able to outrun a car.

I wanted to dismiss the thought immediately but forced myself to think it through.

My car had been running totally *fine* until this evening. I'd been away from the lab all day. Somebody could have messed with it, fixed it so that I'd break down on the way home. Which would mean that someone knew my schedule, my route. I'd been on edge for weeks now, feeling like someone was watching me, following me. I'd been sure I was just crazy. But just because you're paranoid doesn't mean no one's after you.

And just because you get attacked doesn't necessarily mean you're the target. What if Rich's kidnapping hadn't really been about him at all? That whole scene had just been bizarre. Awful, but so apparently *random*. If he'd fallen prey to some true nut job, wouldn't the guy have killed him? Why trap him and leave him there with all the animal blood and gore unless you knew something else was supposed to be out there? Something for which such a set up should be the perfect bait. I was later than all my predecessors in my change. If I'd already shifted, almost certainly I would have been compromised and revealed myself.

Maybe there was no pattern. Maybe independently it all meant nothing. But taken together I couldn't help but consider the possibility—what if a hunter had found me?

The thought made me go cold, despite the scalding water.

According to the journals, there hadn't been a hunter involved in three generations. But what if the hunters hadn't actually disappeared or lost track of us? What if they'd just gotten smarter and more subtle about how they went about the whole process? I mean, they'd have to, right? Forensics had gotten way better over the last several decades. They'd have to be a lot more careful about killing to avoid getting caught.

But how the hell could he have tracked me down? Everything about our lives since we got the letter had been about staying below the radar. We changed our names. We moved. I gave up friends, hobbies, a life. I avoided the internet. I did *nothing* to draw attention. The entire point was to avoid being found. Had all this hell been for nothing?

I was changing anyway. I'd long ago resigned myself to the fact that if it happened, I would have the strength to take myself out of the equation before I could hurt someone. To end the line with me, so no one else had to go through the nightmare. I'd just always thought it would be on my terms, my schedule.

I snapped the towel off the rack.

Damn if I was going to let a hunter decide it for me.

If this was all some kind of game intended to draw me out and verify that I was a werewolf, the hunter was going to be sorely disappointed. So far I hadn't reacted the way he expected. Surely that bought me some time.

But time for what? To wait around for the next attempt on my life? That was hardly practical. It could come at any time, in any form. What if the next time I wasn't alone? Who

else might be endangered just by being near me? Dad?
Sawyer? The thought of either of them being hurt made me
nauseous. I wasn't willing to risk anyone's life but my own.
    As I looked in the mirror I noticed with fascinated horror
that the abrasions on my arm were already half healed. The
change was coming. Sooner or later, the hunter would hit
upon something that would confirm his suspicions. And he
would try to kill me for real.
    Now was not the time to stay passive and quiet.
    I had to leave.
    The contingency plan was in place. Had been for months.
I just hadn't honestly expected to have to use it. Certainly it's
not what Dad would expect me to do with all the training
he'd put me through. For him, I think that was more about
vicariously saving Mom or something. We never talked
about it. He'd be pissed if he knew I'd been squirreling
supplies away for this long. But he taught me to be prepared
for anything. He couldn't be mad that I'd taken him
seriously.
    I'd need a day or two to put things in place. Figure out
how to tell Dad. Or not. No matter what we'd prepared for, I
didn't think he was actually ready to let me go. So maybe a
letter explaining things would be better. Otherwise he'd try to
stop me. Or come with me. And the whole point of this was
to draw the hunter away from him. It was my turn to protect
him.
    I had to say goodbye to Sawyer. There was an ache under
my breastbone at the thought. He'd become so important to
me so fast. We were just friends—I'd known that's all we
could ever be. But after this morning, I'd let myself entertain
the idea that we could be more. That just made the whole
thing worse, probably for both of us. He wouldn't
understand. He'd think he scared me off with what he'd said.
What he didn't know was how lucky I was to have had him
in *my* life. Even if it was just for a few weeks, he made me
feel normal for the first time in four years. But I had to go. I

couldn't possibly put him in a position to lose someone else, even just a friend, the way he'd lost his mother.

There was a soft knock on my door. "Ellie?"

Dad stuck his head in. I could just make out his outline silhouetted by the hall light.

"Yeah?"

"We got your car. I had it towed to the garage. Jim's gonna take a look at it tomorrow, figure out what went wrong."

"Okay. Thanks."

He hesitated. "Are you okay?"

No, I was most definitely not okay. No amount of training could prepare me for what I was going to do. But it would give me a fighting chance, and that was more than my ancestors got. I had to make the most of it.

"I'm fine, Dad. I'll see you in the morning."

Elodie

"Bleach?" Sheriff Beasley's caterpillar eyebrows lifted, creating a whole different set of wrinkles in his weathered face.

"Yes, sir," said Jim. "See, it accelerates the rust process in the gas tank, and in an older car like hers, it added to years of normal wear, so that the rust particles gunk up the engine and make it stop. The engine's probably toast, and the gas tank will definitely have to be replaced."

"How long would this process take?"

"Usually a few days, but in a car that old, hours."

Sheriff Beasley nodded at that. "So the bleach could've been added sometime between yesterday morning and, say, lunchtime?"

"Probably," agreed Jim.

The sheriff turned his attention to me. "Is there anybody you can think of who might want to prank you?"

Before I could respond, Dad interrupted. "Someone deliberately sabotaged my daughter's car and then nearly ran her down." He was barely keeping it together. His hands were curled, white knuckled around the edge of the sheriff's desk and his voice shook with the effort not to shout.

"Now hold on Nate, let's not jump to conclusions." Sheriff Beasley looked back at me. "How about it, Elodie? Is there anybody who might want to . . . retaliate against you by sabotaging your car?"

I froze and hoped my eyes weren't bugging out of my head. The sheriff knew about my run-in with Amber. And judging by the look on his face, he knew I knew he knew.

"Don't be ridiculous," said Dad. "My daughter isn't the type to get into fights or piss people off enough to do something like *this.*"

Had Amber filed charges? Was this the part where my dad finally found out that I broke protocol and stood up for myself in a totally excessive manner? I looked at the sheriff, begging him with my eyes not to rat me out. His expression seemed to say, *Do you want to tell him, or should I?*

Shit. I swallowed.

"There's this girl at school," I began.

I felt Dad's gaze swivel toward me and knew I was getting The Look. My hand fisted around the scrap of Sawyer's t-shirt in my hoodie pocket. I could get through this.

"She's never liked me. I don't know why." Truth. "The guy she likes was hitting on me earlier this summer, and she didn't like it." Understatement.

Damn, Dad. Turn down the laser vision, I thought. I could practically feel his eyes searing my face.

"I wasn't interested, and I blew him off, but she didn't care much about that. She backed over my bike in the parking lot of Hansen's."

"You didn't report it," said the sheriff.

"It was a bike," I shrugged. "I figured she would consider that payback and be done with it."

"But she wasn't," said the sheriff.

"She seems to think that my saving his life means I'm actually interested in him."

"You mean Rich Phillips."

Surely I was getting a pattern burned into my cheek as hard as Dad was staring. My nose flared as I caught the scent of his anger. So. Not. Good.

"I'd have gone on the search no matter who was missing. You know that. Rich might be an arrogant jerk, but he didn't deserve what was done to him."

"Let me get this straight," Dad began. "You're telling me that some girl poured bleach in your gas tank, destroying your car, because of some guy?"

"It's a possibility," I admitted. I glanced up at Sheriff Beasley, waiting to see if he was going to make me finish it. He was. Damn it. "I kind of got into a tussle with her yesterday morning."

"You what?" On no. That low, careful enunciation was never ever good.

"She was provoked according to Bob Hansen. Apparently this young lady has been harassing your daughter for a long time."

The toes of my shoes were suddenly very interesting.

"Elodie?" demanded Dad. "Is this true?"

I bobbed my head once.

"How long?"

"Since eighth grade," I mumbled.

"You've managed to avoid getting into a fight with her for this long. What did she say to provoke you?" Dad asked.

I shook my head. No way did I want to get into this.

"Elodie."

Damn it. He had to pull out the Don't You Dare Refuse To Answer Me Parent tone.

"She insulted Mom," I said softly.

"What did she say?"

Her filthy words scrolled back through my mind and I wished viciously for Sawyer to be there to wipe them away again. I shook my head again. "It's not important. Amber is a hateful bitch and she finally found something that would get a rise out of me. I'm sorry." I looked to the sheriff. Might as well take my medicine. "Is she pressing charges?"

"No. I didn't hear about it from her or her parents."

"Then who?"

Before either of us could speak, Dad's beeper went off.

"Damn it. Barn fire out of hand at MacLellan's Dairy. I have to go. Is she actually in trouble?"

"Not with me."

"Okay. Do you need—"

"I'll finish taking Elodie's statement about what happened last night. Then we'll drop her wherever she needs to go."

"Thank you." He turned to me, and I dared to actually lift my head to look at him. Oy, not good. "We'll talk about this at home, young lady."

"Yes, sir," I said meekly.

Jim left with him.

"I am so dead."

"He'll get over it," said Sheriff Beasley.

Who knew the sheriff was such a fan of the power of positive thinking? He so didn't know my dad.

"So who told you?"

"Bob. He figured Miss Cooper probably would press charges and wanted to make sure the real story got told."

I had a feeling whatever details Mr. Hansen shared probably still had some measure of editing. Silently I blessed him for it.

"So this vehicle last night. Did you recognize it?"

"No. It was dark, and I was blinded by headlights. Then I was kind of too busy running for my life to pay attention."

"Tell me what happened."

So I did. Leaving out the part about being rescued by a wolf, of course.

"Your dad said you were injured."

I shifted in my seat, wincing at the ache in my back. "It looked worse than it was." In truth, all the abrasions were healed this morning. It's why I was wearing a hoodie and jeans in freaking *July*. So Dad wouldn't see. "Just some bruising mostly."

"You were pretty lucky. Do any of Miss Cooper's friends have a vehicle that could fit the description of the one from last night?"

"Sheriff, it's small town Tennessee. Everybody and their brother has a truck or an SUV here. Half the high school parking lot could fit the limited description of what nearly ran me down. Maybe a quarter if you limit it to those with V8 engines."

It suddenly seemed completely ridiculous to think that last night's encounter had been a hunter. Amber was beyond pissed. She'd have found some lackey or other to give me a good scare. And the bleach thing, well we could blame our chem teacher for showing that episode of Mythbusters last semester.

"I'm sorry I don't remember more."

"That's all right. Something might come to you. I'll have a chat with Miss Cooper and let her know that further hostilities on her part won't be tolerated."

I wasn't sure whether that was a good idea or not, but I thanked him anyway, wanting nothing more than to get the hell out of here and find Sawyer.

"I'll have a deputy drive you home."

"Work," I corrected. "I'm very late."

I finished signing whatever paperwork they had for me, and got into one of the cruisers with a fresh faced deputy I remembered as being a senior when I was a freshman. Geez, they recruited them young.

"Where to?" he asked.

I gave him directions to the research station.

He pulled out of the parking lot. "You're Elodie, right? Fixin' to be a senior this year?"

I nodded.

"I remember you."

Well whoopty doo. I didn't remember his name, just his face. He'd never bothered me, so I'd had no real reason to notice him. For purposes of polite conversation, since he obviously wasn't going to let the ride go in silence, I wracked my brain for something I remembered about him.

"You played baseball, didn't you?" I asked.

"Short stop. Yeah."

I thought he smiled. I wasn't sure because I wasn't actually looking.

"You look . . . different."

Something in the tone of his voice had me turning from the window, looking at him with one brow lifted. "Different how?"

Color stained his cheeks. "Oh I just mean . . . I don't know . . . older. More mature. More confident. It's really . . . attractive." He cut himself off with a kind of choking noise and looked firmly back at the road. "Sorry. That was inappropriate."

What was it with everybody thinking I looked different? Rich had acted like he suddenly thought I was sexy. Amber said something about my look being different, as if I was trying to look like a girl. And now this deputy thinks I'm attractive? What was up? All I saw when I looked in the mirror was the same old me. Maybe part of the change nobody wrote about was some kind of spike in pheromones or something.

The remainder of the drive was the epitome of awkward silence. At least he didn't try to actually hit on me or something like Rich had. Given everything that had happened, I definitely was no longer the girl who could stay

134

submissive and suffer through unwanted attentions, and I really didn't want to find out how far I might go to stop them without someone to stop *me*.

Sawyer was out the door of the lab before the cruiser was fully parked, his face a thundercloud. Because I'd learned to read him, I knew his anger wasn't at me, but at any potential threat, so I shot out of the car to intercept him.

"What happened?" he asked, shifting to put himself between me and the car. He hadn't actually looked at me yet, his attention still fastened in a narrow-eyed gaze on the poor deputy, whose name I still didn't remember.

I curled my hand in his, tugging to get his attention. "I'm fine." I looked back at the deputy. "I'm good. Thanks for the ride, deputy."

He gave me a salute and avoided Sawyer's eyes as he got back in the car and drove off.

Sawyer swung around and pulled until I bumped solidly into his chest.

"Where were you?" he demanded. "I was worried."

It took me a bit to work up actual words for an answer because my brain was too busy short circuiting at his nearness and urging me to press closer. "Um, I emailed your dad that I'd be late." The chest beneath my hand was broad, the muscles toned and taut. My mouth seemed to be at war over whether it wanted to drool or go bone dry.

"I saw your car last night. What happened?"

Car. Explanation. Right. This was really going to go better if he wasn't touching me, so I stepped back until there were at least a few inches between us. I didn't matter. I could still feel the heat of him pulling at me. Jesus.

"Broke down." I herded my remaining brain cells together. "Someone poured bleach in my gas tank."

"What?" The word rolled out in a growl, and I found myself stroking his arm.

"Probably Amber, as payback for yesterday morning."

"There's more." It wasn't a question. I guessed he was learning to read me too.

"Yeah. I kinda sorta nearly got run over on my walk home."

No *what?* to that one. Just a glower. He lifted a hand to my cheek, "Are you okay?"

Yes, I'm great, as long as you never, ever stop touching me.

"I'm okay," I breathed. "Look, Sawyer, there's something I need to—"

"Elodie! Good to see you made it."

Sawyer stepped back as Patrick circled around, his pack in one hand, keys in another.

"Everything okay?" he asked.

"Sure. Fine. Just had some car trouble. Prank gone wrong. Dad wanted me to report it this morning."

"Kids these days. No respect for personal property." Patrick shook his head, then shoved his glasses back up the bridge of his nose. "Well, c'mon you two, load up! Big doings today!"

"Later," I mouthed.

Sawyer nodded, and I pasted on a smile. "Great! Let's go."

~*~

Elodie

I collapsed onto the top of one of the picnic tables across from the research station, my feet perched on the seat. "I'll move again sometime next year," I promised as Sawyer collapsed beside me.

"I think Patrick secretly found a way to bottle a little kid's energy and he mainlined it," observed Sawyer, watching the man in question drive away. David and Abby drove out after him. Dr. McGrath was up in Knoxville for the day, doing something with a colleague at UT, so we were, at last, alone.

Carefully, because my back was aching again, I eased back on the tabletop.

"Good idea," said Sawyer.

He lay back himself. He was too tall to fit as I did, so he had to readjust diagonally, angling so his head fit sort of between my head and shoulder. I didn't mind. It was comforting to just close my eyes and be surrounded by the scent of him. If I'd had more energy, I might have rolled a little to snuggle him or brushed my fingers through his hair. Which would embarrass us both, so it was a good thing I couldn't actually move.

It was strange, really. I wasn't a touchy feely kind of person. Dad and I were not what you'd call demonstrative with affection. At least not since the letter. So this perpetual need I seemed to have to *touch* Sawyer was weird. I mean, it worked out. He was a touchy kind of guy. Not in a gross, gropy kind of way, but he was just one of those people who communicated through touch. The brush of his arm. His hand on the small of my back or shoulder. The easy way he curled his fingers in mine.

God, I was going to miss that.

With that thought, any vestiges of relaxation disappeared. I was supposed to leave. Say my goodbyes and disappear. Because even if Amber was behind the car and last night's hit and run attempt, I still couldn't shake off the idea that Rich had been bait.

"Whatever just popped into your head, forget it," said Sawyer.

When I tipped my head to look at him, his eyes were closed.

"Your tension is practically vibrating the table," he said.

"Sorry," I said.

He snaked a hand up and tangled his fingers with mine. "Did your dad give you shit about the car?"

"About the car, no. But he's probably going to murder me over my fight with Amber."

One eye cracked open. "He found out?"

"It was either I tell him or the sheriff would. He got called in to work before he could finish flaying me alive with a lecture. Don't expect to see me tomorrow." I swallowed back the knot in my throat. Christ, I was *not* going to cry in front of him again.

Sawyer's hand tightened. "You think he'll make you quit?"

"I don't know what he's going to do. I currently have no means of transportation, and he would so not be okay with the idea of one of my male co-workers picking me up for work. For the job I totally lied about having."

"Maybe if we steal the club he uses to bash you over the head before dragging you back into his cave by your hair, we could knock some sense into him."

I snorted a bit of a laugh at the heavy sarcasm. "It's moronic, yes, but he has his reasons. I'll probably be grounded the rest of the summer as it is. Breaking that Rule in front of him will get me under total house arrest."

"Don't tell me he's pulling that old jewel of 'I know how teenage boys think. I used to be one.'"

"Well considering that's exactly how I came about . . ."

"I think it just means your parents were too stupid to use protection."

"Oh, thank you so much for that mental image. I need to go bleach my brain."

"Not that I'm complaining since I'm glad you're here. Still, it's not fair for him to punish you for their mistakes or treat you like you're too stupid to learn from them."

"I think it's less about punishing me and more an attempt to protect me. Then, of course, there's the 'It's not you, I'm worried about. It's *them* I don't trust.' Which also, conveniently translates to driving, as it happens."

"A multipurpose parental smackdown. Right up there with 'Because I said so.'"

"I'm guessing that stopped working on you a long time ago."

"Oh yeah."

He shifted, actually tucking his head against my shoulder. After a moment's hesitation, I leaned my head against his, reveling in the feel of his soft hair against my cheek. We lapsed back into a comfortable silence in which he played with my fingers.

"Do you think your parents really loved each other? I mean like, the really *it* kind of love. Or were they just a couple of crazy teenagers?" he asked. "Do you think you can find *it* that young?"

I thought of how, when Dad had to change our name, he'd chosen Rose, after her. Rosalind. "Yeah, I think they were it," I said softly. "He's never so much as looked at anybody else. And she went through absolute hell for him. I don't know what-all my grandfather threatened to make her reveal who my father was, but she never breathed a word. She would have done anything to keep him safe. I never understood that before."

For the first time, I began to consider the possibility that she'd left to protect us. That maybe she was beginning to give in to the madness and feared she'd hurt Dad or me. Maybe her suicide hadn't been an act of cowardice as I'd always thought, but of strength, as I believed my own might have to be.

Sawyer paused in the midst of drawing his thumb down the length of mine. "You get it now?"

"Yeah. Now I get it exactly." *Because I'd do anything to keep you safe. From a hunter. From me.*

I knew then that my decision was made. No matter how much I wanted to stay, I wasn't willing to risk Sawyer getting hurt. So I would take these next few minutes for the gift that

Kait Nolan

they were, even though my heart was bleeding with every brush of his fingers. Then I'd be gone.

Sawyer sat up, tugging to bring me with him, so we were swiveled toward each other, knees touching. Not until he reached out to brush his thumb over my cheek did I realize I was crying. Damn it.

I started to reach up, to scrub the tears away, but he captured my hands. "Don't"

I didn't know if he meant don't cry or don't try to pretend I wasn't crying, and I didn't get a chance to figure it out because my brain totally short circuited as he leaned in and brushed his lips over one wet cheek. Shock kept me immobile as he shifted to kiss the other cheek. I inhaled one sharp breath, which was good because I'm pretty sure I stopped breathing after that.

Sawyer's lips, those marvelous, beautiful lips, curved into a smile as he hovered a few inches away. He stayed there, his gaze dropping to my mouth then lifting back to my eyes and waiting, as if asking permission. Or maybe he was waiting for me to close the distance between us. I wanted his mouth on mine. I had almost from the first time I saw him.

I shifted a hesitant inch forward.

It was enough. He closed the distance between us, touching his mouth to mine.

How could a body that hard, that strong, be so soft and careful? The contrast left me weak and dizzy. I swayed toward him, unintentionally deepening that bare brush of lips. One of his hands slid into my hair, cradling my head, tipping it a bit for better access. My free hand slid up the planes of his chest—dear God, what did that feel like without a shirt?—and came to rest over his heart. Though it thundered beneath my palm, he kept his mouth easy, still testing.

I drew in a breath, smelled his arousal. The scent curled around me, through me, waking something other than terrified nerves in response. My hand fisted in his t-shirt and yanked him closer. One of us, maybe both of us, growled.

140

Suddenly his arms were around me, under my knees, dragging me into his lap.

Oh yes, yes, this was good. My hands found their way into his hair, and it was soft, as his lips had been soft. They weren't soft now. They were hungry. He was hungry. For me. He actually wanted . . . me.

My body seemed to pulse with heat, desperate for more. More heat. More skin. More everything. If this was all I was ever going to have, I wanted as much as I could get.

"Get your hands off my daughter."

I froze, my hand splayed against Sawyer's back beneath his t-shirt. Something that sounded suspiciously like a gun clicked behind me.

"I'm not gonna say it again."

We broke apart, panting. Sawyer stood, set me on wobbly feet, and shoved me behind him. I was still busy trying to force my brain cells to fully engage and my leg muscles to properly hold me up when he said evenly, "Mr. Rose, put the gun down."

"Jesus!" I rushed around Sawyer. "Dad, stop it!"

Dad's attention shifted briefly from Sawyer to me, and his face went bone white. "Elodie. Get in the truck."

"What? What is it?" It wasn't pure anger in his expression. Now there was straight up fear.

"Get in the truck!" he shouted.

"Not until you put the gun down."

Sawyer stepped in front of me again. "You don't have to go with him. He's obviously not safe to—"

"Not safe? *Not safe?* You touch my daughter and you think *I'm not safe?*" The skin across his cheeks seemed pinched, too tight over bone.

I'd never seen him like this, and it scared me. "Dad, put down the gun. I'm not going anywhere until you put it down." I tried to keep my voice even, soothing.

"Get in the goddamned truck!"

The gun never pointed at me. It was fixed steadily on
Sawyer. I stepped in front of him and the gun wavered. "Put
the gun down, and I'll go with you."

"Elodie—" started Sawyer.

"Don't," I said, not looking at him. "Dad. The gun."

Dad's horrified gaze fixed on me. That same *My
daughter is a monster* expression I'd caught right after he'd
read the letter and the journal, but so much more than I'd
ever seen. As if I was turning before his very eyes.

"I won't let you hurt him any more than Mom let my
grandfather hurt you."

Dad's face spasmed, but he lowered the gun. "Get in the
truck," he croaked.

I didn't dare turn back to Sawyer for any kind of proper
goodbye. Dad was way too unstable right now.

"I have to go," I said quietly.

Saywer's hand shot out to grab mine as I stepped away.
"Elodie."

"I have to go," I repeated, squeezing his hand and not
looking at him. I pulled away and walked to the truck.

Once I circled the hood to the passenger side, Dad broke
the standoff. In contrast to my quiet, careful closing of door,
he slammed the driver's side, shoving the pistol roughly into
the holster on his belt. I hoped he'd put on the safety. Then
he cranked the truck and jammed it into reverse, making a
rough three point turn.

I chanced one last look at Sawyer. He looked predatory
and furious as we drove away. Then Dad got the truck turned
around and slammed his foot on the gas.

"How could you?" he demanded.

"How could I what? Be human?" I demanded.

Furious, he slammed the passenger side visor down.
"Look at that and tell me you're still human!"

What the fuck was he talking about? I tilted the mirror to
get a look at my face. My lips were red and swollen from
Sawyer's, my cheeks still flushed. Everything looked totally

normal for somebody who'd been making out on a picnic table for who knew how long. Until I got to my eyes. I gasped. My irises were a pure, glowing gold.

"You're shifting," he said. "Just like she did."

Chapter 9

Sawyer

"**Elodie!**" Panicked fury ricocheted through my chest as the truck sped away, tires slipping on gravel, carrying my mate to danger.

I sprinted after it. I had no plan, no clue what to do, just a desperate need to get to her. My legs burned, as I pushed faster, beyond human limits, the wolf rising within me. Almost there . . . My hand stretched out, the tailgate almost within my grasp, when Elodie's father looked up. His eyes met mine in the rearview mirror and narrowed. The engine roared and the truck sped up, taking the bed of the truck—and Elodie—out of my reach.

"No!" I roared.

Where was he taking her? Home? I could cut through the woods and possibly beat them there. Be on the offensive when they arrived. But what if he was taking her somewhere else? I couldn't risk losing them. Losing her.

I veered into the woods that edged the road, ripping off my shirt. I was fast like this, but not fast enough. The wolf came roaring forth, my limbs twisting and popping, muscles screaming with too fast a change. I stumbled as I landed, tripping over shoes and shorts before gaining my paws again and racing after them.

It was the same path I'd run last night, following the curve of the road where it cut through the mountain. I hadn't been panicked then. Not even when I'd found her car, abandoned, the flashers lighting up the night with an intermittent orange glow. I'd been concerned. Frustrated with her carelessness of not having a backup plan for a breakdown, and determined to see her home as a faithful shadow. Then I'd seen the truck stop. A dark figure got out, peered in the windows of her car, then got back in his own vehicle. And sped off too fast for a mountain road.

I felt more terror now.

Elodie's dad wasn't driving dangerously fast. I could see the truck below me through the trees, and I was grateful for all the switchbacks through this section because my back leg was still aching from being clipped. Last night had been a sprint to beat the driver, to get to Elodie before he could. This was a distance race. Even though I wanted to run all out, I just had to keep up, to find out where her dad was taking her so I still had something left when we got there.

I cursed myself for not paying more attention last night. I should have noted what the driver looked like, what the truck looked like. Could it have been Elodie's father, already coming unglued? I didn't know. My focus had been only her, on getting to her, on saving her, on making sure I hadn't hurt her when I knocked her into that tree. Then I'd stayed with her, made sure she got home safely.

I'd thought her home was safe.

Mr. Rose's driving seemed less erratic the closer we got to town, as if he recognized that he didn't need to get pulled over. Where was a deputy when you needed one? I relaxed an iota when he took the turn by Hansen's. He was going home. Thank God. I peeled off then, putting more distance between us so I could keep to the trees for cover. If I was fast enough, maybe I could get inside before they did.

And then what, dumbass? You think her dad isn't going to shoot a wolf in his house on sight? Okay, so maybe I needed to rethink that approach. There was no way I could get near her as long as he had that gun.

As the truck bumped into the driveway, I crept along the side of the free-standing garage, keeping to the shadows. Mr.

Rose still had the gun on him as he circled around the truck, but it was holstered now. His movements were still stiff and jerky, but he seemed less . . . psychotic now. Elodie walked ahead of him, shoulders hunched. In that moment I despised him for making her look defeated.

Neither of them said a word as they went inside.

I made my way around back to the picture window in living room. I could go through it if I had to. They squared off as they had during that fight after the search, across the coffee table. But this time Elodie looked exhausted and miserable.

"How did you find me?"

"The deputy who dropped you off. I went back by the station when you weren't at home. He told me where he'd let you out. Exactly what have you been doing this summer? Not working as a guide as you told me."

"I've been working as an intern for a biologist in the park."

That seemed to trip him up. "Why?"

"Because I was interested. And because it would look good on college applications."

"You know you're not—"

"No, Dad, I don't *know* anything of the sort. You're the one who refuses to consider that I might have a future, that I might have something of value to offer the world. You want to keep me in a cage."

"Obviously I should! Look what you did when you went out on your own."

"I want a *life!*" she shouted. "For all my hard work in school to actually *mean* something. To lead to a career and a future where I actually live beyond sixteen."

Wait, what? She'd said it so matter-of-factly, as if she'd lived her entire life expecting it to be over already. Why? How? Disease? Suicide like her mother? Something else? I thought of her paranoia, her sense that someone was watching her, and wondered if that was somehow connected.

"I thought when I made it through this year, that I had a shot. That you'd finally get past this insanity and let me be *normal.* So that I can finally have friends and people who care about me beyond an obligation because I'm some kind of burden to them."

"Is that what you think you are to me?" Her father had to choke the words out.

"Aren't I? You've hardly been able to look at me since we got Mom's letter explaining things. I am this *thing,* this *problem* you have to contend with because I share half your DNA."

"Everything I've done, I've done to protect you," he whispered.

"Yes. Protecting me. You threw yourself into this . . ." She waved her arms, as if she could pluck the right word out of the air. "—lunacy when I couldn't even believe it myself. Why is that? Why should an otherwise totally rational man actually believe it when the mother of his child writes that she was a werewolf and charges you with stopping the same thing from happening to me? Why didn't you think she was crazy?"

Stopping it? What the hell was she talking about?

"Because I saw her."

"What?"

"I saw her as a wolf."

Elodie sank down onto the couch. Clearly this was news to her.

"It was months before you were born, and I didn't know it was her. Not until years later when we got the letter. But she had this birthmark on her back. A sort of crescent moon shape. The wolf I saw had a patch of fur exactly the same shape, the same location. It couldn't be a coincidence. And I couldn't risk ignoring her orders on the chance that it wasn't. And why would she go to all that trouble, all that effort to make arrangements for the lawyer to find us thirteen *years* later?"

"Why didn't you tell me?"

"It was so much for you to cope with. For both of us to cope with. And a part of me did want to believe she was out of her mind. But there was always the possibility . . . So I did absolutely everything possible to stop it. Everything she recommended. And I prepared you as best as I could to survive under any circumstances."

Okay, that explained all the Survival Family Robinson training.

"Meanwhile, I've been preparing myself for how to die."

Mr. Rose's face went white again, but Elodie pressed relentlessly on. I had the sense that this explosion was a long time coming.

"Do you think this has been easy for me, Dad? To live this life where I'm half a person, a shadow in school, in town. Completely isolated, blowing off every single person who shows even the slightest interest in me? To live with the knowledge that, at the very least, I have several centuries' worth of crazy in my family tree and at worst, I'm going to turn into some kind of psychotic monster? To live with the responsibility that I might have to *put myself down* like a dog before I can hurt someone else?"

My legs actually gave out. I sank to my belly on the concrete outside the window and wrestled with visions of the knife. Jesus, God, the knife I knocked out of her hand the day we met. It had been a goddamned dress rehearsal.

Elodie

"You've been . . ." Dad couldn't even finish the sentence. He collapsed into the chair. Even now he was doing everything in his power not to look at me.

"You can say all you want about helping me survive, Dad, but you won't let me live. So yes, I lied to you about my job. I lied to you about a lot of things. We've both been lying. To each other. To ourselves. This year has been borrowed time. I should be dead already."

It was strangely liberating to say all of this out loud.

"Oh God, Ellie," he moaned.

"I should have turned last year. We both know that." I stood again, squaring my shoulders. I was going to be honest about all this for the first time in my life. No more deception. "I think a hunter knows it, too."

What little color had returned to my father's face drained out again. "What?"

I sighed, struggling to organize my thoughts. I needed to *move*. It felt like all the muscles beneath my skin were electrified, twitching at once, begging for action. *Not now. This is so not the time.* I rolled my shoulders, trying to release some of the tension. "Someone's been following me for weeks. Since I found Rich. That entire scene was freakish, and totally pointless from a kidnapper or serial killer's standpoint. Rich was left as bait. I think it's someone waiting for me to slip up and show what I am."

Dad sat bolt upright at that. Now he *was* actually looking at me. "Wait, you've known someone was following you, suspected it was a hunter, and yet you take everything we've done the last four years to keep you safe and *throw it away* for some *boy*? Getting involved. Making yourself a target?"

I bristled, feeling the aggression I was starting to associate with being wolfish. Sawyer wasn't just some random guy I'd gone out and picked up for kicks. Given the look on Dad's face, I guessed my eyes had changed again. "Were you 'just some boy' to Mom?" I demanded. I didn't bother to suppress the growl in my voice. "I have done every goddamned thing right. I've followed your Rules. I've cut myself off from every part of a normal life for *four years*. And you know what, Dad? It's happening anyway. I started changing before I ever laid eyes on Sawyer."

Sucker punch, I thought, as he sank back. If he'd been older and less fit, I might've been worried about a heart attack.

"How long?" Dad whispered.

"Just before my birthday." I shoved both hands through my hair and gave in to my body's need to move, pacing a tight path in front of the sofa. "I think the history had it all wrong. The entire cock and bull story was just some twisted morality tale passed down from one ignorant fool to the next, and I am apparently *the only* member of the entire female line of the family going back three hundred years to have the self restraint to figure that out. I don't think this has a fucking thing to do with a curse. It's genetics. I am a werewolf because Mom was a werewolf. She was because her mother was, and her mother before that, all the way back to Brynne. I'm turning, Dad. And I sure as hell haven't slept with Sawyer or anyone else to cause it."

He was silent, still processing this total alteration in the "facts" we'd been living by since the letter.

"You're deluding yourself. Because you want this boy."

"Please. I am not being ruled by my hormones." I thought fleetingly of that desperate kiss, then squashed it. So not germane to the current argument. "I've been thinking about this for years. Magic is nothing but science that people didn't understand. They used to think that thunder was caused by a god. It makes sense that they would see werewolves as a curse, not as the introduction of new genetic material."

"It doesn't change anything."

"No," I agreed. "It doesn't. There's still a hunter. I suspect there have always been hunters. I don't think they disappeared all those generations back. I think they got smarter about not getting caught."

That thought had clearly never occurred to him. "We have to go. The essentials can be packed in a couple of hours.

We'll leave the rest," said Dad, pushing up out of the chair.
"I've got a contact—"

"No. *We* don't have to go anywhere. *I* do."

"No." Dad's voice was ragged as he lurched toward me.
"I won't put you in danger by staying here. I won't put
Sawyer in danger either. What you saw was goodbye. My
mind was already made up."

"What exactly is your plan, Elodie?" he challenged.
"Run? Hope the hunter follows? Where? For how long?"

"I will draw him away from here. From you. I've been
ready for this for a while." I gave a bitter smile. "You did
teach me to always be prepared. You know exactly how long
I'm capable of surviving in the mountains. You trained me,
after all."

"And then what? Play some game of cat and mouse with
this guy and hope he doesn't win?"

"I don't know," I admitted. "The important thing is
getting him away from here. What happens after that is
between him and me. But I have no child. So one way or the
other, this entire nightmare ends with me."

Naturally the fight didn't end with that dramatic
pronouncement.

"Over my dead body."

"That's exactly what I'm trying to avoid."

"This is ridiculous. It's a foolish plan. You have no way
of knowing that the hunter will follow you, no way of
knowing he'll disappear if you do. You don't even know if
you're *right*."

"You didn't know if it was right when you dragged me
here and made me give up my life, but you were willing to
take the chance. So am I."

"And what exactly am I supposed to say about you to
people who ask? You can't just disappear with no
consequences. People will come looking."

"Not if you tell them I've gone to see family.
Grandparents or something. People don't really know us

here. If you tell them I've gone to stay with my grandfather for the rest of the summer, no one will question you. They don't know grandpa died two years ago."

He looked infuriated that I had a practical response to that.

"What if you're wrong? Are you just going to stay in the mountains for weeks, waiting? At what point do you decide it's safe to come home?"

I felt my face spasm. "We both know it won't be safe for me to come home. Whether the hunter finds me or not, I'm on the verge of shifting. It won't be safe for me to be around you or anyone else once I do. Better for me to be in the wild where I'm less likely to hurt someone."

This was not, in fact, my plan. I had no delusions that I would be able to live in the wild, even in uninhabited areas, as some happy little lone wolf. None of my ancestors had survived long enough to confirm whether their humanity, their ability to reason, would stay intact for long after the shift. I was prepared to end it before it got to that point.

I hoped.

He stared at me in apparent anguish. This was more emotion than I'd seen him display in years. "Do you honestly think I'm just going to let you walk away? You're *my child.*"

"I may be yours, but I haven't been a child for years. This is the responsible decision. You wanting me to do otherwise is selfish."

"*Selfish?*" he choked out.

"You'd rather make me stay and risk unleashing me on the world. Yeah, I say that's selfish."

We went on that way for a while longer. I didn't manage to wear him down, which is unsurprising. No parent is going to be willing to let their kid deliberately walk out to face death. Or worse.

I was losing patience and the light, so when he got in my face again to reiterate his point, I twisted my hand in his shirt, lifted him off his feet, and thumped him against the wall.

Increased strength. Check.

"You aren't going to stop me," I snarled.

Using what I was to press the advantage against him left a sick taste in my mouth.

The look of stunned betrayal on his face seared me to the bone. As if even after everything he'd seen, he hadn't truly believed that I was turning.

I let him slide down to the floor. "I won't have your blood on my hands."

This time when I turned to go, to pack, he didn't come after me.

Even the long day of summer had worn away by the time I stepped out the back door. The sky was dark, pinpricks of light studding the sky. Not ideal conditions, but I could find my way even in this. As I crossed the yard, I half expected Dad to tranq me in a last desperate move to stop me. But I made it into the woods unscathed.

A small part of me wept at that.

The temptation to take the direct route to the cave was strong. It was only about four miles as the crow flew. I was tired. Bone deep exhausted, both from the work I'd done that day and from the fight. But laying a direct path to my hideaway would be foolish. Dad might try to come after me. He might alert Search and Rescue to find and bring me back. And I didn't know if the hunter had actual tracking skills, but it made sense to try to confuse him too. Since the last search, I'd taken some time to learn something about muddying scent trails. That should confuse things well enough to give me at least a couple of days to figure out a more solid plan.

Miles to go before I sleep, I thought.

I didn't look back at the house. What was the point? Goodbyes? Regrets? I'd had enough of both. It wouldn't change anything. I was well and truly alone now.

Elodie

My pack officially weighed eight hundred pounds. That's what it felt like at least. I leaned back against a boulder, letting it take the weight from my shoulders for a bit as I rested, taking a swig from my water bottle. I'd lost track of how far I'd hiked and how long. I'd been moving for hours, laying trails, crossing them, erasing them. I'd taken to the river three times, hiking in bare feet. Note to self: newly acquired werewolf powers did not include impenetrable soles of human feet.

Part of me kept moving in an effort to escape the bruise that had been spreading through my chest since this afternoon. That attempt was an epic fail. Physical pain didn't distract from emotional pain. Not when the emotional was so much bigger.

The moon had passed its apex and was on its descent for the night, and that meant it was time to go to ground. I considered just pulling out my sleeping bag and setting up a minimal camp right where I was. But it was too exposed for my taste, and I really wasn't in the mood to string my supplies up to prevent bears from messing with them. It was only a couple more miles to the cave from here. Once I made it in, I'd set up my camp and sleep all day tomorrow if I wanted. It might take that long to recover from the day I'd had. And let's face it. I hadn't had a decent night's sleep since the change started.

Sleep. Right. I was ready to get right on that. I tipped my back, resting against my pack and my eyes closed against the monochrome world of night. I'd stand up again in a minute.

I didn't want to stand up. I didn't want to keep walking. I just wanted to sit down and bawl my eyes out. Because that was such a practical response to the fact that I'd gotten exactly five minutes of *life* before having it ripped away in the worst possible way I could imagine. Okay, nobody died or got shot. Second worst.

I thought it would be worth it to kiss Sawyer. To have that memory to take out and look at, like a secret treasure. But God, *God,* it was so much worse. To feel that much, to know what I was leaving behind. And, thanks to Dad, to have been denied my proper goodbye. Not that I'd been planning on telling him the truth exactly. Before my father showed up, I hadn't expected to be leaving so soon. I'd thought I had more time.

But that was the theme of this summer, wasn't it? Every moment was borrowed. And each one had a higher price than the last.

Whoever said it was better to have loved and lost than never to have loved at all was smoking crack. This *sucked.* Maybe if there was a chance of living until I was old and gray, when I could look back from the distance of years with some kind of rose colored glasses, it would be true. But that wasn't in the cards. So now I just got the pain. Great.

I really needed to get going. Time was wasting, and I was totally exhausted. How many miles had I hiked? Twelve? Fifteen? I felt like somebody was sneaking bricks into my pack with every step. Okay there was nobody out here left to lie to, so if I was really honest with myself, I was weighed down by way more than gear.

I'd felt alone for years. In so many ways, it felt like Dad checked out once the letter came, once we changed our life. Regardless of what he said, I was a duty more than a daughter. But I hadn't truly known what alone meant. Not really.

Was this what Mom felt like when she disappeared? Had she planned to escape to protect us and then been crushed under the weight of the reality? Unable to cope? From the stories Dad used to tell, Mom was vivacious. A real social butterfly. She was used to being the center of attention, so the prospect of doing . . . well, exactly what I was doing now, would have been really hard for her to bear.

I wanted to think I was stronger than that. Or at least better prepared.

But what if I wasn't? What if I found myself in exactly the same position where the knife started to look like a more attractive option? And if this was even crossing my mind now, when I'd only been gone a matter of hours, what would I be like in a few days or weeks?

The snapping of a twig had my eyes flying open. I twisted my head, listening hard, trying to isolate the sound. Was it near? Far? Predator or prey? My hand curved around the hilt of the knife I wore on my belt. The same knife I'd used for my trial. Not among my top ten choices for ways to off myself, but practical from a survival standpoint. Of course I'd more had it in mind for carving spears for fishing and cutting branches, not fighting off a bear or something.

I didn't move from the boulder. It protected my back. But I slowly swiveled my head to either side, scanning the surrounding woods. Yet I saw nothing. Damn it, I couldn't hear for the pulse beating thick in my ears. What use was this stupid hearing if I couldn't control it?

Something fell on my shoulder from above. I went rigid, hardly daring to breathe. No way was I lucky enough that that had been a bug. Something was on the boulder above me. Because it was the only thing I could semi-reliably control, I widened my nostrils and inhaled, sifting through the scents. But the wind was blowing straight toward me. No help there. I was going to have to look.

Degree by painstaking degree, I tipped my head back.

My wolf stood above me, pale fur shining in the moonlight. I have no idea why I thought of him as mine. He obviously wasn't a pet. But it was the same wolf who'd saved me last night. I knew that as well as I knew my own name.

My breath whooshed out in relief. I stepped away from the boulder and turned, staggering a bit under the weight of the pack.

"Way to scare a girl," I said. I was pathetically glad to see him, grateful for a familiar face, even a furry one.

He leapt down, huffing on the landing. I winced for him as his right flank buckled under the weight.

I started toward him, intending to check last night's wound, but he bared his teeth in warning, so I stopped short, raising my hands in surrender. Okay, good reminder that he was a wild animal and wasn't going to submit to my attentions outside extreme circumstances. I would almost swear he gritted his teeth as he forced himself to stand again.

"Stubborn aren't you? Well you're in good company."

He blinked at me.

"So what are you doing here? Is there something horrible in the woods? Something else for you to save me from?" I looked around, tuning the rest of my senses into the night. I heard the soft flutter of an owl and the tiny scream of something that became its dinner. I smelled something I thought was a possum. But mostly the area was empty. No bears. No hunter.

"Or maybe you're just here to keep me company." I took a few steps and he followed. "Thanks for that. It's been a long night. Long day, too."

He gave me a look that seemed to ask why the hell I was still up and out here at all. I don't really know why I felt compelled to answer. "Long story. I had to confuse my trail. I'm heading for camp now."

I was too tired to keep up a stream of nervous chatter like I did last night. If he was going to come, he was going to come, whether I babbled on or not. It's not like I owed him some kind of explanation for why I was out here. Either way, there was no way I was going to be able to stay vertical too much longer. The wolf fell in beside me with just a slight limp.

We were moving slow, so it took nearly an hour before we crested the ridge into the hollow. I was so happy to see the brush screen over my cave, I nearly wept with relief. My legs felt like jelly as I stumbled down the rise. I hauled the screen aside. While I dug out a flashlight, the wolf went on in. Apparently he was all about making himself at home in my space.

I switched the flashlight on, squinting at the sudden glare. Once my eyes adjusted, I hunched and went inside. With the extra height of my pack, I had to stoop at an awkward angle for the first dozen feet or so. Then the space opened up. I played my light over the ceiling and walls. Nothing seemed to have made its way inside in the last couple of days. Thank God. The last thing I wanted was a startled bat dive bombing my head.

I shrugged out of my pack, groaning in relief. "Oh, thank you, God." My flashlight caught the white flash of fur from the back. My friend seemed to be circling around, looking for a comfortable spot at the rear of the cave. There was a sort of alcove back there, partially blocked off from what I thought of as the supply area. It's where I had planned to lay out my sleeping bag. Well I guessed he was gonna be staying a while. That was probably a good thing. As tired as I was, I wouldn't be on as high alert as I should be.

Out of long ingrained habit, I unpacked, stacking and organizing supplies, setting up camp, though it was only a couple of hours until sunrise. That's when I saw the other pack leaning against the cave wall.

Unease trickled through me. Playing the light around it, I saw other gear. More water. More foodstuffs. Another set of cookware. A sleeping bag.

"What the fuck?" I scrambled over, my hands fumbling to open the pack, searching for some kind of identifier. But I already knew what I would find. "No, no, no. This isn't mine."

My location had been compromised. It was no longer secret. No longer safe. I had to go.

"It's mine."

I whirled, dropping the flashlight. "Fuck!" I dove for it, my hand closing around the shaft, already testing the weight for a weapon as I snapped the beam up and toward the back. It lit on hands fastening the button on a pair of low-riding jeans. I drew the knife with my free hand, rolling into a defensive crouch. The light slid up a bare, muscular chest before moving up to land on a squinting face.

Sawyer.

"I'm coming with you."

It was a dream. I was asleep on my feet and hallucinating. It was a product of exhaustion and desperate longing. A cruel trick of my brain. Because there was no way that Sawyer was standing at the back of my cave. Except that he looked pissed in that way only Sawyer could manage, with rage practically seething beneath his skin. Really shouldn't my fantasy be glad to see me?

"I'll take that," said Sawyer, striding over and plucking the knife from my hand. "You clearly can't be trusted with it." He flung it, without looking, directly into a twenty pound bag of rice.

I stared at my empty knife hand, feeling the tingling fingers, and I flashed back to that day in the clearing. Except now that fury was directed at me. Sawyer advanced, mouth curled into a snarl. "You lied to me."

Automatically I retreated a step. "Excuse me?"

"You had every intention of using that goddamned knife. For *no fucking reason!*"

My own temper sliced through exhaustion. "You don't know anything about my life."

"You don't know anything about your *own* life. You've been so stupid. I can't *believe* how fucking stupid—"

I felt a burst of adrenaline through the anger, felt the rising within me, and I backed away from him in a hurry as a

160

growl began to vibrate in my chest. "Sawyer, you have to go, " I managed. "Just shut up and go."

"I'm not going *anywhere*. You're running around thinking you're going to be turning into some kind of slavering monster and have to be put down like a fucking dog."

Shock knocked me back another step. "How . . . how do you know that?"

"I heard you talking to your dad, and you're both, like, completely insane."

I was pressed against the rough cave wall now. Nowhere to go. Nowhere else to escape as he kept coming toward me. Where was the wolf?

"Look, you shouldn't have heard that. You really need to go." I closed my eyes because I knew they must be glowing and I couldn't bear to see him look at me with the same revulsion my father had.

My body was trembling with the effort to hold back the reaction.

"Elodie, you need to look at me."

"No." I shook my head. "You need to go."

Sawyer stepped into me, caging me with his arms against the cave wall. I could feel the heat of his chest just inches away.

"Elodie, look at me." His tone had softened, no longer angry.

I felt tears burn down my cheeks and shrank back as far as I could against the stone. "I don't want to hurt you," I whispered.

His hand brushed the tear from my cheek, then tipped my face up. "Look."

I opened my eyes and looked into his. The same bright, glowing gold as my own.

Chapter 10

Elodie

It was a trick of the light. My eyes were somehow reflecting in the dark of his. Or I was straight up hallucinating, whether from exhaustion or hereditary madness, it really didn't matter. I was seeing what I wanted to see, not truth. My mind was clearly a cruel and masochistic place.

I tried to turn my face away. *It isn't real. None of this is real.*

And then his other hand was there, framing my face, wiping more tears.

"Elodie." His soothing voice didn't work this time. "Don't you see? Don't you understand? I'm like you."

"You're not. You don't know—"

"I *do* know," he insisted. "I am a werewolf. From a very long family line of werewolves. I know exactly what you're going through." His voice had a calm, patient, talk the crazy person off a ledge tone.

Was this a sick joke? Establish some kind of common ground and humor me until he thought he'd talked me down from suicide and could haul me off to the nearest mental ward?

He didn't *know*. He wasn't *like me.* How could he be? How could it possibly be true and he still be *here?* Alive? Sane? No. It flew in the face of everything I knew, everything I was.

I clenched my jaw but couldn't hold back the growl. "Everyone who knows what I'm going through is dead. So don't *pretend* you have any idea what I've been through, what's happening to me."

The hands cradling my face slipped down to grip my shoulders. "You think I don't know what it's like? Being overwhelmed by senses that are suddenly sharper than they should be? All those scents, the sounds. They're enough to make you want to vomit. For the first couple of months, you can't control it. The headaches? Sometimes they're enough to nearly blind you with pain. The night sweats and fevers? Well you probably haven't gotten to those yet. You're a bit behind on the usual shifting schedule."

They could be guesses. Good ones. He was observant. He could easily have noticed the change in my behavior. And my being late shifting, well I'd said that myself in the conversation he'd apparently eavesdropped on earlier tonight.

"What about the short fuse and uncontrollable aggression?" he continued.

Oh, like it took a genius to figure out I'd wanted to kill Amber.

"If I'd been closer to my first transition when my mother was killed, I'd have completely lost it. As it was I nearly killed a guy at school for making a smart ass remark about my mother leaving. Because we couldn't release the truth, that she'd been shot as a wolf. That's why I was expelled. Because I put the guy in the hospital. In traction. I was lucky to avoid prison."

If he was a wolf, he was doing nothing but proving my point. If he was a wolf, as I was, then we *were* violent, we *were* dangerous. There was every reason to cut things off before they ever got to that point, before I could lose control.

"Look, Elodie, I don't know what kind of fucked up information you've been living with, but there's no reason to kill yourself because of this. What you're experiencing is perfectly *normal* for a werewolf. You'll go through transition and then you *learn to control it.* You won't be a danger."

It was almost like he was in my head, reading my jumbled thoughts. A frightening prospect in and of itself. But what he was saying, what he was offering . . .

"It can't be true," I whispered.

"Why is it so hard for you to just accept this?" He actually shook me, his voice snapping with frustration.

"Because it invalidates my entire family history! It makes every goddamned piece senseless and horrible," I shouted. "Because it means that eighteen bright, vivacious women *died* for nothing. Suffered for *nothing.*"

The frustration left his face, replaced with a dawning realization. "Not just them, but you."

I jerked free of his hands and spun to pace. "Yes, me. If I believe you, then everything I've done, everything I've sacrificed and denied myself meant nothing. I've lived this way for *nothing.* My whole life, I've tortured myself for *nothing.* I might have *killed myself for nothing.*" Oh my head ached. I shoved both hands in my hair, gripping, pulling, I didn't know which. I just wanted the pain to go away. All of it.

"Just believe what I'm telling you, and all that stops. Just believe me and put all that behind you." The calm, reasonable tone cut like a knife, through my beliefs, through my fears. And just like the knife, I shied away from it.

It's not that simple.

"Yes, it *is* that simple."

Something burst inside me. Whatever dam I'd built to hold back the tide of emotion so I could keep moving, keep functioning, simply shattered. My legs buckled. I started to fall, but Sawyer caught me, taking my weight, tucking me close as the full body quakes hit. I shook so hard in his embrace I wondered that I didn't break. My chest felt tight, my throat raw, and I couldn't *breathe.* I realized I was crying.

Great, wracking sobs, without making a sound. A silent sort of scream while my world completely imploded.

In a nuclear explosion, after the blinding flash of light, there is a shock wave that wipes out everything in its path before the accompanying sound ever catches up. For that span of time, it's like the world is deaf because the shock travels faster than the speed of sound. Silent destruction. I don't know how long I was caught up in my own shock wave before I realized that Sawyer, currently the only solid thing in my reality, was speaking.

I couldn't understand words at first. Didn't try. It was easier to focus on his tone and stay curled into a ball around the center of my pain. The rumble of his voice vibrated into my cheek, my side, everywhere I pressed against his chest, until degree by bare degree, my body began to unknot. The shaking began to ease. And my ears started to work again.

"You're not alone anymore," he whispered into my hair. "I'm here."

I lay still against him. Listening.

He kept saying it, over and over. And it was the most beautiful, wonderful thing I'd ever heard. Screw poetry.

I opened my eyes. We were on the floor, with me cradled in Sawyer's lap. Somewhere along the way I'd dropped the flashlight. It was pointed off toward the back of the cave, so when I lifted my head, his face was in shadow. The eyes that studied me now were brown, no longer wolfish. He ran a hand down the length of my hair.

"Hey," he said softly. One corner of his mouth crooked in a smile. "Welcome back."

My hand shook when I reached out to touch his cheek. I was so far beyond exhaustion it wasn't even funny. But I feathered my fingers along his jaw, brushing the unsmiling corner of his mouth, which curved in response.

I wanted to say something to express my gratitude for what he'd done, for his persistence and his belief in me. For

changing my life. For *saving* my life. But I couldn't think of
the words. So I kissed him instead.

Just the barest brush of lips. Almost as if part of me was
afraid he would disappear if I pressed too hard. As if I'd find
out this was all a dream. But his hand slid up my back and
into my hair and he pressed closer. Not a demand, just . . .
solid and real. His mouth slanted over mine and I lost myself,
happy, for once, not to have a plan or know what comes next.
Just content to be here, with him.

Eventually he broke away, brushing the hair back from
my face, tracing his thumb over my lower lip. "One of these
days I'm going to kiss you when you're not crying."

I choked out a laugh. "I'm sorry."

He pressed another kiss to my temple and ran a hand
down the length of my back. I found myself arching into his
touch, comforted.

"I propose we get more comfortable for the Q and A
portion of this program."

It occurred to me then that he was sitting on the floor of
the cave with no back support.

"Oh! Yeah."

I wish I could say I scrambled up, but the truth was my
legs were wobbly as a newborn foal's. It took a couple of
attempts. Sawyer was the one who grabbed the sleeping bags
and headed for the alcove in the back. He was already
unzipping his when I picked up and redirected the flash light

"What are you doing?"

"While you had the good sense to bring a mid-weight
sleeping bag in which you will not roast alive, I grabbed what
was immediately available. I'm from Montana, remember?
This puppy is for sub-zero temps. Which kind of sucks in
Tennessee, except that it means more padding."

"Oh."

He flipped it out, then reached for mine to do the same.
Crawling to the middle, he stretched out and patted the space

beside him. "C'mon. I don't bite. Usually." He flashed a cheeky smile.

I really should not have had the mental energy left for the thoughts that remark conjured. To hide my embarrassment, I knelt to untie my boots. I stepped out of them and stripped off my socks, wincing as my bare feet hit the hard floor. With luck this miraculous sped up healing would clear up those stone bruises and cuts by the time I woke up tomorrow. Today. Whatever.

I tried not to think too hard as I crawled across the sleeping bags into Sawyer's open arms. Too much had passed between us tonight for this to be awkward. If he was okay with the fact that I'd just totally fallen apart, I wasn't going to question it. So I snuggled in, as I'd often dreamed of doing, and he tugged me even closer, tangling our legs. It felt so freaking good to be off my feet, I nearly moaned. His chest was warm beneath my cheek and surprisingly smooth. I totally would have expected a werewolf boy to be really hairy. Thankfully I had enough brain cells left to prevent myself from voicing that observation out loud.

"So you're . . ." I didn't even know how to ask the question.

"A wolf. Like you. Yes."

More mental implosions. Sawyer was my wolf. The wolf who had risked his life to save me last night. The wolf who had bled in my kitchen. As billboards for interest and affection go, those were pretty damned big ones.

"I never . . . I didn't even think . . ."

"Don't tell me that brilliant brain of yours rejected the notion of a curse in favor of genetics and never went beyond that to think that there were more of us."

"More?" I said faintly, my brain drawn back to the impossible situation in which I found myself. Not the last. After all the isolation, the notion that there were more just didn't seem possible.

"Sure. I mean, we're not, like, rampant, but there are pockets of us here and there. At least a few hundred across North America."

The rumble of his voice against my cheek tied pleasant knots in my belly.

"A few *hundred?*" I squeaked.

"Sure. Dad could tell you more about it than I can. He's always been more interested than me."

"Wait, your *dad?* Then you didn't inherit this from your mother?"

"From both of them. Which is the *normal* way of things. The fact that you come from a lengthy matrilineal line with human fathers is nothing short of . . . miraculous. I've never actually heard of that before. And it probably explains some of your quirks."

"Quirks?"

"Why I didn't know right off what you were. I should've been able to smell you. Though that may be because you haven't shifted yet. The thing is, when we met there was nothing about you that tipped me off. Except for—" He cut himself off.

"Except for what?" I asked.

"You calm the beast," he muttered. "My beast, I mean. The wolf inside me. It's restless. And when I first came here, it was angry. But even that first time I talked to you it . . . calmed. A—another wolf might have been able to do that. But a human? No."

It felt like there was something else there, something he left out, but he was still talking.

"By rights I should have stayed away from you. Far away. But I just couldn't. And then I started seeing signs here and there. Little things. Nothing I could definitively say yes or no about. So I . . . Don't get mad."

"After what you've done for me, I think you get some latitude," I observed.

"I followed you."

My body went immediately tense, as if he'd plucked a bow. "Oh." I couldn't think what else to say to that. It explained how he'd found this place. "So that whole conversation we had about me feeling like I was being stalked?"

He was stroking down my back again, trying to soothe. "Some of that was probably me. But not all of it. Not after last night."

I groaned. "Okay I vote the topic of who's trying to kill me gets tabled until tomorrow. I don't have enough brain cells left for that."

"Fine with me."

I relaxed again. "When did you know for sure?"

"Your confrontation with what's-her-name. You're not normally aggressive. That on its own would have been evidence that the wolf was ascending, but your eyes were the clincher. I was planning to talk to you about it this afternoon before . . . well before your dad showed up and things got out of hand."

I tried to imagine what that conversation would have been like and failed.

"Do you think he'd really have shot me?" Sawyer asked.

"I wish I could say no, but I don't know for sure. I haven't ever seen him like that before. Ever."

"I thought he was going to hurt you." Now he was the one with tension thrumming under his skin. "You got in the truck and I couldn't *do anything*. I thought I was going to be too late. And then when I got there and I heard—" He shuddered. "I can't . . . lose you."

I was too tired to process the implications of that, to think about ramifications or what it meant for us beyond this moment. So I said the only thing I could. "You won't."

~*~

Red

Sawyer

I heard the growling before I was even fully awake. A low, menacing rumble that had me rolling, covering Elodie with my body as I answered in kind, looking around for the threat.

Then I realized that the rumbling was my stomach.

I blinked, pushing the wolf back, and looked down at Elodie. She lay very still beneath me, eyes now very wide and awake, fixed on me. I could feel the shallow rise and fall of her chest against mine and the wolf came back for entirely different reasons. I wanted her mouth, to drown in the taste of her. I wanted my hands on that lithe, lean body, to lose myself in the feel and scent of it. I just plain wanted her. My mate.

Too soon. I shoved it back again. "Sorry. False alarm." I rolled off her and waited for the backpedaling and awkwardness.

She exhaled. "Nice to know you're on guard." She sat up and did some kind of yoga shoulder stretch that plastered her t-shirt against her breasts.

I looked away.

My stomach lodged another protest.

"I was going to ask if you were hungry, but your stomach is speaking for you, it seems."

I widened my nose to read her. No fear, no discomfort. She just smelled sleepy and comfortable. And my scent was on her from head to foot. My mouth curved in smug satisfaction at that. Didn't matter that nothing had happened but sleep. She was mine. And apparently she was okay with it. Would she be if she knew what that actually meant?

Her mouth split in a jaw-cracking yawn. "What time's'it?"

I checked the digital readout on my watch. "Seven."

She jolted. "AM or PM?"

"PM, I think."

171

"Holy crap, we slept for fifteen *hours?*"

"I'm guessing we needed it. You in particular. Why? Did your escape plan include a schedule? Are you supposed to be somewhere right now?"

"No. I just . . . I never sleep that much. That's the best sleep I've had in months. I actually felt . . . safe."

She gave me a sweet smile before leaning over for a quick kiss. I tried to grab her as she rolled away, because one kiss, one taste wasn't enough, but she only laughed and said, "Hungry!"

I didn't think I would ever have enough of Elodie. I snagged her around the waist and pulled her into my lap, pressing my lips to her throat. "It can wait." God she tasted good.

My stomach growled again and called me a liar.

"You were saying?" I didn't imagine the breathless tone of her voice.

I smiled and let her go. With an exaggerated put-upon sigh, I said, "Fine. Feed me, woman."

She made a beeline for the stuff I'd brought and began picking through the cans and packages.

"Beef ravioli? Mac and cheese? Corn beef hash? *Beanie weenies?* Have you *ever* been camping before?" she asked.

"First, don't knock the corn beef hash; it's good. Second, I told you I was in a hurry and grabbed what was available in our kitchen. I wasn't taking time for a supply run when I left."

"An all male kitchen is a truly frightening place," she said. "Do y'all eat *anything* that qualifies as real food?"

"We are men. We eat meat. I didn't think you had a fridge installed in the back of your getaway cave. Plus when we're out like this, we usually hunt for game."

Elodie went a little pale at that.

"You're not one of those *don't kill Bambi* girls, are you?" I asked.

"No. I'm perfectly at home with my carnivorous nature. I just prefer not to meet my dinner face to face. It's gonna be a long time before I can look at any kind of fresh kill and not see what was done to Rich."

I wrapped my arms around her from behind, absorbing the shudder that ran the length of her body. "The concept will feel less weird after you shift. The hunt is part of our instincts."

"All the same, I think I'm going to stick with fish for fresh food while we're out here. The river isn't too far. It's got good trout fishing."

"Fishing, huh?"

"Unlike normal girls, I'm not squeamish about cleaning and gutting them. I do know how to use this for other things." She plucked the knife out of the bag of rice, where I'd flung it last night and slipped it back in the sheath.

My fingers itched to take it away again. I didn't think she was really in danger of using it anymore, but just having it near her made me twitchy.

"How did you do that anyway? That's the second time I've seen you get rid of it with freakish accuracy. Did you do knife throwing as a hobby back in Montana?"

"Not so much specific training as heightened reflexes," I shrugged. "I can teach you. You're probably already showing signs, you just haven't noticed yet."

"Cool. Maybe we can do a session after dinner. Grab the camp stove and cook pots."

We set up our makeshift kitchen at the mouth of the cave. Within five minutes, Elodie had coffee percolating on one of the two burners and a pot of . . . something that smelled really awesome on the other.

"Are those spices?" I asked. "You actually packed seasonings in all your emergency survival gear?"

She gave me a bland stare. "What? Just because I'm on the run, I'm supposed to eat flavorless crap?"

"You probably even know which mushrooms are safe to eat, don't you?"

"No. Dad wasn't into mushrooms, so that wasn't on his list of Must Teach. Speaking of dads, yours should be back from Knoxville. What exactly did you tell him? Please say you at least left a note before you came after me."

"Of course I left a note."

"Which said . . . ?" she prompted.

"That I needed space, and I'd be back in a few days."

One dark brow winged up.

"What?"

"And you habitually just disappear like that for days at a time without him calling out a search party?"

I shrugged. "Not usually for days. But we're at a point where we're having dominance issues being under the same roof. He'll get it."

"Uh-huh."

I really hated the skeptical way she said that.

"And where did you leave your Jeep?"

I thought about it. "It's still at the lab."

"You think your dad isn't gonna know something's weird since you didn't take your Jeep? And didn't apparently leave from home?"

"Not if he assumes I left on four feet." I shrugged. "I don't know. It'll cover my ass for as long as it'll take us to get back."

"Get back?" She stopped stirring whatever was in the pot.

"Of course. You know the truth. There's no reason for you to stay out here and keep running."

"No reason— Sawyer, did you forget the fact that *someone is trying to kill me?*"

"Of course not. But it seems to me that it would be a good idea to bring in somebody else to help. There's no reason for you to face this alone anymore."

I wasn't what you'd call thrilled with bringing in my dad. We still had a ton of unresolved issues between us. But I wasn't about to let my pride or ego or whatever the hell get in the way of doing whatever I could to keep Elodie safe. If that meant tucking my tail and seeking out his guidance, I'd choke it down.

"And who would we bring in? The sheriff? Some other authorities? What would we tell them? That there's a lunatic out there who is the latest in a long line of lunatics who are determined to exterminate my family line? Because that's what this is, Sawyer. This goes back eighteen generations. We may have had the details about what we are completely wrong, but it doesn't change the fact that someone's been trying to wipe us out for the last three hundred years."

"How can you trust anything you think you know about this?" It was so . . . ludicrous. And yet I couldn't deny that someone had absolutely tried to run her down.

"Because unlike the specifics of turning into a werewolf, death records can be verified. Most of my ancestors were slaughtered by now, at least the ones who didn't die in childbirth or by suicide. And I can only assume that I'm still here because my dad ran and changed our names and did every possible thing to keep us from being found."

"Except that apparently it didn't work. Look, I understand you not wanting to go to the authorities, but my dad could help. He has contacts—"

Elodie was already shaking her head. "No. I'm not bringing anybody else in on this. I'm not *risking* anybody else. I don't *want* to risk you, but I know precisely where you'd suggest I shove it if I tried to send you home, so I'm not wasting my breath."

"At least we're on the same page about something." I paced out into the hollow. This was so *stupid* and reckless. How could she not see how reckless it was? How could she not care?

I paced back. "What exactly is your plan then?" I knew I was echoing her father, and I could tell by the mutinous look on her face she didn't appreciate it. But it was a valid question.

"I don't know," she said quietly, adding some more liquid to the pot—was that chicken stock?—and giving it another stir. "I admit I hadn't thought further than leading him away from Dad. From you. Rich was bait, Sawyer. I know it in my gut. I have no idea *why* the hunter would choose him. But that whole scene was a trap meant for me. By extension it could have revealed you."

The muscles across my shoulders tightened with the memory of fighting the wolf for control and nearly losing.

"How do you know it was meant for you? You've said yourself Rich wasn't someone important to you."

"Maybe that didn't matter. Maybe he was convenient. Or maybe the hunter saw Rich hitting on me and mistook that for us being involved. I don't know. But you said it yourself. It was on the freaking anniversary of Mom's disappearance. That's a pretty fucking big coincidence."

"Then how would the hunter—" I felt ridiculous calling him that, but I didn't have a better term, "—know that you'd be the one to stumble upon it?"

"Presumably because he knows I'm into search and rescue."

"And how would he know *that*? Unless—"

"Unless he's been tracking me for a long time."

The thought of someone researching her, learning her interests, her habits, all the things you should know about your prey, made my blood boil.

"Dad picked a small town because strangers would stand out. We'd hear about anybody who was around for longer than a few days. Anybody who didn't act like a tourist to the park. I think whoever this is has been around longer than that."

"You think it's someone you know?"

Elodie shrugged. "I don't know. Maybe." She swapped out the coffee pot for a skillet. "All I know is that by leaving I draw him out."

"Not if he doesn't know you left. Or thinks you left town."

"I'd planned to lay a trail. Deliberately draw him in once I have it sorted out how I wanted to handle things. That way I become the bait, and maybe I get a chance to stop him."

"Stop him how?" I knew the answer, but I needed to hear her say it.

She raised her eyes to mine, her face grim. "There's only one end to this. Either I die and my line ends with me or he does."

"And you're prepared to kill someone other than yourself?" I knew the answer to that too, and I felt like an asshole for pushing her. But maybe it would cause her to see some sense, to agree to go back.

Her movements were lupine when she rose from her crouch and paced the same circuit I had minutes before. I wasn't surprised to see her eyes flash gold when she turned back to me. "No. Of course I'm not. How can I be?" she demanded. "How can I possibly take another life and not become the very thing I fear most? How does that make me anything other than the monster he hunts?"

I could explain to her how it worked. How, as a wolf, you still mostly retain your human reason, human faculties. How, with training, she'd be able to control it. But she wouldn't believe me. Not yet. Not until she shifted and felt it herself. I caught her as she stalked within arm's length, tugging her close and wrapping my arms around her because I needed the contact and she needed the comfort. "You aren't a monster. And defending yourself doesn't make you one."

Her wolf faded as she looked up at me, replaced by a look of miserable skepticism. She may have believed everything I told her last night, but after how she'd been raised, she had a long way to go before she actually accepted the truth of it. If I had anything to do with it, she'd never be put in a position of having to make that life or death choice that I wasn't entirely sure she could live with.

"What if there were another way?" I said, my brain taking the seed of an idea and turning it over, enlarging it.

"What other way?"

"Well, you think that the person who's after you is the same person who kidnapped Rich and his sister, right?"

"Yes."

"Kidnapping is a major crime. If we could find evidence to link him to that, figure out who he is, we could let the actual cops take over. He'd be prosecuted, convicted, and put away. Then he couldn't touch you."

It was skepticism rather than hope I saw kindled in her eyes.

"And what kind of proof could we find that they couldn't?"

"The cabin. Rich said they were held at a cabin. The cops never found it."

I could see the wheels of her brain starting to turn.

"If we could find it, there's bound to be at least trace scent left that would help us identify who it is." She curled her hands in my shirt, and began speaking faster. "And maybe there could even be some kind of actual physical evidence. It would give the cops more leads, a means to focus their investigation. We might even be able to give them a name." She threw her arms around me. "Sawyer, you're a genius!" She gave me a hard and fast kiss then raced back into the cave, probably after maps.

I wasn't so sure about genius, but it gave her hope, and that was a valuable commodity just now. And at least it gave us something to do other than just running. Something resembling a plan. I knew she'd feel better with one. I wished I did.

~*~

178

Elodie

"Rich and Molly disappeared here." I made a tiny X with my pen on the topographical map I'd spread across the top of our makeshift table. "We found Rich here." I leaned over and made another X. "Neither of which is wholly useful for locating this cabin because a vehicle was involved in both cases. We need to know where Molly was found. That cave was in walking distance of wherever they were kept. Neither of them could have gotten too terribly far in the condition they were in."

Sawyer leaned in beside me. "Rich said it was a cabin by the river. Which river?" He reached out and traced his fingers over the myriad of tributaries that snaked through the park.

I crossed my arms. "Rich isn't the kind of guy who would differentiate between a river and a stream and a piddly little creek even under the best of circumstances. The police combed the banks of the *actual* river and found nothing, so I'm betting it's along something smaller. They might not have actually seen it, just heard the running water."

"Which narrows things down to . . . oh, thirty or forty square miles or so?"

I bumped him with my shoulder. "Hey, power of positive thinking. If we can narrow down where Molly was found, it would help a lot. You were there when the call came in. Do you remember anything of the call?"

"Mostly just 'We found her.' I was pretty focused on getting loose to come find you."

"*Think*," I prompted. "They would've been giving coordinates, saying something about landmarks, trailheads, *anything*. Eileen would've had to update the logs."

He frowned, thinking. "I want to say I remember something about Endicott. But that was probably one of the searcher's names."

I leaned back over, studying the map. "Could it have been Kennicott?"

"Maybe."

"Kennicott Ridge is within spitting distance of the Tennessee-North Carolina border."

"How far is that?" he asked.

"Maybe thirty miles by car. On foot, as the crow flies? Just under fifteen. Still within our county. I think."

"You know, the fact that you say that as if it's a city block really scares me."

"Wuss," I teased. "It gets to be pretty rough country. It'd be a day of hard hiking to get there. Two if we took our time. We've got ample supplies. If we leave within the hour, we could get to the halfway point here," I tapped the map, "in plenty of time to relax and set up camp before sunrise."

"You want to travel by night?"

"Why not? We avoid running into any other hikers, and let's face it. We're awake. What else are we doing to do all night?"

His face shifted and I quickly laid a finger over his lips. "Don't answer that."

He chuckled and leaned back over to peer at the map. "Bristol Falls?" he asked.

"Nature's shower."

"Hey, what're you trying to say?"

"That I'd love to get clean and it's a beautiful place to do so."

Sawyer linked his hands behind my back, eyes going gold. "So tell me, Miss Prepared, did you pack a bikini in all of your get away gear?"

"Wouldn't you like to know?" Of course I had. But it was fun to tease him, to see that wolfish grin curve his lips and feel the accompanying heat thrown off by his body as he tugged me closer with a playful growl.

He nipped at my throat and made my knees go weak. Before my resolve could follow, I pulled away, though my hand lingered in the soft waves of his hair. "Time to pack."

"Slave driver. Just for that, we'll do more reflex training on the way, as payback."

"Great. So you can whap me in the head with more aluminum plates?" The surprise lesson at the river during dish duty had not gone well.

"You're suppressing your wolf, so you're not getting access to all of your senses. You've got to stop being afraid of it."

I began sorting supplies for a multi-day hike. That was easy for him to say. For him this was totally normal, not a sign he was becoming the devil incarnate. For me . . . Well it was one thing to accept that I didn't have to kill myself. I hadn't wanted to do that in the first place. But moving past years of false belief, years of *fear* was something else entirely.

Sawyer moved behind me, running his hands down my arms to capture my hands and wrapping himself around me in a move that left me goosebumply and aching for him.

"You stopped being afraid of me," he said softly.

"I was never afraid of you specifically. I'm terrified of how you make me feel."

"And how is that?" he asked.

"Electrified," I said breathlessly. "And wolfish. When I'm with you I want—" Needs and desires tangled my tongue, and my skin, where he touched it, was on fire.

"What do you want?" he asked, lips against my throat.

"You," I whispered, closing my eyes to ride the sensation. "Just you."

He was my ultimate forbidden fruit. And if what he'd told me was true, he wasn't forbidden anymore. If he'd turned me then, if he'd kissed me, I think I'd have been lost. Thankfully at least one of us had some self-restraint.

With no small amount of effort, he set me away from him. I didn't turn to look at him. When he spoke, his voice was ragged. "We have to go."

It was obvious enough that if we didn't, what control he had left was going to slip as well. I swallowed hard, though it did nothing to wet my parched throat. "Maybe you could go pack up the camp stove." Which was outside.

Sawyer walked out without another word. Which was totally fine. Because if he'd spoken again, the sound of his voice might have overcome the reservations that were hanging on by mere fingernails, and this was so not the time for that. I knew he wasn't angry. I could smell that much. We both just needed a little time to find our equilibrium again.

Right. Equilibrium. That was it.

I was starting to understand exactly how my ancestors had gotten into trouble. If they'd felt a fraction of this kind of desire, this *need*, it was easy to see how sense had been over ridden. Because in the moment, nothing else mattered but the heat.

Hoo boy.

Packing didn't take long. Both of us were motivated to get going and work off this frustration. Or maybe just to get to the falls and get under that icy water. Nature's *cold* shower.

We hit the trail with the white elephant of our attraction stomping between us. I threw myself into the hike, setting a pace that most people would have difficulty matching. Sawyer, of course, was right behind. We marched up hill, over dale, until my legs screamed for relief and my shoulders started to cramp. Then it wasn't just my shoulders, but my back and my legs, until I fell to my knees in a full body Charlie horse.

"Elodie." Sawyer was there, pulling off my pack. "Breathe," he ordered.

But I couldn't breathe. I curled my body, trying to stop the siege on my muscles, but it fought against me, arching back so hard, I cried out.

"You gotta breathe." His hand grabbed mine, and I clamped on, as another spasm hit.

I rolled my head and saw the muscle in my shoulder swell and writhe like a snake beneath my skin. A keening noise built in my throat. It spilled out on the next wave as my legs jack-knifed and slammed into the ground. I curled, rolled to my hands and knees, retching, though nothing came up. It felt like my vocal chords were stretching, straining, breaking.

Then it was over as suddenly as it had begun. I lay panting, on the ground, my hand still clamped around Sawyer's. My cheek was pressed against his thigh, and he stroked my hair back from my face.

"What the fuck was that?" I wheezed.

"Body cramp. I didn't think you'd be getting those yet. They'll start coming more often the closer you get to shifting. It'll get worse before it gets better, I'm afraid."

"Greeeeeeeat." I lay there until my harsh breathing evened out. "Is shifting always like that?"

"No. Eventually it gets easy. More like a full body stretch than . . ." He seemed to search for a word..

"Labor," I supplied.

"Huh?"

"It's like labor. Giving birth from one form to another."

Even from upside down in the moonlight, I could see the vaguely queasy expression on his face at that comparison. Typical guy.

"You okay?" he asked.

Obviously he wasn't gonna touch that one with a ten foot pole.

I took inventory. My muscles seemed to be more or less back to the size and shape they were supposed to be. I guessed I was done with the freak routine for a while. But everything ached. "I hurt. There's ibuprofen in my pack."

"Of course there is. Where?"

"Top left side pouch."

He leaned over and rummaged around, grabbing the painkillers. He helped me to sit up and handed me three pills and a canteen. "Prescription dose. You're gonna need it."

I knocked them back, then just sat. "Shit, that takes a lot out of you."

Behind me Sawyer put his hands on my shoulders, big, strong fingers digging into knots of muscle. I let out an incoherent groan. I kept waiting for the heat, for a different kind of knots, but this wasn't sexy, just straight up therapeutic. And that was . . . a relief. Like I was finally free of the chokehold of desire. For now.

"So if you decide college isn't for you, your future career as masseuse is pretty well set."

"Exercise helps too. I ran miles every day during the months of my transition."

He moved on to my left arm, kneading from the biceps all the way down to my forearm and fingers.

"Months?" I said. "How long does it usually take?"

"From the time the first symptoms appear? Six to eight months?"

"Six to eight *months?* But I don't understand. I've only had symptoms for, like, a *month*. Since right before my birthday."

"Huh." He moved on to my right arm. "Well, I have a theory."

"By all means, enlighten me, Obi-Wan."

"I don't want you to feel weird or pressured or anything."

"Okaaaaay." Where was he going with this?

"Werewolf transition is a lot like human puberty."

"Gawkiness, hormones, and ridiculously unfair acne?"

"Transition means we're of mate-able age."

"Ma—Oh."

Sawyer's hands stilled on my shoulders, then fell away. "You've spent so much time . . . cloistered, avoiding that part of things because of all the rules and your false beliefs, I think you kind of unnaturally delayed a normal transition. And then I showed up."

"And then you showed up. What does that have to do with anything?" I asked, turning to look at him.

He rubbed at the back of his neck, not quite looking at me. "Once your transition actually started, I think I accelerated it."

"I don't understand. How?"

"You remember how I said being around you quieted my beast?"

"Yeah?"

"That would only happen under one condition."

Why was he beating around the bush? "And that is?" I prompted, waving my hand.

He took a breath and met my eyes. "Because you're my mate."

My mouth opened. Closed again.

"Wolves tend to mate for life," I heard myself say.

"Yeah." He seemed wary, as if waiting for me to freak out.

Mates. My brain circled around the idea, turning it over like a new taste on my tongue. I was his. He was mine. And if I understood him correctly, he was implying that my delayed change was now happening faster because I'd found him. As if the dam holding things back had broken, and now things were happening in a flash flood because my wolf recognized him for what and who he was, even if the rest of me hadn't quite caught up.

"Well that explains a lot."

Sawyer let out the breath he was holding in a whoosh.

I thought of Mom and that lightning strike, love-at-first sight of Dad. "So if we hadn't been under the impression that Dad should be getting me to a nunnery, would I have fixated

185

on some human guy and started my transition early? Or at the normal time or whatever?"

"I don't know. Your family is the only one I've heard of that mated consistently outside wolfkind. Maybe that was due to an absence of suitable males. Maybe not. But you told me about how lots of your ancestors kind of went crazy. And I think that's why. We're genetically meant to mate with our own species."

"What, like mating with humans is like marrying your cousin for several generations kind of crazy?"

His mouth curved a little. "No. It's a control mechanism. When we're young, our wolves are tempered by the mated pairing of our parents. Once we're past transition, they're tempered by our mates. So as you settle my wolf, I should, in theory, also settle yours. Your control should be better with me."

I considered this. "So basically my ancestors didn't have that tempering influence because they chose mates who were human and their wolves ran amok?"

"That's my theory."

"And if you hadn't been there to talk me down, I might have actually killed Amber?" My stomach twisted at the thought of how much I'd enjoyed having my hand around her neck, hearing the choking gasps in place of insults.

"I don't know. You might never have been that aggressive if I hadn't kickstarted things to begin with."

That really wasn't making me feel any better.

"You didn't kill her, Elodie. Don't start punishing yourself for what you might have done. You didn't do it."

"And how do you know I won't do it again? To her or someone else, when you're not around. You can't be with me twenty-four hours a day."

"Until you're through transition I can. And until then, I'll be working with you on more control. You've already got an iron will. I think that's part of how you got this far on your own."

"And after transition?"

"It won't be so hard."

"I mean where will you be?"

"Right here. You're my mate, Elodie. I'm not going anywhere."

It was a good thing, I reflected, to belong to someone who believed in me that absolutely. Because I wasn't at all sure I believed in myself.

Chapter 11

Sawyer

"**I** can't believe you're making us set up camp first," I groused, eying the moonlit lake behind us while I slid tent poles through the sleeves of our tent. "We've been hiking for *hours.*"

"Yes, we have," she said, patiently stirring the pot of whatever she'd decided to cook for dinner while I was on tent-duty. "And when we're done with our swim, we aren't going to want to do anything but fall into the tent and sleep. This way we *can* do that."

I kept my mouth shut since I was pretty damn sure I'd want to do more than sleep. So not gonna push that. I shoved the next pole through, arched it, and inserted the pin to hold it. "Sometimes you are a disturbingly practical woman." It was disturbing because it was like my dad. He was always the practical one.

"It's a curse," she replied.

I shoved the final pole through and attached the anchor pins. Suddenly, we had a tent. One final circle around to drive in stakes and we were set. While she dished up dinner, I unrolled the sleeping bags, laying them out as I had last night, so we'd be cushioned by mine and covered by hers. The packs were next. I arranged them to the sides, out of the way as best as they could be in a tent that was really only meant for one.

"It'll be pretty tight," she observed as I emerged.

I stood up and took the plate she offered. "I don't mind."

189

She gave a tired smile. "I don't suppose I do either."

We inhaled the beef stew.

"Swim now," I insisted.

"Nope. Dishes first. Dirty dishes mean ants."

She stood and headed for the edge of the lake.

"Fine," I called. "Then we're doing more reflex training. Think fast." I winged my aluminum plate toward her like a frisbee.

Elodie dodged and the plate whizzed by her, landing with a clang and rolling almost into the lake. She turned and glared at me. "Did you just fling your dirty, gravy-coated plate at my head?"

"Whatcha gonna do about it?" I asked, grinning.

Her plate came flying toward me, slamming into my hand somewhere on the level of my throat.

"Ha! See? Your accuracy improves when you're pissed. You let your wolf out to play then."

"So your super masterful training plan includes getting gravy in my hair to piss me off so I'll try to behead you with a plate?"

"Can't say as I gave it that much serious thought, but, yeah, something like that. It worked, didn't it?"

She just shook her head. "Wash your dish, McGrath."

Once the dishes were scrubbed and stowed, I said, "Now, is camp set up to your satisfaction?"

"I suppose so."

"Then we can swim?" I asked, kicking off my boots.

She bent and unlaced her boots. "Now we can swim," she agreed, stepping out of them.

"Excellent."

She squealed in surprise as I scooped her up. "Sawyer what are you doing?" Then she saw me headed for the bank. "Oh no. No, you're not going to—"

With a running leap, I cannonballed both of us into the lake. I caught a foot to the chest for my trouble. At least I think it was a foot. Elodie wriggled free, surfacing with a growl of outrage, even as I whooped.

"Holy crap, that feels good!" I shoved my dripping hair back from my eyes.

"Sawyer I'm still *dressed*." Elodie's eyes flashed gold.

"I had noticed that. Me too. I figured we could help each other out with that." I grinned and snagged her around the waist.

She shoved back with both hands, popping free of my wet hands. "Do you have any idea how long our clothes will take to *dry* in all this humidity?" God she was cute when she was irritated.

"All the more reason to let them get started now," I said, tugging my wet t-shirt off and hurling it toward the bank, where it landed with a wet plop. "Besides, we both have changes of clothes in our packs. I watched you pack them."

I disappeared beneath the surface to take care of my shorts. They landed in a heap a couple feet from the shirt. That shot had to be worth two points. "There. That's better."

Elodie was a few feet away when I turned back around, eyes round.

"What?" I tread a quick circle, searching the bank for threats, but saw nothing.

She'd stroked another few feet back by the time I made it around.

"What's wrong?"

"You seem to be missing a rather important piece of apparel," she said.

"What's that?"

"Swim trunks."

"Don't have any. I was in a hurry when I packed, remember? Besides, I'm a werewolf. Naked's just another state of being. Plus, swim trunks completely defeat the purpose of skinny dipping."

Even in the monochrome night lighting, I could see the blood creep up her neck to her hairline. Huh. Apparently lack of modesty was a socialized trait, not a biological one. That was going to be an adjustment for her.

"Never been skinny dipping, huh?"

She lifted one brow in that prim, superior way that made me want to nibble her lips. "What do you think?"

"Well, you, my dear girl, have been missing out. And there's no better time to try it than the present." I lifted my arms to encompass the lake and its very empty surroundings. "We're in the middle of nowhere. Nobody around to see."

"You're around."

"Well, yes, but it's night and therefore dark, and I swear I won't look."

The eyebrow went up again.

I lifted three fingers. "Scout's honor."

"If you were a Boy Scout, then I'll lose my shorts."

I grinned. "Dropped out before Eagle Scout, but Mom was troop leader for four years."

"You could totally be making that up," she said.

"You want proof? Okay. Boy Scout oath: On my honor, I will do my best to do my duty to God and my country and to obey the Scout Law; to help other people at all times; to keep myself physically strong, mentally awake, and morally straight." I repeated that last bit to myself as a reminder that I was the one who had to keep things from getting out of hand.

Elodie swore.

"Lose 'em, Rose."

She bobbed for a minute or so, head dipping below the water, but she eventually came up with her shorts. With a narrow-eyed glare at me, she lobbed them to the bank.

I stroked lazy circles around her. "Now . . . what else can we bet your shirt on?"

"I am not a betting woman," she said. She huffed out a breath. "Turn around."

I did as she ordered, listening to the splashes as she wiggled out of the rest of her clothes. Even when I heard the wet thwack of them hitting the bank, I stayed where I was, studying the moonlight as it sparkled on the waterfall. All joking aside, I knew this was a big thing for her, so she got to set the pace from here.

"Okay."

When I turned Elodie was treading water just enough that her chin touched the surface, her hair fanning out behind her. Nervous. I didn't need to catch her scent to know that. She needed distraction, something to make her forget she was naked.

"How good a swimmer are you?" I asked.

"Pretty good."

"Great. Then I challenge you to a race. First one to the waterfall wins."

"Wins what?"

"Choice of breakfast. Loser cooks. And I warn you, if I win, I want corn beef hash."

Elodie made a face.

"On your mark, get set, g—"

She exploded into motion before I could get out "Go!" For a moment I could only watch her. Because she'd lied. She wasn't pretty good. She was amazing. Instead of cutting through the water with a powerful crawl, as I would, she flew in one of the smoothest butterfly strokes I'd ever seen, like some kind of freshwater mermaid. She was four lengths ahead of me before I threw myself into the race.

I'd intended to let her win. Not by much, but just enough to boost her confidence. As it turned out, even my all out wasn't enough to catch her. She flew through the curtain of water and slapped a hand on the rock wall a full three strokes ahead of me. As she turned toward me, her face glowed with triumph, her eyes gold. Her wolf was coming easier now. That was good. I wondered if she realized it.

"I'm not sure that was entirely fair," I protested.

"Hey, you got to 'go'. Not my fault you're slow off the line."

"I'm not slow. You're freakishly fast. Are you sure you're a werewolf and not some kind of sea creature?"

"Well, in the name of full disclosure, I have to admit that you're looking at the All-State silver medalist in butterfly for the 6th grade." She looked smug.

"Silver medalist? Swim team? In *Texas?* Shit. I didn't stand a chance. I'm amazed your dad let you compete."

"I swam competitively for five years . . . before." The light of victory instantly faded and so did her wolf.

Shit.

"Before what?"

"Before . . . this. Before we found out what I was."

"Wait, what? You didn't grow up knowing?"

"No. I got to be normal until I was thirteen. That was the year I got the letter from my mother."

Letter? Then I remembered what I'd overheard of her fight with her dad. "Right, the attorney. Why the delay of so many years?"

"I guess she thought she was doing me a favor letting me have a normal life for as long as possible."

I heard what she wasn't saying. That knowing what she was missing sucked a helluva lot worse.

Okay, time for this train to jump the depressing track. "Well, clearly the time off hasn't hurt your technique. You kicked my ass. Though I'm not sure you did yourself any favors."

Her mouth quirked in a partial smile. "I got out of eating corned beef hash. I may be a werewolf but I refuse to eat dog food, and that's exactly what corned beef hash smells and looks like."

"To each their own, but in the name of full disclosure on *my* side . . . I can't actually cook."

Elodie feigned surprise. "What? With such astounding staples in your pantry and the pizza delivery place on speed dial?"

"Either you've been spying on me, or that's a sexist remark."

"Sexist but true. *I'll* cook breakfast. You get dish duty."

"Shake on it," I said, offering my hand. She took it, and I yanked her closer. "Sealed with a kiss is better," I told her. "I haven't kissed you in almost nine hours. I'm in withdrawal."

"Point conceded."

Her mouth was smiling when I took it. I meant to keep things easy and playful. The whole point of this swim was to lighten the mood, make her forget her worries for a while. But the kiss spun out, riding on the vestiges of adrenaline remaining from the race, heating, deepening. Her body fit flush against mine, our legs tangling with a delicious friction as we each kicked to stay above water.

Her arms twined around my neck, hands sliding into my hair. I gripped her hips, hitching her higher, glorying in the slide of skin against skin. She shifted beneath my hands, lifting her legs to wrap them around my waist. Her low purr of approval stripped away my sanity and left me desperate for more. Somewhere amid the tiny gasps and growls of pleasure, a trickle of something else snaked out and wrapped around the fist of need. I tried to shove it away, to lose myself in the taste of her and the feel of her body against mine. But it took root and yanked me back.

I tore my mouth from hers. "Stop."

She tried to kiss me again, but I pressed my forehead to hers. "Elodie, stop. We can't."

With a noise of frustration and a little wiggle, she made it very clear that if I'd just shut up, we most definitely could. I prayed for strength.

"We're not prepared for this. I don't have any kind of protection with me and despite the fact that you're prepared for nuclear winter with all your provisions, you're not prepared for this either."

Elodie said nothing, but the breath that had been hard and fast began to slow. She unwrapped her legs, and I nearly choked on my own breath as she slipped back down to a less precarious position.

"Besides," I choked out. "If we do this now, before you shift, no matter what I've told you, there will always be a part of you that wonders if I was wrong."

She pulled back and I let her go because I didn't trust myself to keep touching her. My body felt cold without her pressed against it.

"You're right," she said quietly. "You're right." She took a breath and sank beneath the water.

Nature's cold shower, I thought.

Nearly thirty seconds passed before I started to worry when she hadn't come back up. Then I heard the splash well beyond the waterfall.

"Elodie."

I dove through the falls to go after her. She was already halfway to shore.

"Elodie, wait."

But she didn't slow. If anything she moved faster. Before I reached the halfway point, she was scrambling up the bank, grabbing her clothes and sprinting for the tent.

Damn it, damn it, damn it. I should have stopped us sooner. I should never have kissed her in the first place while we were both wet and naked. She was too much temptation. But she'd looked so beautiful in the flickering lights beneath the waterfall and I just couldn't resist.

I was the worst kind of ass. I'd promised myself I wouldn't put her in a compromising position. With the life she'd led, she was beyond inexperienced, responding with instincts and feelings she didn't know what to do with yet.

And now she was upset.

Damn me.

I grabbed my wet shorts on my way out of the lake and stopped to put them back on. Well that was all kinds of uncomfortable. But no way was I going to make this situation any worse than it already was. I took my time approaching the tent, ears tuned for that hitch of breath that meant tears. Mostly I just heard zippers and the sound of stuff brushing against nylon. Elodie drying off and getting dressed probably.

When the sounds of movement stopped, I spoke. "Elodie, I'm sorry. I—" What the hell did I need to apologize for the most? Being the practical one? The voice of reason? Taking advantage of her? Not saying no sooner? Did she think I rejected her?

"I don't know how to fix this," I said miserably. "I didn't mean to upset you."

"I'm not upset." Her voice was muffled somehow. Like it was pressed against a pillow or something.

"You're not?" Could've fooled me.

"I'm—" The next word was unintelligible.

"You're what?"

"I'm *mortified*," she snarled.

Wait . . . this was all because she was embarrassed?

"But . . . why?" I asked.

There was a muffled, double thump. Her fists beating the sleeping bags? "Because I needed you to save me from myself. Again."

How the hell was I supposed to respond to that?

I sank down cross-legged at the entrance of the tent, feeling like a moron talking to her through zippered nylon.

"Which part of this bothers you most—that you think you're a danger to yourself or that all this is happening so fast? Because we'll slow down to a snail's pace if you want. I just got carried away."

"I think it's very obvious what I wanted." Disgust dripped from her voice.

"You say that like a bad thing."

"You don't understand."

"So make me understand. Explain it to me."

Inside she moved. Rolling over, I guess, because when she spoke again, her voice was clearer. "I always thought they were stupid."

Not what I expected her to lead with. "Who?"

"My ancestors. The long, three hundred year line of idiot women who were driven by . . . I don't know . . . hormones and lust. Every last one of them did the exact same thing. And I was *sure* that under the same conditions, I'd be the smart one. The rational one. That I'd never let myself get into that kind of trouble because I'm not an animal," she snarled it, like some kind of declaration. "But I was wrong. Put me in that position and I act like nothing more than—" She seemed to cast around for the right words. "Than a bitch in heat."

For a long moment I said nothing, too busy wrestling with a speechless fury at her parents for helping foster this kind of dysfunctional belief over perfectly normal, perfectly natural behavior.

"And what about me?" I demanded. "I was right there with you. I want you. God knows, I want you sometimes more than I want to breathe. You're my mate, of course, I do. Does that make me an animal?"

"Then . . . how were you able to stop?" She whispered it, and if not for my keen ears, I'm not sure I'd have heard the question.

"Because I love you."

Inside the tent there was a sharp exhalation, like I'd sucker punched her. Okay, maybe too soon for that too, but whatever. It was out now. I bulled on through. "Because you needed me to. And that's okay. I know it's not what you're used to, but you have me now. You don't *have* to be the strong one all the time. That doesn't make you weak. It doesn't make you an animal. It makes you human."

The silence stretched out, and I started trying to figure out how to run damage control. Then the zipper began to move behind me and the tent door slowly fell open. Elodie sat, curled beside the door in shorts and a t-shirt, her hair still wet and slicked back from her face, which was grave. She stared at me long enough that I went back to my damage control planning. Then she leaned forward and laid her cheek against my shoulder.

"Thank you."

Some knot inside me eased. I'd managed to stumble into saying the right thing again.

"You okay?"

She sighed. "Hard not to be. You're here."

I tipped my head back, pressing my cheek to her hair. "We'll figure it out as we go. In the meantime, is there another towel?"

Elodie laughed and tossed a towel and a pair of shorts at my head, and I knew we were okay again.

~*~

Elodie

I didn't sleep late. Beneath the July sun, even under the canopy of trees at the edge of the lake, the tent became an oven. Sawyer's subzero sleeping bag didn't help matters, nor did the boy himself, who threw off body heat like my own personal furnace. Not that I was complaining about being tucked tight against him. It was comforting to know he wouldn't let me go, even in sleep. No matter how prudish, moronic, or otherwise neurotic I managed to be in the span of twenty-four hours.

Because he loved me.

And that was some kind of miracle. That he was here at all, that he'd come after me, risked his life, was like something out of a dream. Only the fact that I was wrapped in his warm, sleeping scent, his breath fluttering against my neck, let me know that I was awake.

I love you.

I don't know why I didn't say it back last night. It's what I felt. It's what I'd felt when I squared off against Dad. *I won't let you hurt him any more than Mom let my grandfather hurt you.* Dad had known what I meant. But Sawyer didn't have that background knowledge of my family to read between the lines. So why didn't I say it for real?

I guess because I was too busy reeling from his declaration and because I didn't want it to sound like a knee-jerk response. Like I was saying it because he'd said it. Somehow it felt like it meant less that way. And maybe that was stupid, but that's kind of how it felt the last several years with my dad. The letter had destroyed our easy affection. After that, his response to my *I love you*s felt more like rote than meant. I wasn't going to do that with Sawyer. It was way too important.

He moved in his sleep, nuzzling closer so that his lips brushed the nape of my neck. My body coiled in automatic response, but he settled back into even breathing. By slow degrees, I relaxed again, wondering if he would always affect me like this. The fact that I could even think in terms of always, of having a future with him was another kind of miracle. It was one thing to go through life, as I had, wanting to live but preparing yourself to die for a greater good. It was another thing entirely to have a real reason to live, to know that death was no longer even on the table as an option. Except for that small matter that someone was out to kill me.

I wanted a life with Sawyer.

And what if that meant I had to take another?

In all my mistaken thoughts about what I was, I was always the danger to others. The idea of killing someone else because I couldn't control the wolf terrified me. It had always seemed like the braver, nobler option was to take myself out of the equation. I'd never thought about it in terms of self-defense. But wasn't that what this would be? This hunter wanted me dead. He probably wouldn't hesitate to use the people I loved against me in ways more gruesome than what he'd done to Rich. Would I not be willing to kill to keep them alive and safe? To keep *myself* alive and safe for the chance at that future?

The obvious answer for anybody else would be, *of course I would.* Straight up logic said the same. If someone tried to hurt Sawyer, hurt Dad, I had no doubt I would rise to defend them.

But what if I hesitated? What if my total abhorrence of killing stopped me at a crucial moment? I mean, it was one thing to say I'd do something, but you never really know what you'll do until you're put in that situation.

I really didn't want to find out. I didn't truly want to know that I was capable of killing another person. So I hoped like hell that we found this cabin today and finally got some answers so that we could turn the whole damn mess over to the police.

It took some serious maneuvering to make it free of Sawyer's arms and out of the tent without waking him. I hadn't planned on an exercise in stealth, but it was good practice. Once outside, I retrieved our food supply bag from the tree we'd hung it in to protect it from bears and hauled the camp stove closer to the lake. Coffee. Nothing said *I love you* to a non-morning person like coffee when you wake up. That I could do. And I'd fix his silly corned beef hash. Gag me. But first, nature was calling.

Given it was broad day, the birds were active, twittering in the trees as I picked may way through the underbrush well away from camp. Something small skittered away as I neared. Squirrel maybe or a rabbit. I didn't manage to catch more than a flash of motion and dun colored fur. Fail. I was a werewolf. I should've been able to tune in better than that.

Coming to a halt, I closed my eyes and inhaled. The dry, musty odor of deadfall. Dirt. The sweet green scent of growing things. And . . . there. That trace of fear overlaying the fading trail of a rabbit. I wondered if it would have been as scared if I were human. My scent was changing. Sawyer

had said it was because the change was nearing. He hadn't
said that was something to worry about, and his explanation
for why it was happening so fast made logical sense, but I
could tell he was somewhat uneasy.

On my way back to camp, I circled around the long way.
I wanted to experiment with what Sawyer referred to as
calling my wolf. It was weird to me how he described it,
almost as if the wolf was a second spirit or persona,
inhabiting the same body. Sort of symbiotic but still separate
in a sense. It was getting easier to tell when the wolf was
present. My vision changed. The acuity was greater, the
colors a little flatter than normal. It took some concentration
to bring it on when I wasn't riled up. Anger made it easier.

I closed my eyes again and envisioned myself slipping
into another skin, a freer skin than my human form. Free
from human limitations and preconceptions. Free from
conventions and logic. Something shifted inside me. An
uncurling and stretching of some mental muscle. When I
opened my eyes, it was like sliding on a pair of specialized
glasses. Everything was clearer, each stick and blade of grass
standing out in sharp relief. Like life in higher definition.

I'd done it.

My impromptu happy dance was interrupted as
something crackled in the underbrush about thirty yards
ahead. Something big and dark was moving through the
trees. I stilled, tilting my head to listen, widening my nostrils.
The thing was cross-wind from me. It couldn't smell me, and
I couldn't smell it. What the hell was it? A bear? I didn't
think so. It didn't sound like a bear's lumbering gait when it
moved. I needed to get closer.

If I could just be quiet . . .

I crept forward, testing each step before I put my full
weight on it. My progress was pain-stakingly slow and my
body hummed with impatience. One step. Another. Until I
was within ten yards of the creature. Something snapped to
my right. I cast out my senses and caught the scent just

before he spoke into my ear with a voice more breath than sound, "It's an elk."

I was so proud for not jolting.

When I met Sawyer's eyes, his glowed gold. His lips curved. I found myself grinning in response. When he bowed and made an *after you* gesture, I continued stalking forward. We flanked the elk's position, and glancing at Sawyer, I realized the game was to see how close we could get.

Twenty feet. The elk grazed between the trees, unconcerned with what was going on around it.

Fifteen. Something small screamed and was silent, captured in the talons of a hawk. The elk, a male, lifted its head, antlers casting shadows in the midday sun.

Ten. The elk turned to look right at me. I froze, captivated by those deep, liquid eyes. I wondered if it would challenge. Then the wind shifted, taking with it my scent, the scent of predator, and the elk whirled, springing into motion.

The game shifted, no longer about silence, now about speed. I didn't pause to see if Sawyer followed. I knew he did.

The elk tore through the trees and down the slope. Without the wolf, I'm sure I'd have fallen. But I was sure-footed as I ran, despite the lack of trail and the presence of rocks. I'd always had good balance, but this, this was amazing. My muscles screamed as I pushed myself faster after it, and I grinned in fierce triumph.

Sawyer shot ahead of me, toward the elk's right flank, driving it in the opposite direction. Its hooves slipped on rock and we nearly caught it before it gained purchase and scrambled into the pass. The sound of its breath was like a bellows, pumping air in and out of its panicked lungs. My own breath was coming fast, but not yet painful. I still had reserves of energy. In some part of my brain I recognized that we could run this elk to exhaustion.

And then what?

My steps faltered.

Something in me tightened, a growl building in my chest.
No.

But the denial was distant, and I knew I wasn't fully in control. My speed built, my strides lengthening.

NO.

I finally understood what Sawyer meant when he described the wolf as separate because mine wasn't willing to relinquish control. I could *feel* her fighting me. She *wanted* that elk, *wanted* the chase. She wanted to take it down.

NO!

I mentally yanked back, almost as if hauling back on a choke chain. The wolf jerked in the opposite direction and I lost my balance going down in a skid. I barely felt the abrasions on my skin because my body was cramping again. Muscles bucked and writhed. I felt my hips crack and realign and let out a scream.

"Breathe." Sawyer snapped out the order in a calm voice.

I tried but my chest cavity expanded with a sickening crunch, and the pain drove the air from my lungs.

"Look at me."

Was he crazy? I couldn't look. If I opened my eyes, they would pop right out of my head from the pressure.

"Look at me."

I managed to force my eyes open. Sawyer crouched in front of me, right at my level and fixed his eyes—his wolf's eyes—on mine. It was a dominant stare, one that my wolf didn't like one bit.

"Let go."

I snarled at him, though I didn't know if he was telling me to give into the wolf or the wolf to give in to me.

"Let go," he repeated.

Focusing on his eyes distracted me from the pain. A little.

"Breathe for me now. In. Out."

I concentrated on taking air in to my newly expanded lungs. On blowing it out. In. Out.

"Try to relax."

He might as well have said, *Try to fly.* But I kept breathing. Kept watching him. And muscle by muscle tried to unclench my body.

It hurt like a son of a bitch.

I could tell muscles and bones weren't their proper length but caught somewhere in between. I didn't even want to think about what I looked like right now. I just focused on Sawyer's eyes and tried to ride it out using some kind of bastardized progressive muscle relaxation technique.

I don't even know at what point it was over. Eventually I just lay on the ground, trembling with fatigue and twitching with aftershocks of pain.

Sawyer laid his hand over mine. "Does it hurt when I touch you?"

I made an incoherent noise in the negative.

"I'm going to carry you back to camp."

Another noise. Affirmative.

Carefully, Sawyer scooped me up. The blinding pain in my head wasn't quite so bad tucked against his chest, so I curled closer.

"It's gonna be okay," he said. "Transition's close. It won't hurt so bad when you don't get stuck."

"She . . ." I cut myself off when my voice came out like a crow's. Apparently my vocal chords were just shredded. "She fought me."

"Your wolf wanted one thing, you wanted another. You did well up to that point. Your stealth is improving and you kept up beautifully during the chase. She was closer to the surface then and wanted to push you."

I shuddered.

"What happens if she wins?" I rasped.

"It's not a contest. You have to accept your wolf as part of who you are."

"But when she's ascendant, I don't feel like I'm in control. I don't feel like I'm the one making the decisions."

"It's still you. Just not a part of you that you're used to feeling."

I thought about that for a bit as he strode back the way we'd come. He carried me so easily, despite the all out sprint we'd done for the last couple of miles. My whole body seemed to have the muscle tension of limp spaghetti after the partial shift. That's what it had been. I'd been caught halfway between two forms. I wondered if anybody ever got stuck permanently in between and shuddered again at the thought. No, that was a fate worse than fully shifting, worse than letting the wolf be in full control. Wasn't it?

"But what . . . what if the wolf wants to do something horrible?"

"Like killing something?" he asked.

"Or someone," I whispered.

Sawyer was quiet for a bit. "I'm not going to lie and say the instinct isn't there. It is. Your wolf's primary drive is your survival. If you feel threatened, she'll come forward and try to protect you the only way she knows how. And sometimes you have to let her because the human side just gets in the way."

I didn't know which I was more afraid of. The idea of losing control to the animal. Or the idea that I wouldn't be able to when I needed to most.

~*~

Elodie

"Let's take a break," said Sawyer.

"*Again*? We just stopped an hour ago."

"You should have some jerky."

"I just had trail mix at the last stop," I grumbled. Since he'd managed to get oatmeal down me back at camp, he'd been foisting food on me every hour or so.

"Werewolves have much faster metabolisms. You have to keep refueling."

He handed me the jerky. I glared at him but tore open the bag and started chewing, more because it seemed to make the strain around his eyes ease a little than because I was hungry. In truth, my stomach was still pretty raw and unsettled after the partial shift this morning. My strength had mostly returned, but I wasn't at all as steady on my feet as I was accustomed and my wolf and I were still wary with each other.

Sawyer was worried. It seemed almost nothing of my transition was going normally. He hadn't said anything about it directly, and I knew that was meant to keep my own anxiety down. But I was learning to read him. He was covering up his fear with this mother hen routine, doing the only things he knew how. But he wasn't pushing me to go back, to consult with his dad. Probably because his dad wasn't likely to have any answers either. Because I and my family line were freaks even among werewolf kind. I wasn't sure how to feel about that. But I was less scared knowing all my ancestors had survived this part. None of them had died in transition. The problems all came afterward.

Since we were stopped, I pulled out the map and checked our location. We were at least two hours behind where I wanted us to be. I wanted to get to Kennicott Ridge tonight. At this point, that meant we'd be hiking after dark. Sawyer would probably fight me on that. But I felt this inexplicable sense of urgency about the whole situation. As if we didn't manage to find the cabin soon, it would all be too late. I couldn't peg down *why*.

There was no evidence so far that we were being tracked or followed. If Dad had done as he'd promised and passed around the cover story, then no one should even realize I was gone. Except probably the hunter, who shouldn't be able to pick up my trail. I guess maybe in the back of my mind, I felt like the longer it took us to find the cabin the more likely any traces of the kidnapper would disappear. As if a month wasn't already enough time for that to have happened. I just . . . needed to keep moving.

I folded and put away the map. "Let's go."

Sawyer opened his mouth to protest again, but I skewered him with a look and he closed it again.

We continued to pick our way upstream, sometimes being forced by terrain to leave the bank but always coming back and following the sound of flowing water. The country was wilder here, certainly not groomed for easy hiking. The heat was oppressive, the sun beating down, making us sweat. Yet I was cold. It got worse as the day grew later, until I could hardly hold back the shiver.

"What's wrong? You're scowling," said Sawyer.

I wasn't scowling. I was gritting my teeth to keep them from chattering.

"Nothing."

"Haven't I told you you're a lousy liar?" Sawyer grabbed me by the arm and put a hand to my cheek. "You're burning up!"

"Actually, I'm pretty sure I'm freezing. It's fine. It'll pass." I wanted to lean into the warmth of his hand, curl into the heat I knew his body would promise because right that moment I didn't feel like I'd ever be warm again. I could call it quits, ask to camp. He'd absolutely agree. But then we'd lose another day.

"You're pushing yourself too hard. You need to rest," he said, tugging me closer.

The embrace was awkward because of our packs, but I still snuggled in, laying my head against his chest, wanting to just lounge there like a lizard on a sun-warmed rock. "I need answers. I can rest when I'm dead."

He stiffened.

"Okay that totally came out wrong. Black humor. Sorry." I pulled back and caught a glint of something in the setting sun. "What's that?"

"What's what?"

I pushed around him to get a better look. It was so covered in vines and saplings that I could hardly make it out, but I smiled in triumph. "A window."

"It might not be it."

"But it might be. C'mon."

We picked our way across the creek and up the other bank. The cabin was nestled high on the ridge with little more than a deer track leading up to it from the water. If the sun hadn't caught that lone bit of window, I doubt I'd ever have noticed it. Kudzu swarmed up the walls and swallowed the roof, which seemed to be some kind of corrugated metal, maybe tin. As we circled the structure, looking for the door, Sawyer began whistling the theme from *Deliverance,* which might have been funny if we weren't looking for a kidnapper's lair. Not that this place ranked high on the Supervillain Lair Scale. I was guessing maybe it used to be a trapper's cabin.

The door was as covered in vines as the rest of the building. I started to reach for the rusty iron knob, but Sawyer stopped me.

"I'll go first," he said softly.

"Oh, because your whistling didn't give it away that we're out here?" I whispered.

He just waved me back. I rolled my eyes, but let him have his way. A door that old, that dilapidated should have screeched on rusty hinges. It didn't. When he twisted the knob and shoved, it swung open with barely a whisper. The entry was so low and narrow, Sawyer had to stoop and twist sideways to go inside. Naturally I could walk straight in. Sometimes being vertically challenged isn't a curse.

The room was maybe ten feet by ten feet, with a line of crumbling stones down one wall that ended in a rubble pile that used to be a hearth. Other than the detritus of the chimney, the rest of the room was strangely clean. It was entirely bare of furniture. I slipped off my pack and set it beside Sawyer's, then wrapped my arms around my torso, already regretting the loss of warmth from the sun.

"Either the raccoons have opened a maid service, or somebody wiped this place down," I said.

Sawyer stood peering through a doorway into the next room—the only other room I saw when I crossed to join him. Here there was an old iron bedstead, canted to one side from age. There was no mattress atop the interlocking wires of the frame. In the corner sat a solid wood chair, one of those hand-carved affairs with a rounded back and arms. The wood was rubbed raw around the arms, as if someone had been tied there and fought to escape.

I inhaled. The scent of the mountain, of the green, growing things that were claiming the cabin for their own came in loud and clear, even though we were inside. Beneath that, the dust of ages, though here, as in the other room, everything was strangely clean. Under that faint traces of something kind of cloying and sweet, almost antiseptic. Chloroform? The reports said Rich and Molly had been drugged. There was something else too. A sharp, peppery odor that I didn't recognize. My head swam a little.

I moved to the chair, bending to get a better whiff of the arms. There were faint traces of blood. Not enough for me to tell if it had been Rich or his sister but enough to set my teeth to aching. We needed to hurry. I was starting to learn the signs, and I'd be having another attack soon. Probably worse this time given the fever I'd had all afternoon. We didn't want to be caught here when I did, with me helpless and Sawyer too worried about me to act with clear thought.

Across the room he checked the wardrobe in the corner. "Anything?"

He was very still, his back ramrod straight with tension. Something was very wrong.

"Sawyer?" I wandered over, laying a hand on his back and trying to peer around him into the depths of the wardrobe.

He held some kind of syringe in the palm of one hand. Except, no, it didn't have a plunger at the end.

"What is that?" I asked.

"Tranquilizer dart," said Sawyer. His voice cracked as he turned his eyes to me. "One of ours."

"What do you mean? Like from *the lab?*"

He nodded.

"So, what, you think one of *our* team is the kidnapper?" My brain couldn't seem to wrap around that idea, that any of the people I'd been working with all summer could possibly have been stalking me for months. That any of my coworkers could have assaulted and kidnapped Rich and his sister.

Sawyer handed me the dart, and I lifted it to my nose. I caught the scent that Sawyer had, faint but unmistakable. Utterly horrifying. Incredulous, I looked at Sawyer. "No. No, that can't be right. It has to be some kind of mistake. Maybe he handled this box of darts in the supply closet or something before it was taken. It can't possibly be—"

"Patrick." Sawyer's voice broke on the name. He wasn't looking at me. He was looking behind me, at the doorway.

Chapter 12

Elodie

I whirled and backed into Sawyer.

Patrick was framed in the doorway. He wasn't wearing his glasses. Which was a ridiculous thing for me to focus on, but they were so much a part of how I visualized him that it was almost like looking at a stranger. His eyes, usually hidden by those Coke bottle lenses, were flat and gray. The mouth usually curved in a slightly amused smile now had a cruelty about it that I'd never noticed. His shoulders, usually slightly hunched, were straight and confident. He no longer looked the part of absent-minded professor, what with the military-style fatigues and the gun in his hand.

Maybe Superman's disguise wasn't so stupid after all, I thought.

The silence spun out, and none of us moved. A bead of sweat trickled down my back, like an ice cube dragged the length of my spine. My body ached with the effort to hold perfectly still so I wouldn't betray the fact that I was burning with fever and my wolf was near the surface. My eyes hadn't changed. Yet. But I wasn't sure how long I could hold out.

And Patrick was standing between us and the exit. With that very wicked looking gun that was every bit as flat a gray as his eyes. And it was still pointed at us, almost like a confession. A blinking neon sign that said *I am the bad guy.*

Still nobody moved.

My fingers curled around the tranquilizer dart. Could I hit him with it? Would it even engage? I had no idea how they

213

worked. Something to do with the force of being fired creating the motion of injection maybe. Would it even start to affect him before he could fire on us?

Bad idea, I thought. Sawyer was the one with the dead eye aim. I'd barely been able to manage whipping aluminum plates like frisbees with any kind of accuracy. If I managed to pass him the dart, would he understand my intent?

"Put the gun down, Patrick," said Sawyer, breaking his paralysis to shift in front of me. I didn't know what was going through his head. He'd known Patrick so much longer than I had. I couldn't begin to imagine the betrayal he must be feeling.

Patrick's attention shifted from me to Sawyer and the smile faded. He looked almost regretful as he shook his head. "You have the worst taste in women, my boy. I really wish you weren't here. It's unfortunate."

He doesn't know, I realized. *He doesn't know what Sawyer is. He thinks it's just me.* I needed to keep it that way if we were going to have a chance.

I stepped around Sawyer, placing myself as a shield in front of him. "It's me you're after. Leave Sawyer out of this."

Patrick swung his attention back to me. "And how exactly do you think that's going to work? You think you're going to come away with me and that Sawyer here isn't going to do everything he can to get you back? You don't know your suitor very well."

I took a step toward Patrick, toward the gun. Despite all my trials, all the time I'd spent facing death, it was a very different thing to face it with someone else in control. My heart rate shot up, and I could no longer totally hold back the trembling. Sawyer reached out and yanked me back, as I'd known he would. And as his hand curled around mine, I shifted the dart into his. He squeezed my hand, and I thought he'd gotten the message.

"Don't do this, Patrick," he said. "Whatever this is about, just let it go."

"My dear boy, I can't let it go. My entire life has been leading to this. To her."

My wolf shoved for release, and I doubled over with a low moan. *Wait*, I begged her. *Not yet.*

Sawyer looked back at me in horror because now was the worst possible time for me to change.

Patrick saw the look on his face and misinterpreted it. "She hasn't told you what she is. Well then, that may change things. Step aside and wait. In a few minutes, you'll see and you'll understand why the beast has to die."

Use it, I thought. *Keep up the act and use the opportunity to get closer to him.*

"Sawyer, don't listen to him," I said, deliberately choking on the words as if my mouth were crowding with extra teeth. "I can explain."

With an agonized look, he shifted toward Patrick, backing away from me. I knew how hard it was for him to leave me unguarded in the face of that gun.

"I'll save you the breath," said Patrick, "since it looks like you need it. She's not human."

"Not human," repeated Sawyer in an *I'm humoring you because you have a gun in your hand, but really you're crazy* tone of voice. "Then what is she?"

He was only a few feet away from Patrick now, still not looking directly at him, doing nothing to telegraph his intent.

"Your lady fair is, in fact, a werewolf."

"A *werewolf?* Like shape-shifting, howl at the moon, allergic to silver *werewolf?*" Given that most of those things were, in fact, *not* true about our kind, his incredulity was fully believable.

"Yes."

Sawyer raised his hands as if to cover his face and stumbled the last few steps to Patrick, who used his free hand to pat Sawyer on the shoulder.

"I'm sorry to have to break it to you, my boy."

"I'm sorry, too," said Sawyer. Then he raised his hand and struck lightning quick, jabbing the dart into Patrick's neck.

Patrick yelled, trying to hit at Sawyer with the butt of the gun, but Sawyer grabbed his wrist forcing the gun up. It fired once, into the ceiling, and I screamed as they both stumbled into the front room. My wolf surged, trying to push free, and I fell to the floor, fighting her.

Not here. Not now. Just give me a few more minutes.

I shoved to my feet and lurched into the other room. They were still grappling for control of the gun. Something was wrong. If the dart had worked, Patrick should have been fading by now. Sawyer shouldn't be having trouble subduing him. He should've been able to take him down even without tranquilizers.

"Elodie, run!" The order was punctuated by a *crack* as Patrick landed a punch to Sawyer's jaw.

Was he crazy? Of course I wasn't going to just *leave him* here. He was my *mate*.

Sawyer slammed Patrick's gun hand against the floor and another shot rang out, ricocheting off the remainder of the chimney. The bullet pinged so close to my head, I actually heard it whiz past my ear as I leapt back and fell hard. As soon as I gained my feet again, I was looking for an opening, some means of launching myself into the fight to help Sawyer. But every time I managed to get near, the struggle over the gun had it pointing in my direction, forcing strategic retreat.

"Go!" Sawyer shouted.

"I won't leave you."

He cracked an elbow against Patrick's nose and blood gushed, hot and bright. The scent of copper curled around me, a seduction my wolf was unwilling to resist. My body seized, muscles tearing, joints popping in a rush of agony that left me blind.

"Elodie!"

216

I wanted to say something to reassure him that I was okay, that he needed to focus on the fight. But my jaw was locked tight. Instead, I turned my sightless eyes toward them, trying to parse out from sound what was happening just a few feet away. Grunt. Scuffle. Roll. Snarl. Thwack.

The gun fired again, and I found myself caught in a fine spray of blood. At the sudden silence, my heart threatened to beat straight out of my chest. Someone drew a very wet, sucking breath. Panic had me scrambling to my feet, despite limbs that were not fully human, not fully wolf. When my vision came back, everything about the scene was sharp and magnified.

Shock and grief were etched on Sawyer's face as he stared at Patrick. My gaze shot to Patrick, searching for the mortal wound. But though blood soaked his shirt, he was backing up, watching Sawyer. My attention swung back as Sawyer fell, collapsing on the too clean wood floors. My eyes moved inch by terrifying inch down Sawyer's chest to the hole spurting a small fountain of blood with each beat of his heart.

Mine stopped.

No.

Sawyer struggled to take another breath, and I could hear the gurgle of blood filling his lungs. He turned his head to find me, his eyes, those beautiful eyes, dark and full of pain. Blood spread out from beneath him. The shot had gone clean through then, hitting God knew how many vital organs in the process.

I was beyond human speech, at the threshold of losing my human intellect, paralyzed by the sight of my mate dying.

"You have to . . ." He coughed, and blood trickled down the corner of his mouth. "You have to go."

No!

"I'm so sorry, my boy." Patrick was on his feet, the gun held loosely at his side. "I didn't want this for you."

Your fault. You did this. My eyes narrowed, calculating distance and speed, wondering if I could get to him before he could get the gun up again.

Sawyer tried to speak again. "Elodie, g..go." He was choking on blood.

I was breaking into a million pieces.

"I l . . . love . . ." He didn't finish. On a bubbling sort of sigh, he closed his eyes.

I love you.

Pain, stunning and sharp, drove past my ribcage and into my chest. I couldn't breathe. There was no oxygen left in the world.

Breathe, I thought. But the order was for him, not for myself.

I stared at Sawyer's blood-soaked chest, willing it to move. But it did not rise. Neither did his hands or feet twitch or his eyes open. He was still. Unnaturally so.

C'mon, heal, damn you! Desperation bound me surely as any chains, waiting for the impossible.

He wasn't getting up from this.

Rage burst through me, an atom bomb of fury lighting up every cell. It burst out of me in a sound of raw anguish that bore no resemblance to a human voice.

Patrick stumbled back from the sound, for the first time apparently sensible of the monster in the room.

He wanted to hunt a monster. I'd give him a monster. I stopped fighting my wolf. At last we were of one accord. My bones popped and lengthened, my body hunching, straining toward four feet.

Patrick was lifting the gun, face grim and full of purpose.

I charged him. Halfway between forms, my loping, limping gait sent me crashing into him. But I was off balance, unable to fully control my body. Patrick was scrambling after the gun that had gone flying, and I had a split second to make a decision.

I could try to kill him here, now, while not fully shifted and not at my peak of speed or strength and risk failing. Or I could do as Sawyer had asked me and escape so that his death was not in vain. So that I could live to survive transition and come after Patrick in full force.

One look at his too still body decided me. Sawyer always wanted me to live.

Before Patrick could get to the gun, I sprang through the door and into the night.

~*~

Elodie

I don't know how long I ran or even where. There was no thought to laying a false trail or doubling back. No careful walking up the river bed. There was just running. Every step was an agony because my body didn't have time to finish shifting to one form or the other, and I didn't stop to let it. I had to put as much distance between me and Patrick as possible. And a part of me desperately wanted to escape the reality lying back there in that cabin because if I let myself think about it, let myself voice the thought, I would break. So I kept running, kept tripping over my feet and falling, picking myself back up and running some more because the pain kept truth at bay.

Until I fell again and just couldn't make myself get up. Couldn't make myself care about the smell of my own blood or the physical aches of shifting and exertion. Breath sawed in and out of my throat, my chest rising and falling in great gusts. And in my mind I saw Sawyer's chest. Blood-soaked and still.

My clawed fingers curled deep into the dirt and leaves, hanging on for dear life, as if the earth was going to give up its gravity and I'd go spiraling into space without some kind of anchor. Lost. Because Sawyer had been my anchor. And now he was dead. Because of me.

Oh God.

If I'd gone back when he asked . . . If we'd consulted his dad . . . Jesus, how had they worked with Patrick all this time and Patrick not *known* what they were? Why was he only after me?

Sawyer was dead.

It should've been me. Never him. It should have been *me.*

My claws dug in deeper and I hung on as the world started to shake. Great rolling heaves that left me nauseous and dizzy and wondering what fault line was acting up. Then I realized it wasn't the ground shaking, it was me. I curled my knees to my chest and held on, helpless against the onslaught of grief.

I was alone. Before him I'd thought I was prepared. I'd thought I was made for this. But it was a lie. Solitude had never been a choice for me. I'd accepted him as part of my life, part of my future, with joy. To know that he wouldn't be there to see me on the other side of transition, to teach me what it meant to be wolf, was a stunning sort of pain.

My limbs convulsed and popped, stretching, shortening, my wolf unable to decide whether to retreat or burst free. She could escape the truth of Sawyer's loss no more than I could. Sharp, hitching breaths gave way to a keening wail that fell somewhere between a sob and a howl. It echoed, long and loud, and I knew it was as good as giving away my location, but I couldn't hold it in. With each breath, the sound continued to roll out of me. An audible manifestation of denial. Of mourning.

When the first howl joined me, I barely registered the tone, harmonic with my own wail. But the second and third got my attention. I choked off my cry, listening as a chorus of four or five other wolves joined in my mourning song. I recognized the voices. The red wolves. The ones I'd been hearing off and on for the last few years. But close. So much closer than I'd ever heard them before. Or maybe that was my own newly acute hearing.

I howled again, waiting for the replies. The next ones were closer. Again. Even closer. They were coming toward me. Answering my call for . . . For what? Comfort? For pack? For all I knew they were coming to evict me from their territory. But I didn't think so. As I listened to the chorus of howls, I wasn't afraid. They didn't sound aggressive. They weren't hunting. They were very specifically responding to me.

When the first wolf appeared over the rise, my heart leapt. Not in fear, but in a moment of joy, of conviction that I'd been right. But the emotion was fleeting, swallowed by the knowledge that if I'd never pursued this, if Sawyer had never met me, he'd be alive now.

Another cry tore free of my throat.

The wolf on the rise lifted its head and howled in answer, a long ululating cry of mourning. I'd always kind of thought that wolf howls sounded sad, but this was somehow different. This was . . . acknowledging a loss. My loss.

He was beautiful. I could only just make out his markings in the dark, but his golden eyes were clear as he came nearer. Different from Sawyer, of course. Smaller, but still broad in the shoulder. Others came from the surrounding woods, approaching me with caution but not aggression. Five in all. Two males. Three females.

The next wail I made was softer, exhaustion catching up with me. Their replies blended with my voice. A beautiful, haunting lament. It didn't make things better, didn't make things easier, but somehow still, it helped.

I expected the wolves to keep their distance. I was not pack. I was not even really their kind. As the howls morphed into far more human tears, they didn't scatter but came closer. I gasped at the bump of the first head against my back, hardly daring to move. One by one they came to me, head-butting, rubbing, and nuzzling me, offering comfort through touch. I was pathetically grateful for the contact and just cried harder.

At length they lay down around me, backs pressed against me in a cocoon of fur that should have been stifling in the heat of the night. But in the midst of my grief, I was still feverish and chilled, and their warmth helped ease some of the ache.

I relaxed into the pile of warm bodies, exhaustion taking its toll, though the last thing I wanted was to sleep and dream. I didn't know why they were accepting me. But I was too tired and too overcome by the events of the night to question it. I'd run for miles. I had no supplies, no maps, no compass. Nothing to rely on but myself. Except, it seemed, this small pack of wolves that shouldn't even exist.

~*~

Sawyer

A six ton elephant was sitting on my chest. It wasn't particularly interested in moving so I could breathe and it certainly wasn't helping the burning pain radiating out from the hole in my chest. At least it was probably staunching the blood. What was left of it. I was pretty sure I'd been bleeding out when I'd lost consciousness.

It was hard to think past the pain. Somewhere in the back of my mind, I was cognizant enough to recognize that pain was actually a good thing. Something about not being dead. I wasn't sure how long that would be the case. But my body was trying to repair the damage. Healing was painful business, and I was stuck between forms. Mostly human, but my insides felt scrambled. I was pretty sure that was the only reason I was still alive. My heart had relocated, shifting over in preparation for becoming a wolf. So instead of a one way trip to hell, I got a collapsed lung. Peachy.

I took the fact that I could hear the whistle of my breath in and out as a positive sign. Not that the accompanying gurgle was good thing. I wondered if there was anyone else to hear the whistle-gurgle of my breathing. I listened for the span of ten shallow breaths. But I was alone.

No one left to finish me off, then.

I paused at that thought, my brain circling around the idea that someone had tried to kill me. I'm sure I should've been alarmed at the notion, but instead I was gripped by a deep sense of unease that I couldn't remember what had happened. Patience was never one of my strong suits, but there was something at the edge of my consciousness that left me simmering with a need to act, to move to do . . . something. Instead I waited for the whistle-gurgle to stop, for my lungs to heal enough for me to draw a full breath and not feel like I was drowning.

I opened my eyes. At least, I thought I did. The pitch black didn't change any, so I really wasn't sure if I'd managed it. Eventually my eyes adjusted enough to see the hint of light coming from a window across the room. It seemed to be mostly obstructed. A bush or tree or something. But I could tell enough to know that it was night.

How long had I been here?

That question lodged in my brain and began to swell with importance. I needed to know how long I'd been here. There was something I was supposed to do.

My body wasn't quite with the program when I tried to sit up. It took several tries, and then I only managed to roll over on my side before I had to rest. I cast my eyes around the room, trying to see if there were any clues in this new direction. Then I saw the tranquilizer dart. It lay beside some rubble on the floor, gleaming very faintly in the dim moonlight.

The dart hadn't worked.

In my mind I saw it lodged in the neck of my opponent as we grappled on the floor, struggling for control of the gun.

He hadn't been the one to weaken. I had. Because he'd been wearing wolfsbane. I hadn't been able to kill him.

Then I saw his face as he stood, gun in hand, watching me bleed out on the floor, regret etched in every feature.

Patrick.

Betrayal was a fresh wound as I struggled to remember why we'd been fighting. Why I'd been shot.

Elodie.

I jack-knifed up, then collapsed again with a wheeze and grunt of agony.

Patrick was trying to kill Elodie.

"Elodie." What I'd intended as a shout came out at barely a whisper. Half a lung's breath wasn't enough to make myself heard. I tried again. "Elodie."

There was no response, and panic had me pushing through the weakness and onto my knees so I could survey the room. It was empty but for the puddle of drying blood where I'd been lying. There was no other body, which was at once a relief and a terror. Where was she?

Inch by painful inch, I dragged myself to the threshold of the other room, nose tuned to try and pick up her scent. It wasn't fresh, and there was no other source of blood, save mine. I collapsed in the doorway when I saw she wasn't here.

So she'd made it out of the cabin then.

But she'd been changing, caught halfway between forms again when I'd last seen her. How far could she have gotten if she didn't run until after I'd been shot?

I needed to get outside to check the perimeter of the cabin, but my body refused to obey. so instead I slumped against the doorjamb and listened outside for any sign that she was near. That she was alive. But there was nothing beyond the raucous noise of the crickets and cicadas. We were not yet into deep night, then, when all fell quiet. Unless. it was the next day.

How long had I been out? Regenerating from a gunshot wound was no small feat. In all reality, it could take days.

She could have been out there, running from Patrick *for days*. In pain from transition *for days*. And I wasn't there to stop him or ease her or protect her.

Mother fucker.

I thought about shifting, but it wasn't magic. It wasn't like in movies or books where shifting miraculously cured all ills. If I tried to go wolf now, I could rip stuff that had already started repairing and speed up my own demise. And shit, being stuck as I was, I hoped like hell things were repairing the way they were supposed to. So as much as every atom of my being wanted to go after them, to find Elodie, and to kill the son of a bitch who'd left me for dead, I needed to sit tight. I wouldn't make it ten feet in the shape I was in now.

Which left me with a whole lot of time and a very vivid imagination that was all too happy to supply the various and sundry ways Patrick could maim, torture, and kill Elodie.

I was half mad with rage and desperation within fifteen minutes.

And why the fuck wasn't I healing? I wasn't dead, but I wasn't hearing any kind of change in the whistle-gurgle. The wound should be fucking closing by now. I was struck by a moment of blind panic. What if it wasn't *going* to heal? What if just not dying had sapped my body's healing resources? What if I was stuck here, lingering and completely useless until . . . until what? My body gave out and died? Until I starved? Until Patrick came back to clean up my body?

My wolf reared up at that, demanding action I couldn't perform. But my nose sharpened and I smelled the bittersweet, evergreen scent of wolfsbane. I shoved back the panic and tried to focus, my nose twitching, searching for the source because it was something *active*, something that kept me outside my head and all the crazy-making going on there.

Collapsed in the doorway, I scanned the floor, which I could see better with my wolf so close to the surface. The moon had risen, giving me a bit more light to work with, and now that I looked, I could see what I'd taken to be grit before scattered over the floor. Not grit, I realized. Dried petals of the plant. Everywhere. It must've fallen out of Patrick's pockets or something as we fought.

Shit.

I had to get out of here.

Moving hurt like a sonofabitch, but that was good. Pain kept me focused on the task at hand. I was too weak to crawl again, so I had to drag myself, shimmying in some parody of a commando crawl across the floor. I damn near passed out again at the halfway point.

Oh no you fucking don't. Get up.

The mental whip didn't get me on my knees, but it got me inching forward again. At one point I had to stop for a coughing fit, spitting up the blood flooding my lung. Maybe it was making more room for oxygen. The notion of a full breath was like the idea of winning the lottery. It felt like an appealing, if distant, possibility. Once the coughing stopped, I was moving again, dragging myself through the fresh blood and toward the door.

Of course it was closed. That in itself presented a whole new challenge. Because getting myself vertical enough to reach and work the knob was like my own personal Everest.

Elodie was waiting.

More importantly, Elodie probably thought I was dead, and given her predilections toward suicide, I needed to get the hell out of here and find her before she decided to go after Patrick and take him out with her.

It took a full five minutes to work my knees under my chest, and another ten using the door as leverage to get myself sort of vertical. But when my hands closed over the iron handle, I felt like crowing. Except, of course, that required more air than I could mange.

I twisted and pulled, falling backward as the door swung inward. The night air rushed in, hot and humid and clean. I flipped myself over and made like the tortoise for the open doorway.

The moment I was fully outside, my head felt clearer. I dragged myself around to the side of the cabin and leaned back against it, already feeling my body beginning to work faster, harder at repairing the damage. Outside at last, feeling progress, at last, I could wait with grim purpose, until my body was well enough to hunt.

I had a murderer to track.

Chapter 13

Elodie

I woke up human with visions of blood and death still etched in my mind. I was prevented from shooting up by the warm, furry bodies draped over mine. The pack had stayed. Some of the blood lust eased as I came fully to consciousness. My body was filthy, covered in blood and scrapes and bruises. But it was mine. My arms. My legs. My aches. The fever, it seemed, had passed for now. I felt raw, inside and out, as if a great claw had reached in and scraped out anything of substance, leaving behind an empty shell.

When I opened my eyes, my entourage was rising, stretching in the dark. The forest around us was cloaked in the relative silence of deep night. I rose with a series of pops and creaks as joints realigned. The pack watched me, but my pseudo-transformation during sleep hadn't phased them. The large male I had seen first gave a yip and the others began to mill around him, restless, making small yaps and growls.

My friends were readying for the hunt.

As much I wanted to do the same, albeit with different prey, my top priority was food, shelter, and figuring out how I was going so survive through transition.

The alpha looked at me with an expression that could only be deemed invitation. Though I felt completely ridiculous doing so, I bowed to the pack. "Thank you. But I have my own business to settle."

I have no idea if they understood me or if my notion of wolf whisperer held outside of my own kind. But the alpha gave a howl of farewell, echoed by his packmates, before they all spun away and disappeared into the dark.

A gibbous moon rode the tree line, lighting the way for my dark-adapted eyes. But there were clouds rolling in. I wasn't going to have light for long. Rousing my wolf, I circled my position until I found my scent trail. Our packs were back at the cabin. While I *could* survive with no supplies, no nothing—I was certainly in better shape *with* supplies. Even if all I could nab was my map and compass, that would enable me to get back to my cave faster. My best chance was if Patrick had left the packs behind when he came after me.

It was a risk. If he had any decent tracking skills to speak of, I could run into him on the way. I was in no shape to fight him right now. I was in no shape for anything right now. I wasn't even sure if I'd hear or smell him coming. Yet I couldn't just stay where I was. If I wanted to stay hidden, I needed to keep moving.

Would he expect that? Of course he would. He'd been stalking me for months. He knew I wouldn't stay put. But had Patrick really learned me so well that he would suspect I might come back? Would he anticipate that I would be that stupid? It *was* stupid. I wasn't so far gone that I didn't recognize that fact. But I thought it might be unexpected enough that it was worth the risk.

But then what? If I actually made it back to the cabin, what would I find? A trap? Sawyer's body still laid out in a pool of blood? Or would the cabin be empty, scrubbed clean again of all traces of violence and death? No sign of Sawyer's sacrifice?

I shoved a hand against my mouth to hold in the whimper.

I couldn't think about it or I wouldn't be able to function. There was nothing I could do to help Sawyer now. All I could do was avenge his death.

With a last look at the trees where the wolves had disappeared, I set off. The going was slower than I'd have liked, not because my trail was faint but because I could barely see beneath the canopy of trees. What little moonlight filtered through the branches was quickly lost before it ever found its way to the ground. Even with my wolf's eyes, I had to keep to a walk and pick my way over rough terrain.

How the hell had I *run* through here in my half-shifted state and not broken something?

The rain began with a drizzle, building up on leaves and dripping down just enough to be an annoyance. Another mile further and the drizzle became a torrent, complete with the growl of thunder that echoed off the mountains. What little light there was came in the sporadic flash of lightning, which did nothing more than foul up my night vision.

I should be taking cover somewhere, not stumbling around in the dark, trying to follow a rapidly disappearing trail. But honestly, it was hard to care. My survival, at this point, had only one purpose, and I was hardly going to die of exposure in a rainstorm in July. Physical misery was far preferable to the emotional that rode in as soon as I stopped. As long as I was moving, I could hold the nightmare at bay.

Within an hour, I'd lost my trail. Visibility was nil, and without a flashlight, I couldn't search for other signs of my passage. I was well and truly screwed, as lost in the mountains as any newbie hiker with no sense of direction. All those years of training, all the careful planning, wasted.

Frustration boiled up in a roar, and I whirled to strike at the nearest solid thing. My feet slipped in the wet leaves and grass and I went down with a crash, striking my elbow on something hard enough to make my vision white out. Then I was falling. Slipping, sliding, rolling, down an embankment, where I bounced off trees and rocks and other unforgiving surfaces that cut and bruised and stole my breath. At last I slid to a stop. Dizzy and sick, I lifted my head.

And saw the creek.

Even in the dark I could tell it was bloated with runoff. Were there other creeks and tributaries? Was this *the* creek? The one that ran below Patrick's cabin? I closed my eyes trying to bring up a mental image of the map, but all I saw was Sawyer's fingers tracing all the waterways. His hand curled around mine. His fingers against my cheek.

I choked out a sob.

Okay, not helping. Not helping. Focus.

I had to look past his fingers, see the map. There was only one other possible waterway that this could be. I'd escaped from the cabin to the northwest. So chances were, this was still the creek I needed. It was action. I needed action. Had to keep moving.

I dragged myself to my feet and headed downstream. One foot in front of the other.

The rain stopped. I only noticed when the moon peeked out from behind storm clouds. There was still a steady patter of water dripping from the canopy of trees. Still I walked. The sky began to lighten, which improved my visibility and unfortunately made me more visible. I moved deeper into the trees, taking the harder path, the more hidden one, though my body cried out for a break. Patrick would give me no mercy. I couldn't afford to give any to myself.

It was the rising sun that tipped me off, as the setting had done just the day before. Light glinting off one of the barely visible window panes on the other side of the cabin. Just the sight of it made my throat close up. I approached cautiously, taking the time for stealth, as I had with the elk. There was no overt sign of Patrick. No sound. No vehicle, though I could now see a narrow track where one had been through. I took my time, circling around. Waiting. Listening.

What if he was in there? What did I think I was going to do? I still hadn't shifted fully. I was faster and stronger than most humans, and I was more agile not stuck between forms, but was I really ready for this? Sawyer hadn't managed to overpower Patrick. In fact, he'd seemed almost . . . weakened somehow. What if I found Patrick now, before I was ready, and failed?

Failure was not an option. Before it didn't matter which of us died because I had no child to carry on the curse. Now that I knew there were others like me out there, this wasn't just about revenge. It was about protecting them too.

"It ends with me," I whispered.

My hands curled to fists, and I crept forward to peer in the window. It was the back room, the one with the bed. No sign of Patrick. I pressed my ear to the glass, listening. Nothing moved inside. If he was in there, he might be asleep.

I crept around to the door, pausing to listen again. Still nothing. I took a breath and held it as I turned the knob degree by slow degree. There was a *snick* as it disengaged, and I nudged the door open an inch, just far enough to press my eye to the slit. The room was swathed in shadows. Still no sign of Patrick. I released the breath and took another before I edged inside.

The room was empty. No Patrick. No Sawyer, though the floor was coated in a sticky residue of drying blood where his body had lain. It looked as if Patrick had started to drag him into the back room, then changed his mind and dragged him out of the cabin. The trail ran right between my feet to the door. Of course he'd have to get rid of the body.

I bolted out the door before I could vomit and compromise the scene, just in case the cops ever actually *did* find this place.

When the heaving stopped, I went back inside, steeling myself to ignore the blood and do what I needed to do. Our packs were still dumped in a pile on the floor. I hauled them both outside. Yes, it was in the open, but I wasn't about to spend any more time in that bloody room than I had to.

There wasn't much to remove from my pack. Sawyer had taken on all the heavy stuff after my half-shift the day before. I shifted some of the foodstuffs, grabbed the water filtration system, and the flint. I left the tent. No way was I making myself a sitting duck by not being able to see what was coming. I pawed through the rest of Sawyer's pack, looking for the knife. He always wanted it out of my hands, so he'd filched it again and hidden it. But it wasn't in the bag. The body chills were starting again, and I couldn't afford to waste any more time.

I slipped out the map and compass and marked the coordinates of the cabin, as I hadn't remembered to do yesterday. If something happened to me, maybe someone would find the map, find the cabin and figure out what it meant. A whole lot of ifs. Studying the topography of the area, I tried to best judge where I could take shelter. I'd never make it back to my cave, so what was my closest option? The X's I'd marked a couple days before seemed to float in my vision. Great, so hallucination was coming next? I wasn't going to make it far.

I pulled my attention back to the X's. Where Rich and Molly had been picked up. Rich said he'd stowed Molly in a cave within walking distance of the cabin. I estimated that maybe they'd have made it two miles in the shape they were in. I drew a rough circle of that radius around the location of the cabin. Rich had said it was near the river. I hadn't seen anything suggesting a cave on the way up, so it seemed my best bet was to continue upstream.

My hands were clammy as they folded the map and stowed it and my compass in an outside pocket. After a moment's hesitation, I swapped my sleeping bag with Sawyer's. I'd want those sub-zero capabilities when I was freezing with fever. With a few more adjustments to the contents of my pack, I slipped it on and headed toward the river. I needed to find shelter before the next round of fever hit.

~*~

Sawyer

The tent was small, one of those ultra-light backpacking numbers that folded up to practically nothing. To the front, a circle of stones marked the remnants of a fire from the night before. Gear, if there was any, must've been inside the tent. Nothing stirred in the long, dawn shadows, but I didn't go any closer. I could move in silence, but I couldn't move fast. Not yet.

My chest wound had closed up in the dark hours before sunrise, the whistle-gurgle blessedly changing to a wheeze. My collapsed lung still hadn't re-inflated, and I'd been coughing up blood off and on for a few hours now. That limited my capabilities of exertion, which meant I had to be smart rather than rash. Rushing the tent and tearing it open without knowing who was inside and how they might be armed would just be foolish. So I bellied down at the crest of the ridge above to wait and rest.

I didn't have to wait long. The buzz of the zipper being dragged open seemed abnormally loud in the morning quiet. Muscles tense, I leaned forward watching the opening. My vision shifted, my wolf rising as a hand emerged, shoving the tent flap down so a man could crawl out.

It wasn't Patrick.

I had to hold in the gust of disappointment. Campers. Just campers. No use to me, just someone else to evade.

A dog trotted out after the man and raced for some bushes beyond the camp to relieve himself. A few moments later, after considerable flopping around, a woman emerged, shoving a pack in front of her.

"I would pay a week's salary for *coffee*," she declared.

"There's instant in the side pocket," her companion offered.

235

"No, I mean, *real* coffee. I bet they've got real coffee at base," she said wistfully. "You know they always keep Eileen fueled."

Base?

"Well they've gotta keep her going. She was probably up most of the night, just in case anybody called in. You know nobody got Nate to actually *stop* looking. I mean who can blame him."

Search party. They're part of a search party looking for Elodie. I was suddenly doubly glad I was positioned downwind.

"I'll grab the radio and report in. See if we have any new orders."

I settled down again. They might not be a waste after all.

The woman dug a walkie out of her bag. "Good morning Base, this is Charlie Team."

"Morning Janet." I recognized the voice as the dispatcher who ran the search for Rich and Molly Phillips. Same team then.

"Sun's up. We're gonna make a bite to eat before we head out. Any news in the night?"

"Nothing."

"Did anybody get Nate to sleep at all?" asked Janet.

"Two hours during the rain. That was it."

"Are we sticking to yesterday's grid?"

Before Eileen could reply, another voice crackled on the line. "Got something."

Elodie's father.

"Found some tire tracks on an access road that seem to match the ones we found on the Phillips search."

"What's your location?" asked Eileen.

Nate relayed the coordinates.

"Sending a deputy your way to take a cast."

An access road to the cabin or somewhere else?

"George will stay. Dr. Everett and I are gonna keep going, see where this leads."

236

Shock kept me frozen in place. Patrick wasn't out skulking around the mountain trying to pick up Elodie's trail on his own. He was with the goddamned search party. With Elodie's *dad*, the person most likely to know what she'd do out here because he's the one who trained her. And Nate had no idea he was practically a walking hostage.

Shit.

I had to get my hands on that radio and a map.

The radio went to static for a bit. Then the dispatcher came back on. "Ken, you and Janet proceed according to yesterday's trajectory. You'll be informed if anything changes." Eileen signed off.

"I hope this comes to better results than the Phillips search. If anything happens to that girl, Nate's gonna lose it," said Ken.

"He won't be the only one. Elodie is one of ours. We've gotta bring her home," said Janet. She put the radio back in her pack. "We can eat and be packed in fifteen."

Fifteen minutes. That wasn't much time for me to come up with any kind of diversion. How the hell was I going to manage to distract both of them *and* the dog? I had absolutely nothing on me. I wasn't at top speed. No way could I just run in and snatch what I needed. What could I do when I was still injured that would draw them away from camp and leave their gear behind so I could get to it?

Still injured . . .

As Janet began pulling out provisions and Ken headed to break down the tent, I edged away from the ridge. My vocal range wasn't far with my limited lung capacity. But I figured I should be able to get just far enough away to call for help. It might not be loud enough for the people to hear, but the dog would catch it. And it would be trained to respond to that. If I was lucky, they'd all come running, and I'd have just enough time to slip around back to camp to nab the map and radio. It was my only shot.

It was difficult to keep my wheeze to a minimum as I moved. I felt a cough welling up in my chest and had to fight to hold it in. I needed the accompanying blood as something for the dog to fixate on when I got to my diversion point.

Don't breathe. Don't breathe. Don't breathe.

Seventy-five yards was about as far as I got before the hacking burst out of me. I doubled over with the force of it. Blood spattered the ground at my feet. Man, how long was I gonna keep doing that?

I took a breath, wondering if I imagined that that was a little easier than it had been.

"Help!" *Well shit, that sounded pathetic. Right on target.* "Help me!"

I fell quiet, listening. No sign that they'd heard me. My next inhale brought on another coughing fit that took me a couple minutes to recover from before I could manage to call again, louder this time. "Help!"

That was it. A bark in the distance. The dog had heard me. I called out once more for good measure then let my wolf ascend, changing my scent as I started circling my way around to come at their camp from the other direction.

Please, please work.

"What is it, boy? Show me, Ripley."

Okay, Janet's on board. What about Ken?

He was still packing up gear when I came around, rolling up the tent and stuffing it in his pack.

Shit. Now what?

I was contemplating whether I could rush him when Janet called out, "Ken! Come here!"

The blood had done its work then.

Ken bolted after Janet, leaving the packs behind. I didn't waste time. As soon as Ken was out of earshot, I slunk into their camp and began rifling through the bags. The radio was easy. Right where Janet had left it. I shoved it into a pocket of my cargo shorts and began rifling for the map.

C'mon, where the hell is it?

I checked all the outer pockets. Nothing.

". . . need to call it in."

Shit. Shit. Shit.

Why were there so many damned pockets? Elodie hadn't carried a pack this size on her rescue. Why were they? I finally found the compass wrapped in a bandana in the top of Ken's pack.

"He's not alerting to Elodie, but that blood is human. Somebody's out here and they're hurt," Janet insisted.

Where was the goddamned map?

I gave up on stealth and tore through the bag. *There!* A corner of paper sticking out of the sleeping bag roll. I tugged. Success.

Who the hell puts a map in a sleeping bag?

I zipped the pack shut and tore out of the campsite, but not before the dog was close enough to hear. He came streaking through the trees after me, barking the alarm. I whirled, dropping to a crouch. The dog skidded to a halt, sniffing, barking, clearly confused at this mix of scents that matched what he had found, and yet didn't. I let my wolf as close to the surface as possible without actually shifting. The growl rumbled out, low and menacing. The dog backed up a couple steps but didn't stop barking. I could hear the crunch of footsteps as the searchers ran toward us.

No time for this.

I reared up, venting my frustration in a bear-like roar that sent the dog skittering back to its people. Then I turned and fled, mentally repeating the last coordinates Nate had reported.

Elodie

It was the scent of old blood that caught my attention. I was weak and dizzy with fever as I knelt to inspect the traces of rust caught at the top of a fissure of rock, as if a hand had grabbed it and been cut. Was it human? I bent to get a closer sniff. My pack shifted and I overbalanced. For a long suspended moment I hung there, arms pinwheeling, struggling to right myself before I toppled over the side and into the fissure.

It was my pack that kept me from plunging to the bottom and breaking bones. I wedged between it and one craggy wall, losing a few layers of skin in the process where my legs banged against rock and my shirt rode up. But I was still whole. And stuck.

I kicked my feet, trying to find something to push off of and climb out, but the space below me widened and I couldn't get my knees high enough to gain purchase against the sloping walls. Within the harness of my pack, I wriggled, unsnapping straps to see if I could get free of the bag itself. It would fall, but then I should be able to climb down and get it, pushing it up ahead of me. The fissure wasn't so deep that I couldn't climb back out again. It took a lot of effort and exhaling, trying to compress my chest like a mouse, but at length I got my arms free of the pack and dragged my body up a few inches.

As predicted, the pack slid down, landing at the bottom with an echoing thump. I made my way carefully after it until I sat at the base of the shaft, gasping and exhausted from something that shouldn't have taken that much effort. The light didn't penetrate too far down here, but I could tell from the echoes that the space continued on for some distance. By some miracle, my flashlight had survived the fall. Its beam pierced the dark, revealing a cave. Nothing so ideal as mine. The floor was rock strewn and uneven. But it was tall enough for me to stand, and it would hide me well enough while I went through transition.

When I slipped my pack back on, I glanced up at the shaft leading to the surface. I wouldn't be able to climb that with paws. If I stayed down here and didn't manage to master the shift between forms, I'd be trapped. But the alternative was to stay exposed, a veritable sitting duck for Patrick and his gun. Leading with the flashlight, I made my way into the cave.

About a dozen feet in, I found the pony tail holder, pink with a little sparkly butterfly. Molly's. Had to be. So close to the entrance. But she was just a little kid. Terrified of the dark. And her brother had put her down here to hide her from the monster. How long had she stayed before she'd ventured out and been found by search teams? I inhaled. Beneath the odor of rock and damp and something I really didn't want to think about being bat droppings, I fancied I smelled her fear. But it was probably just my imagination. I knelt and picked the hair elastic up and slipped it in my pocket, a reminder that she had survived her nightmare.

The cave extended further back than I expected, winding and twisting away into more tunnels. A spelunker I was not. I went in only so far as it took to find a semi-flat space with room for the sleeping bag. The pack fell from my shoulders with a crash that reverberated down the cave. I cringed, waiting for a flurry of startled bats. Small blessings, there were none.

I dug out the small, battery powered lantern and set up my makeshift camp in its pitiful fluorescent glow. Mindful of Sawyer's constant badgering to make me eat, I pulled out some jerky and protein bars, even though I had no appetite. I ate the first bar standing up, more in defiance of my fever weakened state than anything else. Restless, I moved just outside the edge of light from the entrance to the cave and listened hard while I ate my jerky and sipped a bottle of water. No signs of pursuit, just the sounds of the mountain around me.

The part of me that had been running on high alert since last night uncoiled a little, forcing me to admit I was utterly exhausted. I went back to my little camp, tossing the other energy bar back into my bag, and collapsed onto the sleeping bag. Sawyer's scent puffed up around me, at once comforting and nauseating. My throat closed up on a knot of tears. The dull ache of loss flared to life, a vicious, rabid thing. I fought it because I needed to fight something or go mad. But fever and exhaustion took me, and I slid into an uneasy sleep.

Elodie, wake up.

I shivered at the sound of my father's voice. He sounded angry. He never used to get angry before the letter.

Ellie, please wake up.

Nope, I wasn't going to be lulled by the please or the pleading tone. I hunkered down, curling tighter into the sleeping bag, face pressed to the cotton, breathing in a scent that made me sad.

C'mon baby, you have to wake up. We have to go.

Why did he sound so panicked? It was just a letter. Just a sign that Mom was crazy. Why should I have to change my whole life because she was crazy?

"Elodie!" This time he shook me.

The motion made my brain bounce around inside my skull, leaving me dizzy. Could you be dizzy in sleep? I growled in reply.

The hand on my shoulder didn't loosen.

"C'mon, we're going."

My world jerked and shifted, and the pain in my head threatened to drive me back under. But that was bad. There was some reason I shouldn't give in. So instead I fought to peel my eyes open.

I was met with a wall of gray with splotches of black. The splotches resolved themselves into a sort of shield that read *Fire Rescue.* I blinked and let my head fall back. An arm stopped it from falling right off my shoulders, for which I was grateful. Peering up at the blur on top of the t-shirt, my eyes turned it into a face, dimly lit in the darkness of my surroundings.

"Dad?" Was that raw croak my voice?

"I'm here, baby. We're gonna get you home."

There was a part of me that wanted to be angry he'd come after me. But I was so glad to see a familiar face, and I felt so damn awful.

"I don't feel good, Dad."

"I'm gonna take care of you," he said.

Then he brought me into the light and I was blinded. I curled into him, squeezing my eyes shut against the glare.

"Send down the rope. She's too weak to climb."

Something thumped down beside us. Dad shifted me in his arms and I felt a makeshift harness being wrapped around my chest.

"There's something . . ." God I was tired. And so, so cold. "Something I need to tell you."

"It can wait, honey. It's all gonna be okay."

The absolute *wrongness* of that statement resonated through me with enough conviction that I tried opening my eyes again. I was at the base of the fissure, with a rope wrapped underneath my arms. Which made me realize we weren't alone. He'd probably called out Search and Rescue. Why did that idea terrify me?

"She's secure. Pull on up. Easy does it," Dad called.

The rope went taut, digging underneath my arms.

"Wait, Dad, you need to know—"

"Later, Ellie."

I had to force my legs to engage or be scraped against the side of the fissure as whoever was up top hauled upward. My muscles were shaking with fatigue before I was even halfway up. The pain of the rope digging in under my arms and across my chest was the only thing keeping me fully conscious. When I reached the top, arms slipped beneath mine, hauling me to solid ground. Something pressed to my neck as he laid me down.

I turned my head just in time to see Patrick pull the trigger. I felt a sharp sting against my throat.

"Night, night, Elodie."

The scream died in my throat as everything faded to black.

Chapter 14

Elodie

When I was ten, Dad took me on vacation to the beach. It was a rare thing, getting to play in the ocean, and I strayed out too far and got caught in a riptide. I still remembered being tossed like a ragdoll, powerless against the surging current that dragged me, while my hands scrabbled for purchase against the sandy bottom. By the time I fought my way free, I was half a mile down the beach.

Fighting my way back to consciousness was worse than that. Every virtual inch was a struggle, and each time I came anywhere near the surface, the tranquilizers dragged me back under. It would have been an easy thing to let go and just sink into oblivion. But my father didn't know that Patrick was a killer. Who knew what the son of a bitch was doing to Dad while I was off in a drug induced stupor.

That thought made me stop struggling for a bit. What was I going to wake up to? More blood? More death? The body of the only other person in the world who'd ever cared about me?

No!

Panic was enough to boost me the rest of the way. I broke through to consciousness in silence, as though I was breaking through water and had to hold in the gasp that wanted to erupt. No need to alert Patrick I was awake yet. I listened for a while. To my left was a crackling fire. Someone poked at it. I could hear the rush of cinders as some of the logs collapsed. I couldn't hear anybody else.

245

Where was Dad?

"Oh good, you're awake." Patrick sounded conversational.

I froze, though I wasn't aware that I had moved. What had given me away?

"What the hell did you do?" Dad's voice. Groggy. Patrick must have tranqed him too.

"Sorry about that, Nate. But I couldn't have you getting in the way, you see."

"In the way of what?"

I could hear him shift somehow and tried to open my eyes, but they refused to cooperate.

"What the hell have you done to my daughter?" Fury sharpened his voice.

Dad was struggling against something. Ropes, I guessed. My own hands were bound behind my back, my arms numb from the weight of my body.

"She'll come to eventually. I may have overdosed her a bit for her size, but I couldn't have a werewolf shifting before I could restrain her."

My dad went very still. "You're the hunter."

Patrick said nothing, and I had a ridiculous notion that he'd just bowed, like an actor claiming kudos for an especially notable performance.

"Why? What did we ever do to you?"

"You to me? Nothing. It's an ancient feud, really. Puts the Hatfield and McCoys to shame. It all goes back to the first she-wolf of your line. Or her line, really." Patrick's voice took on a lecturing tone. "Our very colorful family history has her as being the spawn of Satan, which I've always thought was a bit far-fetched. Something about some ancestor of mine who was a widower marrying some ancestor of hers who was pregnant by another man. My ancestor raised the girl as his own. And what thanks did he get? She grew up, turned into a wolf, and slaughtered him.

His son by his first wife vowed revenge, to wipe out her and her progeny."

Brynne's step-brother was the first hunter, I realized. That explained why the hunters had always been after my family and not werewolves in general.

"And so it has gone through the centuries. My family were hunters. Her family were beasts. And nobody ever seemed to actually manage to carry out the fundamental mission: to destroy the wolf line. Until me. I was the first one who was smart about it.

"See, I didn't *want* to devote my life to this like my father and his father and his father. But, oh, it was supposed to be some sacred *duty*. I can't even remember all the lies I told my wife while I was tracking down Rosalind. But I figured it out. I tracked her down. And she was already pregnant with your bastard. The next generation already started."

Dad loosed a growl at that.

Patrick paid him no attention, too intent on telling his story. "But Rosalind's father, stupid, stupid man that he was, talked her into giving up the baby. And with that I devised the perfect plan. Get everything over in one, fell swoop. My wife and I would adopt the child—"

"*You?* You were the one who was supposed to take her?" asked my dad in horror.

"Well yes. It was all very straight forward. I'd take care of Rosalind, and afterward, it would have been so easy to make Elodie's death look like a case of SIDS. No blood, no mess. An end to all future generations. Simple. Elegant. And this ridiculous war would be over and I could get on with my life like a normal person."

I couldn't repress a shudder at the casual way he talked about murdering a baby. Murdering *me*. Who was the real monster here?

Patrick shifted his attention back to me. I didn't see it, since my eyes were still refusing to open, but I could feel his gaze upon me. "But it didn't work. Your mother—yes

Elodie, I know you're awake; your breathing changed a few minutes ago—Your mother had you secreted away and then she ran. Oh she was easy enough to track. She didn't have your training, and she was so weak from giving birth. I tranqed her, slit her wrists. I knew your grandfather wouldn't allow an autopsy or a tox screen. He didn't know what they might find, and it would bring up too many questions. So her suicide was really easy to fake."

Dad made a sort of whooshing noise, as if he'd been punched in the stomach.

My brain went into overdrive. My mother didn't kill herself. She didn't abandon me. Abandon *us.* This psycho, sanctimonious, son of a bitch killed her.

"You murdered my mother." My voice sounded faint and very distant to my ears. I still couldn't get my eyes to open.

"Murder implies she was human rather than beast. I put down a threat. It was a public service, really."

"And what about Sawyer? What do you call shooting him?" I demanded.

"An unfortunate accident. It was his mistake choosing to be your champion, something I'm sure he'd never have done if he had known what you really were."

So he still didn't know that Sawyer and his father were like me.

"You really have been so much *trouble.* You've been the thorn in my side. The one that got away. I lost my wife. I lost most of my career. But I couldn't *fail* at this like I'd failed at everything else. It took me *years* to find you. Who knew that when I finally did it would be because of some petty, schoolgirl vendetta on Facebook? Thank God for modern technology and social media. I might never have found you otherwise."

Facebook? Amber's petty, ridiculous smear campaign is what lured this monster to my door? My brain reeled at the ludicrousness of that. But Patrick continued on, since

248

apparently he'd been waiting for quite some time for an audience who could appreciate his villainous monologue.

"Maybe you're wondering why I didn't kill you outright. Well, the thing about it is that I had to be *sure*. You weren't like your mother. You weren't like the others that were described in my records. You should've lost it when you found that boy amid all that blood and gore. But you didn't. So I had to find something else, something to test you, to prove for absolute certain that you were your mother's daughter. I'm not a murderer, you see. I couldn't go off killing girls, half cocked on just a *hunch*. So then I sabotaged your car. It was a risky move. No telling when that old clunker would finally kick it. But that worked out perfectly. And you outran my truck. But just barely. I *still* wasn't sure. And then I *realized*. You're a late bloomer. You haven't actually shifted yet. But judging by that display earlier, you're not far from it. So we're just going to sit here, if you don't mind, until you shift. Then we'll get this unpleasantness over with."

He'd killed my mother in human form. Why should he have a problem with that? Then it occurred to me. "You've never seen it, have you?

"Seen what?"

"Transition." I managed to crack my eyes open to slits, even though my eyelids weighed a metric ton. It was just enough that I could see Patrick watching me from the other side of the fire, a gun held loosely against his thigh. "This isn't about being *sure*. It's about the science. You want to study it. To know how it works."

He inclined his head, his expression a mixture of approval and disappointment. "It really *is* a pity. You truly are a brilliant student. Yes, I'd very much like to see the whole process. It's a pity I can't put you in a lab. Imagine the genetic breakthroughs your DNA might hold."

I was way more interested in imagining my teeth in his throat, but for now it seemed wise to keep him talking while my body continued to throw off the effects of the tranquilizers. Chances were, even fully shifted, I'd never get free of the ropes in time to attack him before he could put a bullet in my brain. But if he was insisting on seeing the transition through, he might be waiting a while. I was close, but this cycle of fevers and body cramps could go on for days more before it finally happened. Maybe someone would find us by then. Search and Rescue was out there. When Dad didn't check in, they'd know something was wrong. Someone could find us.

I just hoped it wouldn't be too late when they did.

~*~

Sawyer

The radio in my pocket crackled to life. I jolted and my hands fumbled to adjust the volume as Eileen's voice seemed to boom out. "Janet and Ken have been found. They are fine. Repeat, they are a-okay."

Well it was nice to know that my stranding them without a map or compass hadn't done them any lasting damage. The tools certainly hadn't helped me any. As it happens, I'm not nearly as good at reading topographical maps as Elodie. My actual starting point and where I thought I was starting on the map were definitely not the same thing, so despite having the proper navigational tools, it took me hours to stumble across Patrick and Nate's trail, evading two other search teams in the process.

According to radio chatter, no one had heard from Nate or Patrick for three hours. This trail was several hours older than that. If Patrick had a vehicle stashed, they could be miles away by now. If he'd found Elodie—

I cut the thought off. There was no reason to suppose he *had* found Elodie, even *with* Nate's help. She was smart and resourceful. I had to believe she'd holed up somewhere to ride out transition. The best thing I could do right now was follow the trail and rescue her father. Elodie would never forgive herself if anything happened to him.

Dialing the volume back even more, I shoved the radio back in my pocket. No need to draw attention to myself. The sun was starting to set, shadows growing longer. I could hear Eileen giving orders for the night. They weren't stopping like last night. Not with two of their searchers being added to the list of the missing. I knew the searchers had changed their pattern, first to try and find Janet and Ken, then to try and locate Nate and Patrick. Since I wasn't a hundred percent sure where I was, I didn't know if any of them was on an intersection course with me. I'd just have to keep quiet, be careful, and hope I didn't cross any of them. The last thing we needed was more casualties in this private war.

The wheeze disappeared by the time I reached the creek. My first attempt at a full breath sent me into a coughing fit that doubled me over until I'd hacked up the last of the blood. It left a sour, copper coating in my mouth. I spat and panted, catching my breath. And smelled smoke.

I didn't think the other searchers would be stopping to make campfires. But would Patrick? Wouldn't he be monitoring the radio as I was? Surely he wouldn't actually stop and make camp with the threat of being found. It was a stupid mistake and Patrick was not a stupid man.

Still, I couldn't risk *not* checking it out.

It'd be faster to go as a wolf. But was it safe to try and shift? My lung had reinflated, the wound closed. I rubbed the heel of my hand over it. My chest still ached. There could still be deep tissue damage. I sighed. Two feet it was.

The trail stayed mostly to the creek. I stuck to the high ground, following the ridge above. I couldn't be sure, but I thought I was north of the cabin somewhere, upstream from where I'd been shot, from where I last saw Elodie. I hoped she was far away from here. Safe. But I knew better. The lingering sense of dread in my gut confirmed it. Elodie would be out for revenge. Unless she was fully incapacitated by transition, she would try to track him. I just hoped I could get there first.

Full dark fell, cloaking me in shadows, covering the sounds of my movement with night noises. And at last I saw a faint glow of firelight through the trees. I made my way closer, picking up the faint murmur of voices.

"*You?* You were the one who was supposed to take her?" The horrified tone rang out clear. Nate.

I'd found them.

Creeping nearer, I could see Elodie's dad struggling to sit up, his arms wrenched tight behind him and bound at the wrist. Obviously Patrick had moved on to the hostage portion of the plan.

Someone shifted to the left side of the fire. "Well yes. It was all very straight forward. I'd take care of Rosalind, and afterward, it would have been so easy to make Elodie's death look like a case of SIDS. No blood, no mess. An end to all future generations. Simple. Elegant. And this ridiculous war would be over and I could get on with my life like a normal person."

Jesus Christ, I thought. *He's totally crazy.* The truly scary thing was that he looked like the same, sane rational guy my dad had been working with for the last few years. His face was placid and just like at the cabin, it was only the gun in his hand that ruined the illusion.

"But it didn't work. Your mother—yes Elodie, I know you're awake; your breathing changed a few minutes ago—"

Frantically I searched the campsite, looking for her. There, on the opposite side of the fire. She lay in a heap, bound like her father, but unmoving. My heart leapt at the sight of her. I could just see the shallow rise and fall of her chest. She was alive!

"—So her suicide was really easy to fake."

What? My brain tuned back in to what Patrick was saying, too late to catch his meaning.

"You murdered my mother."

Oh.

Elodie's voice was weak and a little slurred. Drugged rather than weakened from transition. How long until it wore off?

I circled around the campsite while Patrick kept talking. He'd positioned himself well. The ground here was wide and flat. The creek was several feet to his back, a long drop, which also meant no way to approach. There were no trees within twenty yards, no boulders, nothing to use as cover for a closer approach.

The packs were behind him. He hadn't made camp any further than building a fire. No need to make his prisoners comfortable. One of the packs was open. I could see the corner of some power bars and the white plastic top of a water bottle sticking out of a pocket. One mesh pocket held the map, folded neatly into a square as was his way. The other pocket showed the hilt of a knife. Elodie's knife, I realized with jolt. He must've taken it from our packs before he left the cabin.

He was going over how he had tried to test her, and what the plan was now. That wasn't good. The bad guy never tells you that stuff if he has any intention of letting you live. If I didn't do something, she was dead. They both were. "It's a pity I can't put you in a lab," Patrick was saying. "Imagine the genetic breakthroughs your DNA might hold."

Elodie didn't respond to that. But she'd managed to garner some important information. Patrick was enough of a scientist to want to watch. That bought us a little more time. How much, I didn't know. Hopefully it would be enough that I could come up with a plan to get us out of here alive.

~*~

Elodie

Even behind my closed eyes, I could feel Patrick watching me. I'd tried to fake slipping back into unconsciousness, but either he didn't buy it or he had the attention span of a starving predator. It was disturbing to begin with, but as time stretched on, it became freaking creepy. He was just sitting there on his sleeping bag, gun in hand. Staring at me.

"You know that saying about a watched pot?" I said, slitting my eyes so I could see him. "The same is true of a watched werewolf."

Patrick's lips curved a little, but he didn't take his eyes off me. My skin crawled. Even if I could control my shifting, I wouldn't want to do it under that watchful gaze. He felt like a voyeur. No way in hell did I want to do something so . . . personal in front of him. No. So I did my best to keep my breathing even and my body as close to a Zen state as possible.

The fever came again anyway. It stole over my body, drawing out a slick sweat in its wake, making me shiver at its touch. I held still. Or tried to anyway. I'd long since lost any feeling in my arms and shoulders beyond the occasional, shooting pain. How long did I have? Hours maybe. But I didn't think it would take that long. Because that would mean that something actually went *right,* and absolutely nothing about the last few days had established a precedent for that.

I needed more time. But time for what? It's not like Patrick was gonna get bored with this. Whether it was in the next five minutes or the next five days, he was going to be there to see me on the other side and put a bullet in my brain. No amount of pleading or logic was going to change that. I was completely at his mercy as long as I was bound.

Which meant I needed to get unbound. Somehow. The rope was tight and looped several times around my wrists.

Climbing rope, I thought. I tried wriggling my hands against my bonds, but they were stiff and uncooperative.

Come on, you're a freaking werewolf. You should have the strength to break through even this.

I inhaled a slow breath in preparation for the strain. And saw Patrick lift the gun and level it.

"Not thinking of trying to escape, are you?" he asked, making a tsking sound.

"I was trying to get some feeling back in my arms, actually."

There was no way I could shift and get free in time to kill him before he could fire that gun. Not as long as he was looking at me. I needed some kind of distraction. But what the hell could I manage like this? Trussed up like a freaking Christmas turkey. There was no way I could communicate with Dad, no way I could do anything without giving myself away.

The cramp began in my calf, the kind of Charlie horse I used to think was awful until I experienced the full body version. I flexed my foot trying to stretch it out.

Focus on the breath. I could almost hear Sawyer's voice in my mind, coaching me through this and had to bite back a cry. My mouth filled with the taste of blood from my bitten cheek.

So not helping the situation, I thought, swallowing the warm taste of copper.

In and out. Slow and steady. The cramp moved up my leg. Inhale. Exhale through the pain. I tried to focus on the scents around me as a distraction. Sweat hung sour in the air. Mine. My father's. Our kidnapper's. It mixed with wisps of smoke on the bare breeze. I wondered if I'd ever smell smoke again and not be afraid, after this. Or if I'd ever smell smoke again, period.

The cramp started in my other foot, harder now. I wanted to scream, to scramble up and force the muscle flat. But I held as still as I could and I breathed.

There were green, growing things around us. Old leaves decaying from last fall. Damp earth. And Sawyer.

My legs flailed and my breath exploded in an exhale. I hurriedly sucked in another breath and found the scent again. No. Impossible. It was the fever. I was hallucinating. Conjuring the one thing that could comfort me in the middle of this nightmare. But it woke my wolf. She shoved at my mind, at the edges of my body. My legs jackknifed again, coming perilously close to the edge of the fire.

The fire.

It was the only thing within reach. If I could manage to knock the burning logs into something else, it might be just the distraction I needed. Of course, that meant I had to get control over my limbs.

Focus. Focus.

My wolf snarled and strained in return.

Give me control, damn it. I have a plan.

My body jolted again, my shoulder slamming into the ground with bruising force that let me know what my wolf thought of that plan. Then there was no more thought to the fire, no more thought to distraction. There was only the pain as I began to buck and writhe. I flipped to my stomach and curled in on myself as my body betrayed me and my wolf tried to pursue a ghost.

Mate.

I could still smell the phantom scent. But it was no longer comfort. Rage sizzled through me, a worthy accompaniment to agony as my back cracked and my ribs expanded. I grabbed for it, tried to latch on to the emotion because fury was better than pain. But it slipped away as I spasmed again, my head flying back. Dimly I could hear my father shouting something, but I was too focused on the pain to make out the words. With a loud crack, my hips broke and realigned. My mouth opened in a wailing howl as my legs reshaped, my joints shifting into canine hindquarters.

Someone was . . . laughing.

What the hell?

It was Patrick. Through the red haze of agony I could see him, delighted in the spectacle before him.

The rage returned, and with it, my shoulders cracked, slipping out of alignment. Gritting my teeth to hold in another scream, I rotated my dislocated shoulders forward until my bound wrists lay in front of me

And then . . . everything seemed to stop. Suspended in a moment of exquisite suffering where I was caught between forms. Again.

No!

I lay there, panting, waiting for my wolf to rouse, to continue to push. But she was in as much pain as I, all but blind with it. And exhausted from the effort to change forms.

"Well now, that was a disappointment," said Patrick.

I was beyond human speech, so the only response I could muster was a whine.

"Ah well. That was enough. Even I have enough heart to put a suffering beast out of its misery," he said.

"No!" shouted Dad. He was struggling to his knees. He lurched toward Patrick, coming through the fire, his clothes catching, burning.

No. Oh dear God, no.

He fell before he could reach Patrick, rolling on the ground to put out the flames.

The gun that had shifted toward my dad for a moment moved back to me, pointed directly at my head.

It was over. As I had always promised, it would end with me.

Chapter 15

Elodie

A roar rent the air, a vicious sound, somewhere between a growl and a scream. My eyes flew open to see Patrick jerking the gun toward a new target. He was barely turned before something crashed into him. He went down hard on his back and the gun went off.

The world went to molasses as the sound tried to catapult me back to the cabin, to the blood. I fought to stay present, to stay in the now. And in that long, slow moment, it was Sawyer's face I saw shifting, his half-formed muzzle snapping, nearly grazing Patrick's throat as they fell.

Hope and disbelief rammed into me like a Mack truck. It wasn't possible, wasn't real. Sawyer was dead. I'd seen it happen.

With a rubber band snap, time sped up to normal again and the scene before me played out in a rush. Sawyer missed. Momentum carried him too far and he hit the ground hard, one of his paws turning beneath him. His leg buckled. He rolled with it, and came up fast, snarling and favoring his leg.

He was here. He was *alive!* My brain just froze as I stared, searching for wounds that simply…weren't there. For long moments, I forgot the pain, forgot to breathe. My mate had survived. And he had found his way back me.

A sob ripped free of my throat, buoyed by a fierce joy that eclipsed the pain and the danger. Sawyer was alive.

With a wrenching shudder that was probably all in my head, my world tipped back to its proper axis.

Sawyer stalked Patrick, who had gained his feet and was moving slowly backward. Patrick's eyes were everywhere at once, looking for the gun but trying not to take his eyes off his opponent.

Where the hell is the gun?

The question froze the blood in my veins as I, too, started looking frantically around the campsite. Sawyer was hurt, intent on Patrick, moving forward, but limping. He couldn't possibly be fully healed from being shot, and if Patrick got to the gun first it would happen all over again. And this time he wouldn't have the strength left to survive it.

The terror of that wrecked me, hurt me more than the next spasm of pain from my incomplete transition. *No. No, no, no.* I tried to scream, but the words were all in my head. What came out of my mouth was something horrible, something between a snarl and a sob. Something neither canine and nor human. I clawed the ground, willing myself to change, willing my wolf to rise and finish this. All of this.

I dug my claws into the dirt and pulled myself forward on my belly. It didn't matter that I was caught between forms, that every motion was agony. I just had to get there. I concentrated on the action of throwing out my deformed limbs, digging my claws into the dirt, pulling forward toward the fighting. I was not going to lose Sawyer. Not again.

I could see the moment Patrick's eyes found the gun in the way his body tensed. Sawyer saw it too. He was already leaping as Patrick flipped over in a dive for the pile of gear and Sawyer's jaws snapped on empty air as Patrick's hand closed around the barrel of the gun where it had come to rest against one of the packs. Sawyer turned, coming back for another strike as Patrick swung the gun around.

I tried to scream a warning. A mistake. My strangled howl drew Sawyer's attention to me and Patrick smashed the butt of the gun into Sawyer's head, sending him staggering sideways. His injured leg buckled. He recovered, but Patrick was already on his feet again, leveling the gun on Sawyer.

My field of vision narrowed. Blood roared in my head. Desperate, I tried to lunge forward, my heart threatening to burst in my chest. But my legs buckled and I fell, too far away to stop him. I screamed again, inhuman, terrified, waiting for the shot.

My dad crashed into Patrick. I hadn't even seen him moving. Injured, his hands still bound, his rush was unbalanced. Patrick sent him flying backward with an elbow strike. But the distraction was enough for Sawyer to clamp his jaws around Patrick's gun arm. Another shot exploded, splintering a tree on the other side of the clearing.

Sawyer lunged forward, wrenching the arm like a bulldog, but Patrick used some kind of judo throw, turning Sawyer's momentum against him, flinging him away and scuttling toward the packs. Sawyer tumbled, skidded to a stop and scrambled toward him. Patrick, one hand wrapped around the bite on his arm, fell into a fighter's crouch, a knife in his other hand.

My knife.

They circled. The knife was not Patrick's natural weapon, and he was wounded. He gripped it in his fist, making awkward slashes that Sawyer mostly avoided with ease. Sawyer feinted left and dodged, coming under Patrick's guard to nip at his leg. The deadly dance went on, neither of them gaining ground. Sawyer couldn't go in for a killing strike without the risk of being stabbed. Lunge. Nip. Slash. Again and again. As their stand-off continued, Sawyer started to slow. He couldn't go on like this much longer.

Sawyer's leg gave, causing him to stumble. Patrick charged, swiping wide. The knife flashed. Sawyer danced back, but not before the blade caught him across the chest. Blood spilled, bright and hot, soaking his fur.

And I went mad.

My wolf rose above the tangled snarl of rage and pain, growing, pressing up and out, until my body, my mind, was filled with her. The limbs that were stuck at improper lengths tore into shape with a crunch. All along the length of my skin I felt the prickling sprout of fur. I did not take a backseat to the beast. I became the beast. The gut-wrenching agony faded, replaced by a steadying strength.

I rose to my feet—all four of them—no longer weak, no longer defenseless. And I fixed my eyes on Patrick.

He continued to brandish the knife at Sawyer, driving him back toward the drop off to the creek. Sawyer was weakening, slowed by blood loss. Even as I watched he took another edging step in retreat.

No.

I sprinted toward them and leapt, landing claws extended on Patrick's back. As he staggered under my weight, I sank my teeth into the meat of his shoulder. His scream echoed off the mountain and his blood burst warm and sharp into my mouth, like some kind of exotic fruit. I bit harder, teeth tearing through flesh and muscle.

Patrick whirled, trying to fling me off, but my jaw was locked on his shoulder, my claws digging deeper into his back. With a roar, he raised the knife to slash at me. I saw the glint of the blade coming at me and my stomach clenched with fear. Sawyer sprang at him, mouth closing around Patrick's knife hand, his bulk and momentum driving us all to the ground in a tangle of limbs.

We landed hard, and the impact loosened my hold. Patrick scrambled away from us, bleeding, frantic to find the knife or some other weapon. But we were between him and it. He turned to run only to realize we had him caged between us and the edge of the drop off to the creek.

Gotcha.

Patrick faced us, eyes now wide and white around the edges as he looked from me to Sawyer, hands raised in a universal sign of surrender.

We stalked forward, shoulder to shoulder. I couldn't help but lean over to rub my head against Sawyer's shoulder, just to feel that he was really real and not some figment of my fevered brain. But I met with muscle and fur and heat. Life. It was real. He was real.

"Look, let's talk about this," said Patrick backing up a step.

I cocked my head in a gesture I hope he took for *Really?*

"You don't need to do this. I know you don't really want to hurt me or you'd have done it already."

I wished I had my voice to ask him how he thought that was gonna work. How we could let the hunter live and not expect to be tracked again, constantly looking over our shoulders for the rest of our lives. Been there, done that. This ended here, with me, as I'd always said it would.

My lips curled in a snarl and I paced forward.

Patrick retreated another step.

Beside me, Sawyer faltered. I glanced at him out of the corner of my eye, still keeping Patrick in my sights. As we got even closer, I could practically feel him weakening. He shook his head as if to clear it and continued to step forward.

What was going on? He hadn't bled that much, had he?

Patrick turned his eyes on my mate. "You're hurt, Sawyer. I don't know how you survived being shot earlier, but you obviously can't take much more of this."

I snarled and snapped at him and he lifted his hands in surrender again as he edged back one more step. His foot knocked some rocks over the edge. They tumbled down the incline, bouncing and cracking against the stone face before plopping in the water. It was a long way down. Long enough to break a neck or something else vital.

"Just stand down and I'll go. I'll leave you be."

Right. Exactly like he'd let my mother be.

"You don't want to do this."

No. I didn't. And yet, I did. This wasn't about being an unthinking beast, about being out for blood for the sake of blood. This was about survival. My survival. Sawyer's. Patrick would never give up, never go away. And if he did, someone else would take his place if we let him go. We would never have peace, never have safety as long as he still lived. Because a man didn't give up his entire life, his marriage, and his career in pursuit of a centuries old family feud just because he surrendered one battle.

I wished I could speak, to say what I was thinking.

Even as I thought it, I felt my bones begin to shift. With a yelp of surprise, I fell back to my haunches. Things were moving fast, joints realigning, fur receding, muscles transforming. Painful, but not the all out agony of becoming a wolf in the first place. I looked to Sawyer, knowing my eyes were wide, confused.

A blur of motion caught my attention, and I turned to see Patrick lunging at me. With a roar, Sawyer threw himself between us, slamming a shoulder into Patrick's midriff. He flew backward, arms pinwheeling, searching for balance, even as his feet left the ground and he tumbled over the side. His scream cut off abruptly with a splash and a crunch. Then all was quiet.

Sawyer peered over the edge for a long moment before returning to me. I watched in fascination as he seemed to kind of . . . melt back to human with a great deal more grace than I was managing. Then he was kneeling and gathering me into his arms until we were a desperate tangle of human limbs.

I couldn't touch enough of him. Even as he was trying to kiss me, I was still frantically running my hands over every inch, assuring myself that he was real and here and alive. I framed his stubbled cheeks in my hands. "You're alive. You're alive! How? I watched you die."

"Guess hell spat me back out," he said, one corner of his mouth quirking up.

"Sawyer!" He looked like hell. He was filthy, as I was. The long, shallow cut on his chest was still oozing. And a fresh pink scar puckered just over his heart. I laid my hand over it.

"I was starting to shift when he shot me. Bullet missed my heart. I guess we're a little more indestructible than I realized."

I wrapped my arms tight around him. "Oh God. Oh God, I thought I'd lost you."

"I'm right here."

I pressed my lips to the scar, feeling his heart heart beat strong and true and whole. "I love you."

He made a humming, contented noise deep in his throat.

A groan came from somewhere behind us.

"Dad!" I disentangled myself and raced toward him.

He looked a total mess. Half his clothes were burned, the skin beneath red and beginning to blister. His hands were still bound. A quick search located the knife Patrick had lost in the fight. I used it to saw through the ropes. I was almost afraid to turn him over. But he groaned again as I released his arms, so I grabbed his shoulder and pulled. A livid purple bruise spread across his temple. He'd need to be assessed for a concussion. I quickly checked the rest of him over. The shoulder he'd landed on was dislocated, but he didn't have any broken bones and wasn't bleeding from anything bigger than a surface scrape.

"Ellie?"

His eyes were open, staring at me.

"Hi, Dad. You're gonna be okay. Patrick's . . ." I hadn't leaned over to look. I glanced back at Sawyer for confirmation. He shook his head. "Patrick can't hurt us anymore."

Color was creeping across his face and I started to flipping through my brain trying to figure out what that was a symptom of.

"Ellie, you're naked."

I looked down. "Um. Yeah. Lost my fur."

"Here."

I looked up to see Sawyer holding out a t-shirt. He'd robbed some shorts out of one of the packs for himself. Grateful, I took it and slipped it on. One of Patrick's. He was a pretty small guy, so the shirt barely came to the top of my thighs, but so long as I didn't bend over, all the important stuff was covered.

Dad was glaring at Sawyer. "I don't know whether to thank you or kick your ass."

"You have nothing to kick his ass for, Dad. We didn't— um." Nope, couldn't actually *say* that to my dad. He knew well enough what I was talking about. "We didn't." I repeated firmly. "I was right. It's straight up genetics. And as you can see, he's just like me."

"How is that possible?"

"There's a whole helluva lot that your family history got wrong," said Sawyer.

He bent and began rummaging through the other pack, finding another pair of pants and tossing them to me before helping Dad sit up.

I turned and shimmied into them. Dad's. Naturally they swallowed me. Gripping the waistband, I shuffled over to pick up the knife and the rope I'd slipped out of when I shifted. While I was hacking, I could hear Dad giving Sawyer instructions on how to reset his shoulder. By the time I'd fashioned a belt to hold the pants up, it was done with a crunch and a short scream.

I bent to roll up the legs so I could actually walk, and I heard the *snick* of a chambering round.

I didn't stop to think, didn't stop to consider the impossible or the morality. I just turned, using the momentum of my motion to fling the knife before I even consciously saw my target.

My aim was true. The knife buried itself to the hilt in Patrick's throat. For a moment, he stood there, looking like some kind of undead soldier, broken and twisted, bruised and bloody, the gun wavering in his good hand. Then a thin trail of red snaked down from the knife and he collapsed with a gurgling wheeze.

"That's for my mother, you son of a bitch," I breathed.

There was a beat of stunned silence in the clearing before Dad stumbled over to Patrick. I knew he was dead even before Dad knelt and checked for a pulse. He kicked the gun away for good measure.

Sawyer crossed to me. He didn't try to shield me anymore. Death was an ugly reality, one I would have to find a way to live with. His hands slipped around mine, and as he tugged me close, I finally looked away from the body and up at him.

"It's finally over," he said.

"No," I said, tipping my face up to his. "It's just beginning."

~*~

Sawyer

"Bumps and bruises, some scrapes. No lasting physical damage. You're incredibly lucky, Miss Rose." The doctor laid down her otoscope and pulled off her gloves with a snap of rubber. "We'll be keeping your father overnight for observation. I'll send a nurse back as soon as we get him settled in a regular room. We don't technically need to keep you, but given tonight's events, I don't think he'll sign off on you going home, so we'll arrange somewhere for you, too."

"Thank you."

The doctor fixed me with an amused glance. "I assume you'll be staying, as well?"

I tightened my hand around Elodie's. "Yes."

"Thought so. The sheriff is still waiting to talk to you."

Elodie sighed and dropped her head to my shoulder. She needed sleep, not to be badgered at two in the morning about something that was already over.

"Send him in, I guess," she said.

As soon as the doctor left, Beasley and two of his deputies crowded into the tiny room. The scent of Elodie's anxiety immediately bled through the antiseptic stink of the ER.

"We need to speak to Elodie," said the sheriff looking at me. "Alone."

I tensed, prepared to tell him exactly what he could do with that suggestion, but Elodie's hand tightened on mine in warning.

"No. Sawyer stays."

"Elodie—"

"My father is still being treated, I've just been through hell, and Sawyer saved my life. He stays." Elodie's tone brooked no argument.

"Fine." Beasley nodded to one of the deputies, who had a notepad and pen. "Tell us what happened to you."

Here we go, I thought. *Time to make that cover story fly.* I worried about how this was going to go. Elodie had, thus far, proven to be a terrible liar.

"Four days ago my father and I had a fight."

"About what?" asked Beasley.

"What do you think?" she asked, injecting just the right amount of irritated teenager in her voice. "It was a continuation of the verbal butt whipping he started to give me in your office. He wasn't inclined to get over it that quickly."

The sheriff inclined his head in acknowledgment.

"I was angry, so I packed a bag and left."

"Running away," he clarified.

"Getting some space," she corrected. "I figured after a few days away, he'd realize I'm not a child he can control anymore."

"Why the park?"

"As you are well aware, my car had been sabotaged. I needed to get away on foot. The park is right out my back door, so it seemed the best option."

"Even after someone nearly ran you down."

"I thought that was Amber. Or someone with Amber. And she's got about the same amount of survival skills as a two year old. She'd never come after me there. I didn't think I was in any real danger or I'd never have gone."

"So you entered the park behind your house. What happened then?" His eyes flicked to me, shrewd and questioning. "Did you have plans to meet Mr. McGrath?"

Ah, he'd asked the wrong question.

"No. I just hiked in to do some camping. I didn't know I was being followed." She fell to silence, closing her eyes as if remembering her ordeal. A shudder ran the length of her body and she pressed her face to my shoulder. Maybe she was remembering. I curled my arm tighter around her shoulders.

"What happened next?" Beasley prompted.

Fast forward, I thought.

But before she could continue, a set of running footsteps came pounding down the hall.

My father skidded to a halt in the doorway. He was breathing hard, his hair in disarray, his eyes far more gold than green. I could smell the fear on him.

"Sir, this is a private—" began one of the deputies.

"That's my son," Dad snapped. "Sawyer, are you okay?" There was a whip of temper in his voice, but I recognized the desperation beneath. Only then did I realize what he'd probably been going through since I left.

"I'm fine," I said. I leaned closer to Elodie. "We're both fine. Sorry I worried you." As apologies went, it was about fifty miles shy of what was called for, but with our current audience, this was as good as it was gonna get for now.

He released a breath on a long exhale and nodded.

"If we can proceed?" said Sheriff Beasley.

Elodie took a deep breath. "Nothing happened the first night. But the next day, I ran into Dr. Everett."

"You didn't think that strange?"

"I've been interning for Dr. McGrath and Dr. Everett. We've been out in the park all summer, doing analysis on the feasibility of reintroducing red wolves into the wild here. He said he was doing a prey density analysis in that sector. He wouldn't be the first scientist to work on the weekends."

"Did you feel threatened?"

"No. No, I didn't suspect a thing." Her lips twisted in a bitter smile. "That's what they always say when reporters interview the neighbors of serial killers. 'He seemed like such a normal guy.'"

Dad had gone very still, very pale in the door as he listened to her account.

Elodie took another breath and continued. "He let me go at that point. Said he'd see me at work next week. It was hours later before I realized I was being followed. I thought I was just being paranoid. Until he tried to shoot me." Her voice broke and her hand dug into my arm, her scent spiking to fear.

"It's okay," I murmured. "I'm right here."

One of the deputies handed her a glass of water. She sipped and set it to the side.

"Dr. Everett shot at you," prompted Beasley.

"Tranquilizer darts. I got lucky when it hit the padded strap of my pack."

"Did you know it was Dr. Everett?"

"No, and I wasn't sticking around to find out. I ran."

"Why didn't you try to get out of the park, come for help?"

She glared at him. "I'm sorry, in the process of running away, I kind of lost my direction. Getting away from the psycho with the gun was a slightly higher priority. I lost him, but I couldn't find my way back."

The lie smelled bitter on her skin.

"I found a cave and hid. And I found this." She pulled some pink, girly hair thing out of her pocket. "It's Molly's."

"Then what happened?"

"Well, this is supposition on my part, but he went for the only person who'd be able to track me. My father. It was all under the guise of being part of the search and rescue team."

"So your father is the one who tracked you down."

"He is the one who trained me, after all," she said. "Dr. Everett shot us both with tranquilizer darts right after they found me." Elodie rubbed a hand against her neck, though the puncture wound had already healed. "I don't know where he took us or how long I was out. The next thing I remember was waking up in the woods tied up next to his campfire."

"Did he say anything about why he took you? What he was planning on doing with you?"

"He wanted to finish what he'd started with Rich and Molly before they'd escaped. Presumably that means he planned to wound us and then watch while we were eaten alive by local predators. I really wasn't in a chatty frame of mind, Sheriff."

"And how did you escape?"

This was the part where I jumped in. "I found them. I'd seen Patrick grabbing some tranq guns and extra darts after hours. It was weird behavior, so I followed him. I kept up for a while, but then I lost him, and got lost myself." I did my best to look embarrassed by that.

"Then I stumbled across a radio. One of the ones the rescue team uses. I picked it up and I was standing there thinking about whether or not I was over my head and should call for someone to get the hell out of the woods, or if I still had any hope of finding my own way back. But then I heard radio chatter about Dr. Everett and Mr. Rose searching for Elodie and what direction they were headed. Well, I *was* a Boy Scout, so I start started heading that way and just hoped I wasn't going in the opposite direction. I mean, I still didn't know what was going on with Dr. Everett, but finding out that there was a search underway for Elodie, I wanted to find them and help. I know I should have used the radio," I looked down and scuffed my foot on the floor, trying to look sheepish, "but I wanted to help, not use up the rescue team's resources looking for me, too, and then get sent home.

"Anyway, it was probably more dumb luck than anything that I got anywhere near them. It was smoke that eventually led me to their campsite, and more dumb luck that I was too tired to call out and actually got a look at the situation before giving myself away."

I outlined the fight with as much accuracy as possible, leaving out the part about Elodie and me being fanged and furry, until it came to the end. "He was waving the knife at us, trying to keep us back, and he slipped and went over the cliff." This was the really iffy part. "I don't know if the fall would have killed him or not, but he fell on his own knife."

Before search and rescue had arrived, we'd tossed Patrick's body over the side, staging things to look like he'd landed on the knife. It was the best we could come up with on the spot. If anybody decided to do some serious forensic analysis of the scene or the body, we had no way to explain the reality.

"Then we radioed for help. You know the rest," said Elodie.

"There were bite marks on the corpse," said Beasley.

My stomach twisted into a knot. We hadn't been able to come up with an explanation for this. Had hoped they wouldn't ask.

"Bite marks?" asked Elodie.

"Looks like an animal or something. On his arm and shoulder."

Elodie just looked at him with one brow raised in question. "Would you like to take impressions of *my* teeth, Sheriff?"

"You don't know what bit him?"

"I don't know what may have decided to investigate the body after we left. We didn't stick around to guard it."

Beasley still looked somewhat skeptical, as if he knew something we were saying didn't quite add up, but he couldn't put his finger on what. He opened his mouth to ask something else, but my father interrupted, stepping fully into the room.

"They've given you their statements, Sheriff. It's very late. They both need some rest. You're done here."

I felt the full weight of an alpha behind the order. Apparently so did Beasley because he rounded up his people to go.

As he was walking out, I said, "If you search Patrick's truck, you might find evidence that he transported Rich and Molly."

"I'll get my people on it. In the meantime, y'all don't leave town."

The door shut behind him and we were left alone with my dad. We all listened as the pack of footsteps receded down the hall. Then Elodie slumped, exhaustion taking its toll.

"So how much of that story was actually true?" Dad asked.

When she lifted her head, her eyes glowed gold. "The part about Patrick hunting me like an animal and Sawyer saving my life. Repeatedly."

Dad actually took a step back. He tilted his head, got a whiff of her new scent beyond the antiseptic. His brow furrowed. "You two have a lot of explaining to do. Not the least of which," he said, turning fully to me, "is explaining why you didn't come to me when you were in trouble."

"I wouldn't let him. Patrick and those who came before him have been after my family for a long, long time. I felt like it was my fight, and my fight alone. My bullheadedness put Sawyer in danger, though, and I'm sorry for that. He was nearly killed because of me."

I wanted to snap at her, tell her she didn't have anything to be sorry for. But that didn't seem like the right thing, so I just squeezed her hand.

273

Dad continued to study her. "Because of you? I brought that maniac to you. And my misplaced trust put my son *and* his mate in danger."

We both flinched, surprised, though I probably shouldn't have been.

Dad reached out and took Elodie's other hand. Patted it. "By God I want answers out of you two, but I can wait until you've had some rest. No more secrets," he said, more strongly, pointing his finger at me and giving me the alpha glare. For some reason, it didn't seem as potent as it usually was, and it didn't make me angry.

"Yeah, sure Dad."

"Right now I'm just glad you're okay. I wish you'd come to me for help, but you handled things. You took care of your mate. I'm proud of you, son."

I swallowed, unable to think of a reply. We stood on opposite sides of Elodie and stared at each other for a long moment before he turned on his heel. "I'll go talk to your father and see if he'll consent to letting me check you out to come home with us. You'll rest better outside a hospital." Then he walked out.

Elodie and I were silent for a moment.

"Well, that was intense," I said.

"But it was good, right?" She squeezed my hand. "You two are good?"

"Yeah, it's all good." And I was surprised to find that I actually meant it.

Elodie

The shrill scream of the bell reached into my brain like a claw. Closing my eyes, I dropped my head forward, wishing the cold kiss of metal was soothing to the ache. All around me lockers slammed, footsteps shuffled and pounded down the industrial tile halls in a mass exodus stampede. The sounds ricocheted through me like bullets. I still couldn't control the super hearing on my own.

Happy first day of senior year.

"Elodie?"

I lifted my head to find Rich Phillips about two feet away. He leaned awkwardly against the bank of lockers, less a product of some new lack of confidence than to the permanent damage to his leg. He wore long pants, despite the August heat that our school's air conditioner couldn't combat. A backpack was slung over one shoulder, and his fingers moved restlessly over the strap in a vaguely familiar gesture I finally realized as guitar chords. He still wore that over-powering deodorant to cover the testosterone boy reek, but this time it was laced with an under-current of nerves.

I made Rich Phillips nervous?

"Hey," I said.

He started to say something and seemed to change his mind in midstream. "You look . . . different."

I glanced down at the red tank and khaki shorts. Yeah, I was wearing color. An outfit that couldn't double as military fatigues. I even had on *jewelry*—a set of silver crescent moon earrings and matching necklace from Sawyer. Rich wasn't the first person to give me a second look today, but he was the first person who'd mentioned it.

I shrugged and waited for him to get to the point, which only seemed to make him more anxious.

"Anyway, I just . . . I never had a chance to say thank you. For saving my life. And for . . . you know, the other thing."

"What other thing?" I asked.

Rich looked around and leaned in. "For making sure the son of a bitch couldn't hurt anyone else."

For a moment the hallway faded out and I was back in the clearing, my hand still singing, the blade still quivering in Patrick's gurgling throat. I swallowed against a mouth suddenly dry, wondering when I'd stop having flashbacks.

Rich was looking concerned when my eyes focused again. For the space of a breath, I wondered if he could possibly know the truth of his statement, then shook it off. No one knew who hadn't been there. The Sheriff had accepted our statements. They'd found evidence in Patrick's truck that linked him with Rich and Molly's kidnapping. It was all over.

"I'm sorry," he said. "I shouldn't have brought it up, I just—"

"How's Molly?" I interrupted, trying for a smile and ending somewhere closer to a wince.

"Better since— Better. Thank you."

I nodded, not knowing what else to say.

From somewhere up the hall, a body thumped into a locker and books crashed to the floor. I knew the culprits even before I heard Amber's shrill laugh. Leaning around Rich, I could see the Barbie Squad surrounding some poor girl who was crouched, trying to gather her books to stuff them in a patched messenger bag. I didn't recognize her face, but I recognized the look. I'd worn it long enough myself. New kid. Fresh victim.

My wolf roused.

"Excuse me," I said, moving around Rich and heading down the hall.

Amber didn't see me coming. But Deanna did. The smile slid off her face and she tapped Amber's arm, nodding toward me. Amber turned. There was a fleeting moment of panic that flashed in her eyes before she buckled it down again and assumed her natural haughty expression.

"What are you doing?" I didn't raise my voice. But enough of a crowd gathered that I knew that rumors of our little encounter at Hansen's had to have spread. I could smell the lust for violence on the air.

"Nothing. Just welcoming the new girl. Teaching her what her place is."

My hands fisted and my wolf tried to stretch beneath my skin.

Not now, I told her.

I took a step toward Amber. She took a step back. I took another, then another, until she retreated right into the bank of lockers with a thud. I leaned in close, so I got a good whiff of her fear and bared my teeth in a vicious grin. "The only person here who needs to learn her place is you. Now we talked about this, but maybe you need a bit of clarification. I won't stand for your bullying anymore. Not of me or anyone else. I see or hear any evidence that you're up to your old tricks again, and you will answer to me." I leaned in close, dropping my voice so only she could hear. "And in case you need a reminder, I've gone up against things much worse than the likes of you, and I'm the one that walked away alive."

I stayed leaned in a few seconds longer than necessary, enjoying the scent of her fear and the sight of her pulse beating rabbit-fast in her throat. My wolf had to be satisfied with that.

"Are we clear?" I asked softly.

"C . . . clear," stuttered Amber.

I stepped back. "Now apologize."

"Sorry Rachel."

Rachel, who stood staring from Amber to me, her bookbag clutched messily in her arms, muttered, "Thanks."

Amber shoved through the crowd, bumping into shoulders as she went, her entourage following in her wake.

Everybody's eyes were fixed on me. Where such attention used to make me nervous, now it just made me straighten my back and glare. "Can I help y'all with something?" I demanded.

Someone in the back of the crowd started clapping. Then someone else joined in. And two others. And some others. Until the entire assembled group lit up the hallway with applause and catcalls.

"Way to go!"

"About damn time!"

"You go girl!"

I could feel the blood rush to my cheeks. Okay, so I wasn't immune to all attention these days. I turned from the clapping students to Rachel, who still looked shell shocked.

"Welcome to Mortimer, Rachel. I'm Elodie." I held out my hand.

She took it, shook it numbly. "Who *are* you?"

"I'm the girl Amber's been giving hell since the eighth grade. I grew a spine." Actually, I'd grown claws. "I don't think she'll be bothering you again."

The crowd was starting to disperse, and even amid the competing scents I could smell his approach. Sawyer was grinning as he appeared, slinging an arm around my shoulders and tugging me in for a fast, dizzying kiss. I immediately felt my headache wane.

"You missed some excitement," I said breathlessly.

"Oh no, I heard it from up the hall. Nicely done, by the way." He stuck his hand out to Rachel. "Sawyer. Her other half."

Rachel took it and gazed up at him with the same star-struck, dopey grin that seemed to be the typical female response to his smile. I'd been seeing variations of it all day on practically every girl in school. How evolved was I, that I wasn't even jealous? Much. And, okay, maybe that was because they'd all stared at me with such shock and envy when he'd made it abundantly clear that he had eyes for no girl but me. His mate.

"You good?" he was asking. "Need a ride home or anything?"

"Ah, no," stammered Rachel. "I have to meet with my Latin teacher. Thanks."

"See you around," I said.

With the arm around my shoulders, Sawyer steered me toward the exit. "Well that confrontation went better than you expected. No fangs. No claws. Amber's still breathing."

"It was easier to control this time," I admitted. "So how was your first day?"

In the end Sawyer hadn't bothered to tell his dad about the GED he'd earned. He decided to just stick around and repeat his senior year with me.

"Well Mr. Lester is trying to decide if I'm a delinquent. Mrs. Rabinowitz is convinced I am a zoology genius. And I'm pretty sure I got asked to join every sport at Mortimer High. All in all, pretty good. You?"

I looked out at the emptying parking lot, past the skater guys, across the way to the football field where tryouts were already going and the cheerleaders were starting up practice. I lifted my hand to return a couple of waves as I considered the question. Then I felt a grin stretching my lips.

"It was completely and utterly . . . normal."

And that was all I'd ever wanted.

~*~

Finis.

About the Author

Kait Nolan is stuck in an office all day, sometimes juggling all three of her jobs at once with the skill of a trained bear—sometimes with a similar temperament. After hours, she uses her powers for good, creating escapist fiction. The work of this Mississippi native is packed with action, romance, and the kinds of imaginative paranormal creatures you'd want to sweep you off your feet...or eat your boss. When she's not working or writing, she's in her kitchen, heading up a revolution to Retake Homemade from her cooking blog, Pots and Plots.

You can catch up with her at http://kaitnolan.com.

Looking for more action-packed adventure? Check out Kait's Mirus series (*Forsaken By Shadow, Devil's Eye, Blindsight,* also available in an omnibus edition: *Genesis*), available wherever ebooks are sold. And don't forget to drop by her website and sign up for the newsletter to be notified of upcoming and new releases!

An Excerpt from *Heroes 'Til Curfew* by Susan Bischoff

Joss

Just because you're paranoid, doesn't mean no one's out to get you.

The thought went through my head in my dad's voice—I was that well programmed. That's why I'd varied my schedule, to throw off my stalker.

As I walked down the brick-paved road that ran through the middle of the downtown pedestrian mall, my own boots were the only ones I could hear beating the pavement. The feelings I had weren't the sensations of being followed and watched that I had become familiar with over the last month or so. Tonight was different.

It's not like I'm that kind of psychic. I don't have any kind of extra-sensory perception or anything. It's just that, since I was a little kid, my dad trained me to pay attention to my surroundings. At some point that kind of training turns to instinct—an instinct that warned me something was up.

The economy of our town was not great, and downtown was especially bad. Yeah, here and everywhere else in the country, right? That left a lot of empty storefronts on the mall, a lot of darkened glass windows that showed my reflection as I walked by, a lone, dark-haired girl in a vintage army jacket and combat boots, faking confidence in her stride.

Our store was at the far end of the mall and I had to walk the whole length of it to get home. I was happy when my dad started letting me walk home by myself, because I loved walking it, the feeling of freedom in the night air, the quiet, the glow of the converted gas lights. But making enemies, getting my ass handed to me, getting to walk around with a bruised face for weeks and all the attention that got me…that kind of thing changes a girl, I guess.

I glanced over at the image of the confident girl who moved from glass to glass beside me, at the dark alleyways that opened up every few buildings, the looming, brick store facades, and the shadows under awnings where the attractive but weak lamplight didn't reach. I listened hard to the sound of nothing—too much nothing, it seemed to me—and tried not to think about the cell phone in my pocket and of calling Dylan. Not because I was some useless girl, afraid of the dark and in need of rescuing, but just to hear his voice.

As if I would have the guts to just call up Dylan.

I passed by the fountain that they didn't bother to put water in anymore, even in summer. More than one person had used it for a giant trash can during the day. *Is that really any better than throwing your trash right on the ground? What's wrong with people?*

I don't know what it was that made me take a closer look as I walked by Dog-Eared. Mr. McGuffey closed the shop at five o'clock. He always said that after dinner his customers were all home reading, and he would be too. The lights were on low in the front of the store, like usual. Over the piles of used books stacked against the front windows, the tall bookcases created a maze through the shop and stacks on the floor encroached on the narrow aisles. But I guess that squeezing your way around Dog-Eared is part of its charm.

There was a flare of light. Just a quick something that was gone almost as I noticed it. Definitely not right. Moving closer to the shop, I thought I saw a shadow of movement, so I decided to duck down the alley and see if I could see anything through the windows over there.

Now I'll admit it: it's not a great idea for a girl, alone at night in a deserted downtown shopping area, to go creeping down dark alleys to peep in store windows where suspicious activity may or may not be taking place. But in my defense, I'm not exactly an ordinary girl, and I was just going to have a look anyway.

Through a window I could see the wide aisle that ran across the back of the shop, in front of the door to the back rooms. In that aisle were four boys doing bad things.

I recognized Jeff right off, even though his back was to me. Maybe it was the Neanderthal posture. Standing next to him was a smaller guy who looked vaguely familiar. Probably a freshman. Across from Jeff was a tall guy I didn't know, who looked older than we were. Next to that guy was a sophomore, Nathan, who was in my gym class last year.

Jeff and the freshman each had a pile of books in front of them, and when I say pile, I mean it looked like they'd just gathered up an armload and dumped them on the floor. Nice. They were tossing these books, in sync with each other, into the air in front of the other two. Who would then d-i-s-i-n-t-e-g-r-a-t-e them. No, really, I kid you not. I don't know what Nathan was doing, but his book just turned to dust which floated down to the carpet. The older guy's book burst with a brief flash of flame and then exploded into embers that glowed for a second before they joined the mess of dust and ash on the floor.

I shuddered. *Damn I hate fire.*

And fire in a bookshop? Genius. What a bunch of idiots. Did they want to burn the place down? Start a fire that would rip through all those stacks of books, choking the place with thick, black smoke, trapping them all in that maze of bookshelves as they crawled frantically along the floor, searching for the exit, while the temperature—

I sat down hard in the alley and put my head on my crossed legs, taking deep breaths of dirty, old cement and the smell of my leather boots. It's worth mentioning again: I hate fire.

But what was I going to do, let them burn down the store with their stupidity? Besides the fact that not even stupid people deserved *that* experience, more importantly, there was Mr. McGuffey. He used to bring me some tattered picture book that was beyond selling every week when I was a little kid in the store with my dad. I totally owe my love of reading to my complete lack of a social life and the owner of Dog-Eared. So there was no way I was going to just walk away.

And I couldn't call the police either. Or…I guess it was more like I wouldn't. These guys were Talents. No matter how much I didn't like them, I still had enough *us against them* mentality that I wasn't about to bring in the cops. We Talents needed to police our own.

The cops would just report the whole thing to the *National Institutes for Ability Control*. If NIAC came to investigate Talents in Fairview again, it wasn't going to be good for anyone. We'd already had more kids taken away to the State School in the last month than in the last few years put together, and I did *not* want to draw any more attention to our town than we already had.

I just wished these idiots felt the same way.

I pushed myself back up and moved to the next window, the one that didn't have a view of much of the shop because it was located behind a bookcase and piled with paperbacks. I could see the latch in the middle, so it wasn't a problem to reach out to it with my mind and get it to turn. The fact that it had been painted over at least once required a little mental elbow grease, but I got it. I floated the piles of paperbacks down to the floor before opening the window, so they wouldn't fall and make noise, and then I hoisted myself up and climbed in.

At the end of the row of bookshelves, I peeked around the corner. They were still playing their stupid game.

The first two would count it down, "Three, two, one, GO!" and toss the books.

Then the other two would say, "Ashes to ashes!" and "Dust to dust!" at practically the same time they destroyed the targets.

Losers. I was debating what to say when a girl rushed out of the center aisle into the middle of them to bang on the door to the back room. *Yeah, hon, just step right in the middle of a contest between the guy with the flame and the guy with the—disintegration ray power.* Whatever. It's not always easy to come up with names for some of these Talents.

The door was yanked open and Marco stepped out. My stomach did something unpleasant. Okay, I'll admit I was kind of scared of my nemesis. Call it post-traumatic stress. Mr. I-Can-Bench-Press-A-Steel-Girder did almost kill me not too long ago. When I looked at him, I imagined the feel of his hands around my throat, right before Dylan tackled him and saved my life. I *so* did not want to take Marco on again.

"You're screwing up Angie's concentration, Bella. What do you want?"

"Corey was feeling me up again when I was out of my body."

"What?" came a voice from the stacks. "She wasn't using it."

"Cor, this isn't a date-rape opportunity, it's a job. If you get your rocks off fondling unconscious chicks, get some GHB and do it on your time. Or take Sleepy, here, for a night on the town."

"My name is *Curtis,*" the freshman whined, indignant.

"Like anyone cares," Jeff said.

"Hey, you guys need to get back to business. Now. Angie's still working on the safe. Bella, get your virtual ass back up to the roof and do your job."

"Okay, but I thought you'd want to know that some girl went down the alley and was looking in the windows."

"What?" Marco asked, in a dangerous tone that made the boys sit up, but didn't seem to affect Bella very much.

"Yeah, dark-haired girl in an army jacket? Looked kind of like Joss Marshall."

Oh shit. I pulled back behind the stacks and started to move toward the window.

He came through the bookcase. I mean *through* the bookcase. One minute there was no one between me and the window, and the next there was a shimmer to the air in the form of a body coming out of the books. It grabbed me hard while it was still fading back into Corey Danvers. He smiled at me as he jerked me into the back aisle where everyone could see me.

"And look what I found."

I hope you enjoyed this excerpt from *Heroes 'Til Curfew*. The Talent Chronicles series introduces a world in which kids with supernatural abilities must hide their powers from a government that seeks to imprison them. This second installment, as well as the first book, *Hush Money*, are available in ebook and paperback at many online retailers. A free short story, *Impulse Control*, is also available in electronic form. Please visit http://susan-bischoff.com/talent-chronicles for links and information.

CPSIA information can be obtained at www.ICGtesting.com
Printed in the USA
LVOW08s1931081014

407882LV00011B/169/P